BODY
Language

Kenna White

Bella
BOOKS
2010

Bella Books, Inc.
P.O. Box 10543
Tallahassee, FL 32302

Printed in the United States of America on acid-free paper
First Edition

Editor: Katherine V. Forrest
Cover Designer: Linda Callaghan

ISBN 13: 978-1-59493-181-9

This book is dedicated to the beauty and timeless splendor that is uniquely Venice, Italy. I'll never grow tired of exploring its secrets or the people who call it home.

Acknowledgment

Many thanks to Kristi and Craig for making my last trip to Italy possible. Also to Mario, my knowledgeable desk clerk who knew all the perfect places to eat and how to get there without becoming mindlessly lost in Venice's maze of streets and back alleys.

About the Author

Kenna White lives in a small town nestled in southern Missouri where she enjoys her writing, traveling, making dollhouse miniatures and life's simpler pleasures. After living from the Rocky Mountains to New England, she is once again back where bare feet, faded jeans and lazy streams fill her life.

CHAPTER 1

Joanna Lucas sat staring at the telephone, drumming her fingers on the buttons as she decided whether to make the call. She spun her desk chair around and went to the window of her third-floor office and stared out at the busy street below.

It was a warm summer day in Boston but for some inexplicable reason she felt a chill. She didn't have time for this. She had sixteen student interns waiting for assignments. She also had to restore an exquisite Victorian candelabra she suspected was sterling silver, but some jerk had spray-painted green, a sixteenth century French Bisque figurine with chips that needed repair and a one-of-a-kind grandfather clock that needed cleaning before the museum added it to their collection. She didn't have time for this poor-poor-pitiful-me self-doubt. It was just a chill, probably from the air conditioning.

But it was the same chill she felt Saturday evening as she waited for LuAnn to meet her for dinner. She felt the chill again later that evening when LuAnn suggested they go back to her apartment. The idea of having sex with her had never frozen Joanna in her tracks before. Well, maybe it had, now that she thought about it. Several times in the four months since they met she had noticed that chill. She had tried to ignore it at first, attributing it to early relationship jitters. But as much as she tried, those feelings of apprehension were still there. Not the feelings she expected—the ones of anticipation and contentment over their next kiss or their next rendezvous. The sex was good. Joanna had to admit that. Or as good as sex could be when she looked forward to the orgasm more than the lovemaking.

There was no denying it. Something was drastically wrong. And there shouldn't be. She had a right to expect more. She was tired of forcing a smile and pretending every touch was magical. When she kissed a woman, she wanted it to be passion driven. Not duty bound. Joanna couldn't explain why but dating LuAnn had become a chore, not a pleasure. That wasn't fair to LuAnn or to herself. At forty-one, Joanna wanted and needed more. And she knew it wasn't going to come from LuAnn.

Joanna watched the couples walking the sidewalk, her hand subconsciously holding the collar of her blouse closed to the neck. She returned to her desk and snatched up the receiver, keying in the number. She leaned back in her desk chair and closed her eyes as she waited for LuAnn to pick up but it went through to her voice mail instead.

"LuAnn, this is Joanna. Sorry I missed you. I'm really sorry to spring this on you at the last minute but I won't be able to make it this weekend. Something has come up at work. I know. I know. We've been talking about a weekend in P'town for weeks. Forgive me. Oops, got to go. Another call coming in. Talk with you soon. Bye-bye."

She hung up and heaved a relieved sigh. She wasn't sure she had breathed the entire time she was fibbing and hated herself for doing it.

"Ms. Lucas, you said to let you know when the crate arrived from Baltimore."

Joanna only marginally heard her, the call she had just made still twisting in her mind.

"Ms. Lucas?" The co-ed in the doorway was twirling a lock of her long hair, dragging it across her mouth as if tasting it.

"Yes." When are they going to stop sending me these babies as interns, she thought. They're getting younger and younger. And not just younger, but perkier. Sexier. If life was a baseball game, Joanna knew she'd be the over-the-hill relief pitcher with tennis elbow and rotator cuff damage. The young perky graduate students, like the one draping herself around her doorjamb, would be the league MVPs. Joanna couldn't compete with that. But when had that ever been a priority? God, is it that time of the month again? It has to be mood swings or the birthday she was hoping to ignore next week.

"Ms. Lucas?"

She pushed the telephone back on her desk as if putting the call out of her mind and looked up, saying, "Yes, Haley. I'm on my way."

She sprang to her feet and headed out the door, once again in complete control of herself and the work she had to fill her day. As assistant director of the art objects department of the Straus Center for Art and Technical Studies, she was not only expected to critique incoming art objects for repair and restoration but was instructor to the interns hoping to become art conservators. She was also expected to make herself available for fund-raising opportunities that dragged her to endless meetings and luncheons. All of them activities she'd rather not have to do since they took her away from being an art conservator, something she truly enjoyed.

Haley wasn't moving fast enough for Joanna and she passed her with long purposeful strides, high heels clicking along the polished marble floor and the lapels of her satin blouse bouncing against her cleavage. As she approached the workroom at the end of the hall, she could hear voices, more voices than were usually at work in that room.

"What's up, kids?" she said, her mere presence parting the crowd as she entered. A dozen or so interns were watching two women lift the lid from a wooden crate. The only markings on the plywood box, something larger than a side-by-side refrigerator, were the words CAUTION–EXTREMELY FRAGILE stenciled on each side. She peeled the plastic invoice packet from the lid as they set it aside. She sifted through the papers as another student began the task of unscrewing the long rows of screws that held the front panel in place.

"Is that the only screwdriver we have, Rita?"

A middle-aged Hispanic woman looked up from her perch on a five-wheeled secretarial chair.

"Dr. Heath borrowed our toolbox and hasn't returned it." She shrugged matter-of-factly.

"Anyone have a pocketknife with a screwdriver blade on it?" Joanna asked, scanning the group hopefully. Everyone shook their heads.

"Can't have them on campus," one of the young men offered, as if Joanna should already know that.

"We'll be here all day at this rate." Only two screws had been removed and there were dozens left.

Joanna groaned indignantly as she spun on her heels and crossed the hall to an equipment locker. She returned a minute later with a screwdriver in each hand and gave them to two of the spectators. "Now we have three."

When one of the screwdriver-wielding women broke a nail and gave that more attention than the job at hand, it was all Joanna could do not to grab the tool out of her hand and do the job herself. But she was supposed to delegate. That was part of her position as assistant director. She circled the crate, mentally calculating how long it was going to take to unscrew all the panels at this rate.

"Is anyone going to let us in on what's inside?" a young man asked.

"Something to do with Dolley Madison," Haley replied.

"So?" He didn't seem impressed.

"Robert, what can you tell me about Dolley Madison?" Joanna asked, turning to her job as instructor.

"She was married to James Madison, the fourth President of the United States. It was her second marriage. He was quite a few years her senior and was President during the War of 1812," he said, his arms crossed pretentiously. "She was a large woman. Buxom is the word I think they used to describe her." He smiled chauvinistically.

"That's part of her story," Joanna said. "She also was a survivor. She and her son survived yellow fever that killed her first husband and a large percentage of Philadelphia's population in 1793. Years later she was forced to sell off the family estate at Montpelier to pay debts her son incurred through alcoholism and stupidity. But it's her eye for style and artistic flair that we're celebrating with this piece of history. When the British marched up Pennsylvania Avenue in August of 1814, looting and burning everything in their path, it was Dolley Madison who's credited with saving much of the silver and paintings in the White House. She had White House treasures loaded onto wagons and taken from the city before the building was burned. Even so, many of the exquisite pieces of furniture were lost."

The class was listening attentively. She went on. "As an anniversary present for his wife, President Madison ordered a mahogany writing desk be made nearly a year before. The cabinetmaker mistakenly delivered it to the White House a month early. The First Lady wasn't at home and the President was so busy with the war and the impending invasion by the British troops, he paid little attention to the mistake. But at the last minute, he changed his mind. He had the desk removed and put in storage to be delivered on their anniversary instead of her birthday. But with the burning of the White House it was long forgotten. It wasn't until two years after he left office that the desk was rediscovered. It had been stored in the root cellar of one of the White House staff members."

Finally the front panel was folded down, exposing excelsior packing material surrounding a plastic-wrapped piece of furniture.

"Let's have a look," Joanna said, tossing a wad of excelsior aside. "Watch out for the corners."

She removed blocks of foam protecting the top corners. Several students helped to remove the desk from the crate, lifting it like it was made of glass. As the plastic was removed, the dozen or so onlookers moved closer. Joanna peeled back the last layer and studied the mahogany desk with a slow contented smile. "This is it, kids." She circled the desk, sliding her fingertips along the edge of the desk as if caressing a lover. "Magnificent," she whispered. "Look at the reeded quarter columns and the inlay. It's gorgeous."

"There's a package in the bottom of the crate, Ms. Lucas," Rita said, unwinding the bubble wrap around a wooden cigar box.

Joanna opened the box and unfolded several pieces of tissue paper. They contained six slivers of wood, each about four inches long and an inch wide. There was also a small brass name plate, tarnished beyond recognition. The tiny nail holes were clogged with dirt and grime.

"These must be the damaged parts of a drawer back." She set the box in the top drawer for safekeeping.

"Are we just repairing the drawer?" Robert asked, giving his own circle to the desk.

"We have the privilege of cleaning and restoring Dolley Madison's desk before it's added to the First Ladies' Collection going on tour after the first of the year."

"Whoever had it didn't take very good care of it," he said, looking at it more critically than appreciatively.

"You're a half-empty kind of guy, Robert," Joanna couldn't help but say.

"Well, they didn't. Look at the legs. They're all scuffed up. There is a big gouge out of the back. And it's filthy."

"I'd much rather have it arrive in this condition so we can

restore it properly than have someone do the wrong thing. As far as we know, this is the only piece of furniture to be exclusively owned by Dolley Madison to ever have been in the White House prior to it being burned in 1814."

"That's just a technicality. It wasn't there long enough to count."

God, she hated these pompous young men with narrow minds and narrower educations. He obviously didn't understand the importance of the piece and she didn't feel like arguing with him. The gawkers, including Robert, gave a last look before drifting off to their own workrooms.

"Is she in there?" a gravelly voiced man called from the hall.

"Yes," Haley said as she exited.

"I'm here, Dr. Finch," Joanna replied without looking in his direction. "Come see the desk. It's exquisite."

He worked his way through the departing students. Dr. Finch didn't have the commanding presence of Joanna although he was the director of the Straus Center and Joanna's boss. He was a smallish man in his sixties with gray hair, balding with a deep comb-over. His eyebrows were bushy and unkempt like the tufts of hair sprouting from his ears. He was hard to look at without wondering why his wife hadn't seen to his grooming needs, assuming she wasn't blind or indifferent.

What Harvey Finch lacked in social graces he more than made up for in his academic attributes. He was well-read, well-schooled and well-traveled in anything to do with the conservation and restoration of fine arts. Unfortunately, his wealth of knowledge was smothered by his administrative duties for the Straus Center and the Harvard University Art Museum of which it was part. The politics of fundraising and budgetary constraints had dimmed his artistic interest and to Joanna that was a shame. He had been Joanna's mentor when she was a green intern. In her view, he had sold out. She thought he was much more valuable in the lab than in the front office. But she wasn't naïve. She understood the ascension up the administrative ladder. She also understood the Peter Principle about rising to your level of incompetence.

"What desk is this?" he asked, peering over the top of his granny glasses without much interest. Joanna noticed his eyes had stopped at the deep V of her blouse, wallowing around in the view a moment before moving on to the desk.

"The Dolley Madison writing desk from the Gillenburg estate." She gave him enough information hoping to jog his memory. He only shrugged.

"The one from the White House, Dr. Finch," one of the co-eds said. "The anniversary gift from President Madison."

Joanna hated it when the interns talked down to him like he was a senile old man.

"Ah, yes," he said as if the light had finally come on. "1814. Mahogany with rosewood inlay and brass capital columns."

Atta boy, Harvey, Joanna thought.

"Yes." She blew some excelsior dust from the surface of the desk. "They included the broken drawer back and the brass plaque. I haven't checked to see if we have all the pieces but hopefully we can reconstruct the back."

"What's that?" he said, eyeing something on the front leg. "Surface check or split?"

Joanna tucked the back of her skirt behind her knees and squatted to examine the damage.

"It looks like the wood is dried out and cracked along the grain. The strip of inlay is all there but it's loose." She worked her nail into the crack, careful not to damage it more.

"Weather check probably?" He stooped closer, resting his hand on her shoulder for support as he looked. "Don't let that piece get lost. You might want to take it out, clean the residue off the slot and the back of the inlay then replace it. It'll make for a better fit."

Joanna removed the bottom drawer and turned it over.

"Nice delicate dovetail joints," she said, showing him.

"Marcus Role," Harvey said, squinting critically at the drawer. "Or his brother, Henry. But I'd bet Marcus."

"I was thinking the Hiblinger Furniture Company from Alexandria, Virginia. They worked with rosewood and burled

8

inlay like this. They also used batwing escutcheons similar to these."

"You've got a good point." He ran his fingers along the rim of the drawer pull. "They did occasionally use reticulated escutcheons like these. But I'm not convinced."

"What do you see I don't?" Joanna was relieved to hear her mentor return to teaching if only for a moment.

"In 1805 or so, the Role Brothers started using alternating dovetail widths."

"Do they add to the joint strength?"

"No. It was purely for show. They also used hickory for backup wood. Drawer bottoms and backs. It's a dense wood that works well with mahogany. I doubt Hiblinger would have had the balls to use a lesser backup wood for a piece of furniture going to the White House." He scratched the drawer bottom with his thumbnail then sniffed it. "Yep. Hickory."

"Do we know for certain this was made by the Role Brothers?"

"We do now. You can confirm it by checking the bottom of the piece. If it was Hiblinger's there would be a small rectangular plaque or the shadow where one had been. No one is going to make a piece of furniture for the White House without leaving their mark on it. If it's Henry Role there will be a tiny HLR mark in the corner. Probably hand carved. If it's Marcus, you'll see MR with a circle around it about the size of your thumb. It will probably be a pressure stamp. He was the older brother and had a bigger ego. More ostentatious in his detailing. He was also a more skilled craftsman. I'd bet this is Marcus's work." Harvey gave the desk one last look as if releasing his interest in it. "You can check it later. Now, I need to talk to you. Have you got a minute?"

Joanna replaced the drawer and stood up, brushing off her hands and straightening her skirt. "Sure, what is it? If it's about the luncheon next week, I already contacted the caterer. And I really think you should give the welcoming speech. Dr. Han isn't coming to see me."

"No, no. This has nothing to do with that."

"Rita, you can go ahead and photograph the desk. Get a close up of the right leg. You'll see the split. And take close-ups of the drawer joints. Document anything you find. Check the crate and the packing to make sure we didn't miss anything. And photograph any marks you see on the bottom or back."

Joanna led the way down the hall to her office, Harvey following. It wasn't until she closed the door that he pulled a several-page folded letter from his suit jacket pocket and back-creased the pages.

"Coffee, Harvey?" she asked, stepping to the coffee machine on the credenza behind her desk.

"Sugar, no cream," he said as he flipped through the pages as if looking for something. "I received another letter from the Procurator's Council. Actually it's the proto's office but it's all the same thing. They want an answer, Joanna."

"I thought we gave them one." She set the cup in front of him as he took a seat across the desk from her.

"Thanks," he said and immediately took a swig. "Good. Good coffee." He went back to searching the letter. "You need to reconsider, Joanna. This isn't like a library group that wants you to attend their luncheon. This is Basilica de San Marco in Venice, Italy. Saint Mark's Cathedral."

"I know, Harvey. But I don't have time. You go."

"I'm the director. My job is to delegate. You're the assistant director. Besides, they specifically asked for you." He took off his glasses and tossed them on the desk with the letter. "This is nothing to sneeze at, Joanna. This is a very handsome proposal. A few more grants like this one and we can think about adding that stereoscopic digital scanner you've been harping about."

"Bribery isn't your best posture, Harvey." She leaned back in her desk chair, holding her cup in her hands as if it were warming her on a winter day. "Let's stick to the facts."

"Did you even look at this?" He sounded disappointed in her.

"No. I assumed your doctorate in art history meant you

10

could." She said it with a little smile as she turned the letter on the desk so she could look at it. "Harvey, write a letter to the Procurator's Council at Saint Mark's Cathedral in Venice. Tell them thank you for the consideration but we are unable to accept your grant proposal at this time. Recommend Augusta Wittingham in Houston. She specializes in religious artifacts. If she can't do it she can recommend someone who can."

"Did you see how much this grant pays? Half to the Straus Center. Half to you." He raised his bushy eyebrows and pointed to the figure in the letter. "All expenses paid. Airfare. Lodging. Transportation. Food allowance. They'll even have a computer available for your use. You won't have to take one. Two weeks in Venice, Italy. And don't tell me you don't secretly fanatasize about going to Venice, Italy again."

"Again?"

"Surely you've been." There was a judgmental curiosity in his tone.

"I've meant to." Joanna knew it sounded strange someone in her profession, all but a dissertation away from a doctorate in art history, hadn't been to one of the most historic and embellished cities in the world.

"Joanna, do me a favor. Do yourself a favor. Look it over. Give it some serious consideration. It isn't very often someplace like San Marco asks for an outside opinion. They have in-house advisors and experts. This is big league, believe me. This would look really good on your curriculum vitae. Hell, it would look good on anyone's curriculum vitae. If I were twenty years younger, I might fight you for it."

"You go." She held out the letter to him.

"God, no." He laughed, locking his hands behind his head. "Besides, you are the expert on mosaics. Not me. Think of it as the vacation you keep promising yourself and don't take."

"I take vacations."

"No, you don't. You take business trips. Those don't count. I can't believe you've never been to Venice."

"I've been to Rome."

11

"Not the same. That's Roman, not Renaissance. The art doesn't compare. Neither does the city itself."

He finished his coffee then stood up, hooking his thumbs through the suspenders on his trousers. "Read the letter, Joanna. Give it some thought. As your boss, I can't order you to go. But as a friend, I can strongly recommend it."

"I'll read it," she said, scanning the second page.

Harvey opened the office door then looked back at her. "October. Two weeks. Venice, Italy. Not a bad way to spend the fall."

"I'll read it, Harvey."

"Venice can be very romantic in October." Harvey was showing a playful side Joanna hadn't seen before. "That's where I took Nancy on our anniversary. She insisted, and for once, she showed good sense in selecting a vacation destination. Take someone with you. Make it a real vacation."

"I'll read the letter, Harvey," she said, folding her hands over it.

"I'll need an answer first of the week."

"Okay."

"Monday," he insisted, giving her a fatherly stare.

"Monday."

"Why do I get the feeling something is bothering you, Joanna?" His eyebrows rolled forward, nearly touching the bridge of his nose.

"I have no idea." She straightened her posture convincingly. "I'm fine. There is nothing bothering me other than I've got a boss who keeps harping on me to take a vacation."

"Okay. Then I'll see you Monday morning."

She chuckled. "Goodbye, Harvey. And it might not be first thing in the morning. But sometime Monday, I promise."

Joanna listened to his footsteps down the hall then went to close her office door. As she again took her seat behind the desk her eyes fell across the framed photograph on her desk of herself and LuAnn. She picked up the frame and studied LuAnn's face. It wasn't a good photograph. Their hair was mussed and they looked tired after walking the full length of the Freedom Trail across Boston. Why she had chosen that one to frame was a complete mystery.

She used her finger to block out LuAnn's mouth and nose so only her eyes were visible. The more she studied it, the more she could see someone else's eyes looking back at her, the soft, passionate and sparkling eyes of another. Why hadn't she noticed it before? LuAnn's eyes were the same shape and deep brown color as Chandler's eyes. She quickly removed her finger, gasping at the revelation.

This was not Chandler and Joanna hadn't wanted it to be. The two years she spent with Chandler Cardin had gone from ecstatically happy to painfully ugly so fast it made her head spin, leaving her with an open wound that took months to heal. But heal, it had. And Joanna wasn't going to pick that scab anymore. Nor could she remain in an unfulfilling relationship with LuAnn.

Just as she reached for the telephone there was a knock on the office door.

"Come," she said.

"Rita said to let you know she found a mark on the bottom of the desk you might want to see. She photographed it."

"Thank you, Haley. I'll be right there."

Joanna waited for her to close the door then dialed. While she waited she studied the photograph on the desk. She placed her thumb over LuAnn's entire face.

It is. It's Chandler's body. She even stands like Chandler. How could I have missed that?

"Hi again, LuAnn. Regarding that last message I left, I hope this isn't awkward but I have good news. I was able to shuffle things around and I can make it this weekend after all. Hope this is okay. Talk with you later. Bye-bye."

Joanna hung up. She looked down at the photograph, squinting her eyes to blur the images. She then dropped the frame in her desk drawer and closed it, feeling a sense of relief for the first time in months.

CHAPTER 2

Joanna paid the taxi driver and started for the ferry landing as her cell phone jingled. It was Deena. Undoubtedly calling to check on how things went with LuAnn. Joanna wasn't ready to talk about it. Deena was her oldest and closest friend and she would eventually tell her what happened but it was too soon. LuAnn's bitter words as well as the slap she landed on Joanna's cheek were too painful to discuss. It wasn't until the second call that Joanna opened her phone and answered.

"Hello, Deena," she said, forcing a cheery voice. She watched as a seagull pecked at the remnants of a bagel on the wharf.

"Hey, Josie." The statement hung in the air, an orphan

waiting for Joanna to gather it in and support it. When she didn't, Deena continued. "Are you okay, honey?"

Joanna knew Deena. Her curiosity was about to get the best of her.

"I'm fine. I'm getting ready to step on the ferry." The ferry worker waved passengers to begin boarding.

"I'll pick you up. What time do you get in?"

"Nine, but you don't have to do that. I can ride the bus."

Deena's reply was terse and adamant. "Absolutely not. I'll be there. You are not riding home on the bus at nine o'clock at night. I'll take you to dinner and we can talk."

"I'm not hungry, honey. And I'm all talked out for one day."

"Okay, no dinner. We can go to Brewster's for a drink and no talk. I swear. I won't say a thing if you don't want me to."

"I just want to go home." Joanna heaved a tired sigh. Deena's support was reassuring but she didn't need to spend hours propped on a bar stool retelling the ugly details of her breakup. Joanna wasn't sure it was any of Deena's business anyway. She was a true and loyal friend but they weren't Siamese twins. Joanna was entitled to keep at least some of her private life private. Or as private as she could from a friend who had seen her naked, held her forehead while she threw up after a New Year's Eve party and taught her how to pee standing up while hiking the Berkshires.

"I can't let you go home and spend the night wallowing in guilt and self-doubt. What kind of friend would I be to abandon you in your hour of need?"

"You'd be a wonderful friend. You'd let me take off my shoes, soak in a hot tub and get a good night's sleep. The first one I've had in two weeks. And before you say anything else, I'm not wallowing in guilt and self-doubt. I'm only sorry I let it drag out so long. It would have been kinder to say something weeks ago." Joanna took a seat by the window on the starboard side of the ferry, a habit. It offered the best view as they entered Boston harbor.

"Screw her."

"Deena! Please. Make me a promise."

"What?"

"The subject of LuAnn and talk like that is closed. No questions. No comments. No insults. Promise me."

There was a long silence. Joanna could just imagine Deena's face writhing with desperation at not being able to know every sordid detail of their breakup.

"Promise me," Joanna demanded.

"All right," whined Deena. "You're such a spoilsport."

"Think of it as a gift."

"Giving a gift shouldn't be painful for the giver."

"So you promise?"

"Reluctantly."

"Say it. Say you promise." Joanna wasn't being childish. She knew Deena all too well. She lived by the letter of the law. If she said she would be someplace at six o'clock, she'd be there at six. If she said she would keep a secret, not even bamboo under her fingernails could drag it out of her.

"Damn it. Okay. I promise," Deena grumbled. "I won't say a word about LuAnn ever again in my entire life and for at least three years of the hereafter. Are you happy?"

"Yes. Thank you."

"Josie, I've got to go but I'll be there at the dock to pick you up. I'll park as close to the side gate as I can. Love ya." She hung up.

Joanna closed her phone and held it against her cheek. She stared out at the churning water surrounding the ferry as it backed away from the dock. The more she thought about it, the more she was convinced she had done the right thing with LuAnn. Maybe she hadn't been as tactful or as diplomatic as she could have. But she felt a sense of relief. Yet she felt as if she were leaving a piece of herself behind and that was as painful as anything she had ever done. Joanna closed her eyes, fighting back the tears. But it was no use. She leaned her forehead against the window and cried quietly.

As the ferry pulled up to the dock Joanna was already waiting at the railing to disembark. She wanted off. She wanted to put the unhappy weekend as far behind her as she could. As she descended the gangplank, she noticed a commotion outside the dock entrance. Through the crowd she could see two uniformed police officers struggling with a pair of women. The huskier of the suspects was kicking and fighting with the woman officer who had her trapped against the fence.

The other police officer, a young sandy-haired man in his early twenties, was trying to restrain an older woman but without much success. The female officer ushered her suspect into the backseat of a patrol car then went to help the male officer. She grabbed the woman by the wrist and folded her hand back, instantly driving her to the ground, placing her knee in the woman's back as she wrestled to gain control of her hands.

"Your hands," she warned through gritted teeth as if holding back a fierce temper. "Watch her feet, Keith. Don't let her kick you in the family jewels."

"I got them, sergeant," he said, sitting astride the woman's legs but not before she landed a kick to his thigh.

The sergeant grabbed the woman's hair and pulled, arching her head back, then clicked the handcuffs closed around her wrists, pulled her to her feet and positioned her over the hood of the patrol car.

"Anything in your pockets I should know about?" the sergeant asked, using her foot to spread the woman's legs wide apart. "Anything that's going to hurt me?"

"I want a lawyer," she said angrily. "I know my rights."

"I'm sure you do." The sergeant searched the woman's pockets, pulling out a wad of money, a knife, a small baggie of white rocks and a piece of partially burned glass tubing.

"That's not mine. I'm just holding it for a friend."

"I didn't ask you anything, honey. It'll probably be better if you shut up. We've got all the witnesses we need."

Another patrol car pulled up, its lights flashing.

"Hey, sergeant," a blond female patrol officer said, stepping out and slamming the door. "They've got you working late. I thought you were off duty. Need some help?"

"She's all yours. Officer Edmonds here will give you the details. It's his arrest."

"Thanks for the help, sergeant," Keith said, escorting the second woman into the back of the newly arrived patrol car.

"Anytime. You'll need to Mirandize them, Keith."

The sergeant brushed off her hands and straightened her hat then looked up and smiled. "Hey, Josie. How was the ferry ride? And yes, I know. I won't say a word about LuAnn." She came through the crowd and gave Joanna a hug and a kiss on the cheek.

"The ferry ride was fine but what's all this?" Joanna couldn't help but stare at the two women, thankful they were securely inside the police cars.

"Nothing. Just a couple pros plying their trade."

"Maybe I should get a taxi."

"No, no. This is Keith's arrest. I just happened to hear the radio call and I was here anyway. Come on. I'm parked down the block." Deena took Joanna's tote bag and led her to the patrol car.

"Are you still on duty?"

"Not really. Not till ten thirty. I'm going to help out with traffic control around Fenway. The Red Sox have a doubleheader with the Yankees. It'll be a zoo afterward. It sounds like it's going to be a sweep. That'll bring out the goofballs for sure." Deena unlocked the passenger door and held it while Joanna climbed in and got settled. "Buckle up," she said, smiling down at her.

"Yes, officer." Joanna looked up at her and chuckled but it quickly changed to a gasp. "Oh, my God, Deena. What happened to your eye?"

Deena touched her eye, wincing at the pain. "It's nothing."

"Did one of those women do that?"

"The little one. I misjudged her capabilities." She laughed and closed the door.

"You're going to have a shiner tomorrow, honey. You should put some ice on that," Joanna warned as Deena removed her hat and slid into the driver's seat.

"I'll survive," she said, brushing her cheek nonchalantly.

"Does it hurt?" Joanna frowned sympathetically. She wanted to touch it but Deena wouldn't allow that. Not the macho, independent, self-reliant sergeant Deena Garren.

"Not yet, but it probably will once the adrenaline wears off." She checked her eye in the visor mirror.

"I think we should stop by the hospital and let them take a look at it. That's what you'd say if it was me." Joanna was glad she hadn't mentioned LuAnn's slap. Deena would probably have her arrested for assault and battery. Joanna discreetly touched her own cheek. It was still sore and it was just a slap. She couldn't imagine what Deena's wallop across the eye felt like.

"I'll be okay. Let's get you home before the traffic picks up."

Joanna was grateful for the distraction. The arrest, the black eye and the thickening traffic kept Deena from mentioning Joanna's weekend with LuAnn. In spite of her promise not to, Joanna wouldn't have been surprised for her to find a way to bring it up.

Deena gave the siren a short blast to warn a pedestrian not to cross against the light. She slowed and wagged her finger at the man who looked intoxicated.

"Wait for the light, sir," she shouted through the window. He replied something profane and incomprehensible then turned and went the other way. "What's new at work, Josie?"

"We got that desk in last week. The Dolley Madison one I was telling you about." Joanna was glad to have something else to think about.

"The one found in a basement?"

"Yes. It is truly a gorgeous piece. Would you like to come see it?"

"Naw, you enjoy it." Deena made no qualms about displaying her indifference to what she had no interest in.

"Harvey's been at me to reconsider that grant in Italy." Joanna turned her gaze out the side window, watching the black-and-white patrol car's reflection in the store windows. "I think I'm going to accept it."

"Really? That's good. Where in Italy was it again?"

19

"Venice. Saint Mark's Cathedral. They want me to analyze a section of mosaic floor that is scheduled for restoration. There seems to be some debate over the age of the tessera."

"Tessera? What's that?"

"The individual little glass or marble tiles used to create the mosaics. The glass ones are usually found on the ceiling. Floors are usually marble or granite."

"Oh, yeah."

"You're cute when you try to sound like you understand."

"I understand marbles."

"Not marbles. Marble. Stone. Not the little round glass things kids play with."

"Oh. I was wondering how they got them flat enough to walk on without hurting your feet." She looked over at Joanna and grinned.

"You big goof," Joanna scowled, pushing at her arm. Deena had again taken advantage of her gullibility and made her blush.

"Are there really that many colors of marble? Enough to make mosaics?"

"Yes. Different countries of the world are sources for different color marble. Marble is essentially limestone that has crystallized in the earth's crust from heat and pressure. In its pure form, marble is white. It's the impurities and chemical composition that create the different colors."

"Okay," Deena interrupted, holding up a hand. "Stop right there. I don't understand any of that."

"Would it help if I just said marble is available in almost every color of the rainbow?"

"Yes. Thank you. And I'm glad you're going to Venice. You need a getaway." She patted Joanna's hand. "And you'll enjoy it there. I understand it's full of artsy-fartsy crap." She winked, as if knowing that wasn't a term Joanna would use. Joanna dutifully replied with a smirk.

"Want to go with me?"

"Sure. I can play marbles in Saint Mark's Cathedral." Deena laughed out loud.

"Okay, get a passport and clear your calendar for the middle two weeks in October."

Deena pulled up to a red brick apartment building in mid-block. She put the car in park and rubbed at her eye.

"Don't do that. Let me make you an ice pack. It'll keep your eye from swelling."

"I can't, hon. But thanks. I've got to head across town. How about lunch next Saturday? I've got four days off."

"Sounds good. Where?"

"Mario's. About twelve thirty?"

"I'll meet you there," Joanna said, climbing out then looking back in. "Put ice on that, sergeant. That's an order."

"Good night, Joanna." Deena saluted and motioned for her to go inside.

Like always, she didn't pull away from the curb until Joanna rode the elevator to the fourth floor and flashed her living room lights three times to indicate everything was okay. Joanna had argued she wasn't afraid to enter her apartment. Nor did she need a chaperone to go out at night but Deena insisted. It was just easier to give in and let her have her way. Besides, it gave Joanna a sense of security to know someone was out there looking after her welfare even if she was a little nosy at times.

CHAPTER 3

The summer passed all too quickly giving way to rainy September. Joanna had gotten past LuAnn. She was single again. As much as she didn't want to, she finally gave in and told Deena what happened. It was all Joanna could do to keep her from confronting LuAnn. It wasn't until Joanna explained she just wasn't worth the anger, it was over, Joanna had moved past it, that Deena backed off. Whatever feelings she had for LuAnn were gone and so was she.

It had been weeks since Joanna's and Deena's schedules allowed them time for a leisurely lunch and they both were looking forward to it. Joanna was late, a long-winded client keeping her well past the noon hour. She finally hurried across town and into the restaurant that overlooked Boston Common. Deena was seated at a table in the corner, sipping a cup of coffee and reading the newspaper, her uniform hat hooked on the back of her chair, her patent leather holster and service weapon draped over the seat of the chair, looking ominous.

Deena was an imposing figure of a woman. At nearly six feet tall with dark cutting eyes and thick brunette hair, she was a force to be reckoned with. She held a black belt in karate and Aikido. She taught self-defense at the local Boys and Girls Club. She had been awarded medals for both bravery under fire and for heroism. She had three scars, one on her left wrist, the result of a knife fight with a drunken suspect in a dark alley, another on her right leg from an angry pit bull used as an alarm at a crack house, and one at the corner of her right eye. It was small and almost indistinguishable from the web of crow's feet but had nearly cost Deena her life. If she hadn't flinched, a bullet from a punk who had just robbed a liquor store would have struck her in the eye. She didn't talk about them. For a dedicated police officer, they were just a day at the office. She and Joanna had met while they both attended graduate school at Boston College, Deena in Criminal Justice and Joanna in Art Restoration.

"I'm sorry I'm late, honey." Joanna gave her a hug and a kiss. "I got tied up."

"That's okay. I just got here myself." She held the chair for Joanna. "So, what have you been up to these days? How's the research going?"

"Good. We finally received permission to do a stereophotogrammetry model on the Houser mosaics. I just hope it isn't too late. There isn't much mortar left."

"Is that good or bad?"

"It's bad. Very bad. We can replicate the mortar but we've already lost half of the tessara. The family hasn't been very careful with it. You can't store a two-hundred-year-old mosaic in the attic like it's grandpa's football trophy."

"I have every confidence in your ability to save the, what is it again?"

23

"Houser mosaic. From the Francis Davidson Houser Collection in San Diego."

"Yeah, that." Deena couldn't hide a smile.

"Okay, so you don't have any idea what I'm talking about. Someday I'm going to explain it to you so you'll understand the importance of restoring our artistic heritage."

"So long as you understand it, that's all that matters, Josie."

"How's your day going?"

"Don't ask. Two officers got shot last night. No witnesses. At least none willing to say anything."

"Oh, my. Serious?" Joanna was almost afraid to ask. She hadn't seen any news reports.

Deena nodded and opened the menu. "Both critical. The vest may have saved Officer Hardy. If Martha survives, it'll be a miracle. Drive-by bastards."

"I'm so sorry, honey." Joanna placed her hand on Deena's.

"What's good for lunch here?" Deena asked as if needing to change the subject.

"Everything." They each scanned their menus. "Have you gotten your passport yet?"

"Passport?"

"Yes. Did you get your application turned in?"

Deena stared at Joanna. "I thought you were joking about that."

"No, I'm not joking. Do you want to go?"

"To Venice, Italy for two weeks? Hell, yes, I want to go. I've always wanted to go there. I thought you were just kidding about me going along."

"Then get a passport."

"Really? You'd let me tag along while you go do whatever it is you do?"

"Sure. The hotel has two adjoining rooms that share a bathroom. It isn't big but you'll have your own room with a balcony that looks out over this very picturesque little square. It includes breakfast and is just two minutes from a vaporetto stop. That's like a water bus."

"You're not pulling my leg, are you, Joanna? You'll really let me go to Venice with you?"

"Absolutely. My trip is covered by the grant. You pay your way and you can go. But you need to get moving on the passport. Sometimes it can take a month or so to process."

"I've already got one. I had to escort a female prisoner back from Montreal a few years ago. The department got me one."

"And it's still good. It hasn't expired?"

"It's got five or six years left on it."

"Then you are good to go." Joanna grinned at her.

"What do I need to do? Book a flight? Exchange my money? What?" Deena was instantly all giddy and enthused.

"I'll book our flights. We won't exchange our dollars for Euros until we get there. All you'll need is a guidebook and a good map. You'll be on your own while I'm doing the consult."

"You're serious. I can go with you to Italy?" Deena's eyes moistened. She looked away and swallowed. "God, I can't believe it. What a dream come true."

"We'll have a great time. And yes, I know just how much you need this trip too, honey. We'll put an ocean between us and Boston." She squeezed Deena's hand. She could feel a tremble in the tall woman's strong hand, an ever so slight but palpable tremble.

Joanna hadn't seen Deena display this kind of emotion since that terrible night over a year ago. She knew the psychological scars were still there just below the surface. Deena wouldn't admit it but she hadn't gotten over taking the life of a teenager in the line of duty. The shooting was justified by the department but that didn't diminish the fact. It didn't matter drugs had played a part in the shooting. They didn't discuss it but Joanna knew Deena needed to get away from those memories that haunted her.

"Thank you, Josie. This means a lot to me."

"I know, honey. I know." She looked into Deena's eyes and saw the deep anguish. Joanna would do anything she could to help her through this.

25

She had no interest in Deena as a lover but it hadn't always been that way. There was a time a dozen years ago when she wasn't so sure. Deena's bright eyes and engaging personality had done their job. But before what would have been a brief one-night stand they both realized their friendship was more valuable than meaningless sex. Joanna wasn't what Deena needed. And vice versa. Deena needed someone who understood the pain and frustration of being a police officer in a big crime-ridden city. She needed someone who could love her unconditionally and passionately one minute and hold her while she cried the next. Joanna's needs were simpler. She just wanted someone to love her, faithfully and unequivocally. And here she was, going to the most romantic city in the world, Venice, Italy—alone.

CHAPTER 4

"Knock, knock, Josie," Deena called cautiously, peeking through the partially open door.

"Come in. I'm almost ready. I can't find my umbrella." Joanna was rummaging in the back of the coat closet. Her suitcase and carry-on were waiting by the door.

"Don't ever leave your door open like that."

"I knew you were on your way up."

"I don't care. It isn't safe to leave your door open even a few inches." There was a stern mothering tone in her voice, more so than usual.

"Okay. Never again. I'll ask for three forms of ID, fingerprints and a DNA sample before opening the door to anyone. Happy?"

"I'm not kidding, Joanna. Single women living alone are a prime target for all kinds of scuzzbags."

"Hey, I took that karate class you signed me up for. I'm ready. Mugger, beware!" She gave a karate chop to the air then poked Deena in the ribs but she didn't flinch.

"It's not funny."

"What's this all about? Are you nervous about the long flight? I told you it'll be a breeze." It wasn't like Deena to nag persistently. Her warnings were usually short and to the point, like the message that Joanna's self-defense class started at seven and she should wear something comfortable. It was a class Joanna hadn't considered needing but Deena had made the arrangements so she attended. "Deena, what's wrong?" Joanna studied the pained look in her eyes. "What happened?"

Deena hesitated, taking a deep soulful breath. "A woman was attacked last night. Twenty-six years old. Right in front of her apartment building. Six blocks from here."

"Is she going to be all right?"

"Eventually. She was beat up and raped."

"Oh, God. When?" Joanna gasped. "During the day?"

"Just after midnight."

"Did you catch him?"

"No, but we will. We've got a couple witnesses. We'll DNA his ass to the barn door." Deena straightened her shoulders confidently. "Just don't leave your fucking door open, EVER!"

"Okay. I promise. I won't." She opened the closet and checked the floor behind the shoe rack. "I give up. I can't find it. I've looked everywhere."

"What is that?"

"What?" Joanna continued to search the closet shelf for the umbrella.

"That what. That painting in the bottom of your closet you're trying hard not to step on."

"It's just a painting. Maybe I left my umbrella in my office."

"That's one of hers, isn't it? And don't you dare say who or I'll arrest you for trying to deceive a police officer."

28

"I'm not trying to deceive anyone." She closed the closet door and went back into the living room.

"Then you admit it. It is one Chandler's paintings."

"So what if it is? It's just a painting and I happen to like the asymmetric composition and the color palette."

"It's a picture of a naked woman sitting in a pile of leaves and the woman who painted it is a jerk."

"The woman who painted it is a fine artist. It has nothing to do with our personal history. Deciding to keep it was a purely dispassionate and objective decision."

"Is it at least worth something?"

"Probably, yes."

"Then sell it." Deena grinned brightly. "Spend the money and forget all about her."

"I am not selling it. I told you, I like it. The fact that I once had a relationship with the artist makes no difference in my appreciation of her work. Now can we go before we miss our flight? Maybe I won't need an umbrella," she said, giving one last look around.

"We aren't going to the moon, Josie. I'm sure they sell umbrellas in Italy if you need one." Deena picked up Joanna's suitcase and headed for the door. "Are you ready? It's after three."

"Yes, I'm ready." Joanna checked her watch then collected her tote bag, jacket and purse. She hated leaving something undone. It made her nervous. She liked everything in order and efficient. "Let me check the thermostat."

"Come on, Josie. You've already checked it three times."

"How do you know that?"

Deena just stared at her.

"I'm going to check it anyway." She did then pulled the door shut behind them.

"Lock the deadbolt as well as the doorknob."

"Yes, sergeant," she said as she turned the key in both. "I always do." She poked Deena in the side with her key.

When they got down to the street, an unmarked police car

was parked in front of the building, a woman in plainclothes behind the wheel.

"Are we going to the airport in this?"

"Sure. Gwen was headed that way anyway." Deena placed Joanna's suitcase in the trunk as Joanna climbed in the backseat. "You want to ride in the front?"

"No. You go ahead." Joanna scanned the seat skeptically. She had heard Deena's stories of perps urinating and vomiting in the back of squad cars.

"We just had it detailed," Gwen said, watching Joanna in the rearview mirror. "It's clean." She and Deena laughed as if sharing an inside joke. "God, it wasn't a few days ago. It smelled like a sewer."

"That's nice to know," Joanna muttered, keeping her hands off the upholstery. She looked out the window as they wound their way toward Logan Airport. The chatter from the police radio made conversation impossible. Something about a suspicious vehicle in midtown and a multicar accident on the interstate. Deena and Gwen seemed to know exactly what was going on by the codes but for Joanna it was just noise. Her mind was on Venice and the work she had to do.

By the time they checked in, made their way through security and found their gate, the flight was ready to begin boarding.

Finally seated on the aircraft next to Deena, Joanna suddenly gasped painfully and cupped her hands over her breasts, feeling for the straps.

"What's wrong? Are you air sick already?"

"I just remembered what I forgot." She covered her face with her hands and shook her head.

"What? Passport?"

"Worse than that."

"Credit card?"

"Worse. I washed out the three bras I wanted to bring. They're hanging on the shower pole."

"So? You've got one on. Just wash it out occasionally. I only brought one extra. It's no big deal."

30

"Deena, the one I'm wearing is being held together by safety pins and sheer allegiance to duty. A stiff breeze and it'll probably be down around my waist. I can't rely on it to last two days, let alone two weeks."

"That pink one you told me about?" Deena snickered. "With the one-hook closure?"

Joanna nodded.

"I just put it on while the good ones were drying. I was going to throw it away before I left but I got so flustered looking for my umbrella I forgot all about it."

"Like I said, we aren't going to the moon. I'm sure Italian women wear bras. Buy one."

"I'm quite sure Victoria's Secret doesn't have a store in Venice."

"Go braless." Deena said it loud enough to attract the attention of the woman sitting across the aisle. She smiled coyly and adjusted her blouse.

"I am not going braless," Joanna insisted out of the corner of her mouth. "I'll buy one." She snatched the magazine out of the seat pocket and began flipping through the pages. "But *you* are going with me."

"Why me?"

"Because it's your fault I forgot my bras."

"Why is it my fault?"

"Because you arrived two minutes early. If you had arrived on time I would have remembered to pack them."

"You are so full of it, Josie."

"You're going with me because I'm not going into a store where I can't speak the language to try and explain what I want and what size I need."

"What am I supposed to do? Rip open my shirt and point to my tits?"

Joanna held the magazine up to her face so no one else could hear.

"Deena, what if they don't size bra cups the same as we do? How do I explain a thirty-six C?"

"Tell her you wear an orange cup."

31

"An orange?"

"Sure. You know the universal codes for bra cup sizes. B is an egg. C is an orange. D is a grapefruit. Tell the woman in the store you wear a thirty-six orange. She'll know."

"I am not going to say that." She looked away then back at Deena. "If D is a grapefruit, what is a double D?"

"Cantaloupe," Deena whispered. "And before you ask, an A cup is a fried egg." She chuckled.

"It is not."

"Is, too. God's honest truth." She held up her hand as a pledge. "Where have you been all your life you didn't know this?"

"Well, I'm not telling a salesclerk in Venice, Italy my tits are the size of an orange."

"Have it your way. Of course, you could always just show her. Let her make up her own mind."

"You are *way* too preoccupied with breasts."

"I know." Deena gave a sigh and looked around at the women taking their seats. "I need to get some and soon."

"And you plan on hitting on some cute Italian babes?"

"Of course. Aren't you? You're single again."

"No!" Joanna replied emphatically. "I am not going to Venice to find sex."

"Why not? My guidebook says it's one of the most romantic cities in the world. And I hear the Italian women are very hot."

"You can't meet someone, develop a relationship and fall in love in just two weeks."

"Who said anything about falling in love?" Deena winked.

This is where she and Deena differed. For Joanna, there was a methodical progression to a relationship. Unlike some of her friends who considered sex as expected after dinner as dessert, she never slept with someone on the first date or the second—Cherie Levinsky notwithstanding. They were college freshmen. They were drunk. And they were salving each other's broken hearts at being rejected by first love.

For Deena, love and sex didn't necessarily need to be in the same sentence or the same person.

Joanna said, "I'll be in Venice two weeks. While I'm there I'll offer an opinion on the mosaic in Saint Mark's Cathedral then see as much of the art and culture I can squeeze in. That's all."

"And hunt yourself down a cutie with an Italian accent and legs that won't quit."

"No. Absolutely not."

"But if one does come along?"

"If one does, I'll have her knock on your door. Now, please just drop it."

"If you insist on spending your vacation without human companionship, unhappy and alone, far be it for me to interfere."

"Had you thought about what Venetian tourist attraction you'd like to see?"

"I really don't care. Anything. Maybe the Rialto Bridge."

"We can do that."

"How about you? What do you want to see, other than Saint Mark's, of course?"

"Me?" Joanna smiled at the thought. "Anything. Everything. Maybe something no one else knows to look for. The people. The ambiance of just walking the streets."

"Ladies and gentlemen, please direct your attention to the screen as we point out the safety features of this Boeing 767 aircraft," a voice said over the loudspeaker.

"Did I tell you thank you, Josie?" Deena said, leaning in to whisper.

"You're welcome, honey. I can't imagine going to Venice without you. We're going to have a great time."

Deena sat in silence for a minute, watching the safety presentation then whispered, "What are the Italian words for your place or mine? I need to practice."

Joanna laughed out loud, attracting attention from nearby passengers. "I have no idea."

CHAPTER 5

"Good morning. You're up early." Deena stood in the doorway in her bra and underwear towel drying her hair. Her body was toned and sculpted like an Olympic athlete, the result of years of martial arts training. No wonder she had no trouble attracting a bedmate, Joanna thought. That body just gets better with age. Chandler's body was like that.

"Good morning."

Deena looked over at Joanna's laptop sitting on the desk. It was closed.

"I thought you said they are providing a computer for you to use. Why did you bring that?"

"Because I like to have my own for e-mails and things."

"Then why aren't you on it e-mailing someone about French goo-gaws or Japanese thingamagigs. What's wrong? Don't they have Internet access here?"

"Yes, they do, but something is wrong with my computer. I can't get online. I think my Wi-Fi network card died."

"Then it's a good thing they have one for you to use." Deena leaned over and ruffled her hair. It was thick and wavy, something even her uniform hat couldn't hide. "What time do you have to be at the church?"

"Nine thirty. Francesca said she'd meet me at the entrance."

"I'll get dressed and we can go down to breakfast. I can smell the coffee already."

Deena slipped on jeans and a sweater and accompanied Joanna down to the breakfast room off the lobby of the hotel. It was a bright, wood-paneled room, lined with modern tables and chairs. The buffet table consisted of juice, croissants, yogurt, two kinds of dry cereal and pre-packaged toast squares with an assortment of spreads and jellies.

"Do you see a coffeepot?" Deena asked, claiming a cup and saucer from the tray.

"I think it's this." Joanna read the buttons on the espresso dispenser at the end of the table. "It looks like a do-it-yourself machine. You can choose from hot water, hot chocolate, espresso, caffé Americano, caffé latte, or hot latte."

"I know I don't want espresso. That crap will melt the caps on your teeth. I guess hot latte." Deena set her cup under the spigot and pushed the button. A stream of steaming milk dribbled into her cup, spitting out the last drops. "What's that?" She looked up under the spigot curiously. "Where's the latte? I think it's broken."

"Let me try." Joanna set her cup under the spigot and pressed the button firmly. Again steaming milk dribbled into the cup. "All I got was milk, too."

"Excuse me," Deena said, holding out her cup. "The machine is broken. I didn't get any latte. Just milk."

The girl smiled shyly. "*Buon giorno,*" she said, placing the tray under the cover. "*Si.* Latte."

35

"No. No latte. Only milk." Deena gave the cup a swirl.

"Latte," the girl said touching the rim of the cup. "Hot latte." She pointed to the sign next to the button on the machine. "Latte."

"But it's not giving latte. It's only giving hot milk," Deena argued.

The girl hurried back into the kitchen. She reappeared, carrying a dairy carton with the word Latte on it.

"Latte," she said, holding it up. "Hot latte." She pointed to the machine.

"Oh. Is milk latte?" Joanna asked, realizing what she meant.

"*Si*. Latte."

"So hot latte is just hot milk?"

"*Si*." She smiled. "If you like coffee and milk, push this one," she said with broken English, pointing to the button marked caffè latte.

"I understand. Coffee is caffè. Milk is latte. What is caffè Americano then?" Deena asked.

"Caffè with hot water."

"Diluted espresso, I guess," Joanna said.

"I'll pour them together and see what I get," Deena said, setting another cup under the spigot and dispensing caffè Americano.

"Thank you," Joanna said to the girl. "What is your name?"

"Claudia," she said, seemingly happy to be noticed.

"Thank you, Claudia."

The girl smiled shyly then retreated to the kitchen.

"See, we learned something new already." Joanna filled a plate with a croissant, a package of toast and a peach yogurt.

"What do you suppose *albicocca* means?" Deena read the card in front of the croissant tray. "Pastry?"

"I have no idea. But I'm going to try one. They look wonderful and I'm starving." Joanna tried a bite. "Did you want to come with me today? You can see Saint Mark's and get a lay of the land. We can meet later for lunch or something."

"Sure. The one thing I'd like to find is a police station. I'd like to see what they look like over here. Curiosity tells me it might be different because there are no cars."

36

Joanna sipped the last of the strong coffee. The more she drank the Venetians' idea of coffee, the more she missed her Boston blend. It definitely wasn't for wimps. After two weeks of this she expected to see hair growing on places she didn't want hair.

"I looked in my guidebook and the Italian term for police station is *stazione di polizia*. I think there is one right in Saint Mark's Square."

"Signora, you require *polizia*?" Claudia asked, overhearing their conversation as she refilled the yogurt tray.

"Yes."

"Is everything all right with you?"

"Yes. Everything is all right. I just want to visit a police station."

"You want to visit Italian police *stazione*?" Claudia seemed skeptical.

"Yes. I want to see what they look like inside."

"You're going to have to tell her," Joanna whispered. "She thinks you're a crazy terrorist."

"I am a law enforcement officer," she said but Claudia still stood staring down at her. "Police." Deena patted her chest.

"You *Polizia*?"

"Yes. Police sergeant Deena Garren."

Claudia drew a deep surprised breath as her eyes widened. She thought a moment then brightened. "You have *pistola*?"

"A pistol? Not with me, no."

Claudia seemed disappointed the American wasn't packing heat. "But you have *pistola*?" Her curiosity and the subject of her questions made Deena uncomfortable and Joanna could see it.

"Yes. I have one at home."

"And you shoot this *pistola*?"

Deena hesitated, wiping her mouth with her napkin. She looked over at Joanna, a sudden and desperate pain shown in her eyes.

"Sometimes." She stood up. "We better get going if you have to be there by nine-thirty, Josie."

"Yes, we better. Let me go up and get my coat and purse."
Joanna knew Deena needed an escape from this conversation.
She took the last bite of her croissant and followed Deena across
the lobby. Deena vaulted up the stairs, taking the steps two at a
time, Joanna hurrying to keep up with her.

"Deena, I'm sure Claudia didn't mean anything by it. She was
just curious. You know how young people are." Joanna followed
her down the hall.

"It was no big deal." Deena disappeared inside her door,
closing it behind her.

She may have said it was no big deal but Joanna knew better.
Deena was a good cop. Fair, honest and dedicated. She took her
job very seriously. It was that dedication to duty that made her
decision to draw and fire on another human being that much
harder. Joanna went into her room and collected her things,
giving Deena a moment alone. Finally she went through the
bathroom and leaned her forehead against Deena's door.

"Are you okay, Deena?"

A minute later the door opened and Deena reappeared, her
smile bright as ever.

"You ready to go?"

"Sure." Joanna smiled back at her. "Are you okay, honey?"

"I'm fine." Deena widened her smile. "Let's go be tourists."
The doom and gloom that Claudia had uncovered by her
questions were gone. Deena was her happy self again.

It was a cool blustery day, making Joanna glad she brought
her scarf. She and Deena blended into the crowd along the Ca'
Maddalena on the way back to the vaporetto stop. They validated
their travel cards by scanning them in front of the meter and
waited on the landing for the number one water bus.

"How do we know which way to go?" Deena asked, reading
the charts on the wall. "We are here. And San Marco is here. I'm
turned around."

"The train station is that way," Joanna said, pointing up the
canal to the right. "Saint Mark's has to be the other way. So is the
Rialto Bridge."

"So we take the vaporetto coming from the right, going to the left?" Deena leaned out, looking in both directions. "It might be fun to get lost in Venice." Deena folded her collar up around her chin to the cool breeze blowing down the canal.

"I'd rather not get lost. I brought my map and my guidebook and I'm not afraid to use them." She patted her purse.

A cumbersome metal boat pulled up to the platform, bumping it ever so gently. The passengers waited while the attendant lassoed the metal post on the landing and opened the railing, then stepped off. Joanna, Deena and six other passengers made their way onto the crowded deck. Once they were loaded, the attendant slid the railing closed, untied the rope and the vaporetto lumbered away from the dock. Joanna and Deena pushed their way through the crowd to the middle of the boat.

"This must be the morning commute. Do you want to sit in the back or stand?" Joanna asked, struggling to keep her balance.

"Let's sit. It's too crowded to see anything." Deena led the way into the passenger compartment in the back of the boat and found two seats by the window. The vaporetto was filled with camera-toting tourists ogling at the sites and locals carrying grocery sacks and briefcases. Deena pulled her camera from her pocket and snapped a few shots. Joanna was satisfied to watch, soaking in the ambiance.

"Look! That must be a police cruiser," Deena said, pointing at the passing blue and white power boat marked *Polizia*. "And there's a woman in there. Good deal. Venice has female police officers. Nice uniforms."

"Can you see the uniforms?" Joanna squinted through the condensation on the window.

"No. But I can use my imagination." She grinned.

"I should have known better than to ask."

"I guess everything has to be moved by boat. People, packages, produce, trash. Everything." Deena was fascinated with the canal traffic. "That must be a moving van." She pointed at a barge piled high with furniture and boxes.

Joanna studied the buildings and architectural details along the canal as Deena watched the boats and people. The boat moved from one vaporetto stop to the next, discharging and taking on passengers in a constant stream of activity. As they approached the Rialto Bridge they could see dozens of tourists looking down, pointing and taking pictures.

"Look, Josie," Deena said, elbowing Joanna and pointing to the young couple at the apex of the bridge, locked in a lover's embrace. "Looks like a good place to kiss."

Joanna watched until they slipped under the bridge and out of sight. The guidebooks were right, she thought. The top of the Rialto Bridge is a popular lover's hangout. She sighed and went back to watching the buildings. The farther down the canal they went, the more crowded the boat became.

"How many more stops before we get off?" Deena asked, snapping a picture as they floated past a lavish looking hotel with a balcony dining room. Joanna pulled out her map.

"Three more."

"Maybe we better start moving up through the crowd."

They began maneuvering up the aisle, working their way into the crowded standing area.

"I can't see anything," Joanna said, grabbing onto Deena's sleeve so they wouldn't get separated. "This is like riding the MTA at rush hour."

"We're almost there," Deena said, shuffling toward the railing. "Hold onto your purse, Josie. Keep it in front of you."

The boat bumped the dock hard, bringing on gasps from the passengers. As soon as the railing was opened a flood of people poured off the boat. Like water through a ruptured dam, Deena and Joanna were carried along with the crowd. Joanna lost sight of Deena. She followed the crowd onto the sidewalk, afraid to stop and look for fear she would be trampled.

"Over here, Josie," Deena called, waving from a safe position near the seawall.

Joanna waited for the crowd to dissipate then crossed to her.

"That was just like Boston," she chuckled. "Keep moving or get run over."

"No kidding. Come on. Let's find this Saint Mark's Square you've been talking about."

"It should be ahead and to the left around that building."

They walked past a row of curio booths selling everything from key rings to feathered Venetian masks. The San Marco stop seemed to be a central hub for vaporetti from all directions, clogging the entrance to the Piazza San Marco with a thick crowd of curious spectators and greedy vendors. As soon as they rounded the corner and found an open space to breathe, Joanna looked up and stopped dead in her tracks, causing Deena to run into her.

"Oh, my heavens," Joanna gasped, staring at the huge ornate domes and gothic architecture that was unmistakably Saint Mark's Cathedral. "Look at that, Deena." She stood with her mouth open, transfixed by its sheer size and presence. "Basilica di San Marco."

"Okay but can we move out of the way. We're holding up traffic here."

"Let me just look for a minute." Her eyes darted from one onion-shaped dome to the next then to the statues perched across the roof. "Look at that. Byzantine gothic. The chiesa d'oro. The church of gold."

"Looks kind of gingerbready, doesn't it?" Deena said, squinting up at the detailing.

"Ornate isn't the half of it. It's been embellished and ornamented with more riches than some third world countries own. Venetian merchants plundered and pillaged all over the world to decorate this church. It's a testament to thievery." Joanna smiled over at Deena. "You should appreciate that. Almost everything on and in this church was stolen from another country." Joanna started up the piazza toward the mammoth church.

"And we're going to pay to see it?"

"No, it's free. At least the sanctuary is. The upper-floor museum has a fee. That's where the bronze horses are. The real ones. Stolen from Constantinople in 1204. Those on the roof are reproductions."

41

As they made their way up the pavement, past the ornate pink-marbled Doge's Palace and the over three-hundred-foot-tall Campanile, Deena seemed impressed by the sheer number of people filling the immense square. Everyone seemed to be doing the same thing, gasping, pointing and taking pictures of the awe-inspiring buildings.

"God, Josie. There must be thousands of people here."

"And they are all here to see the same thing we're here to see."

A line had formed from the center door of the basilica back to the corner of the building but it was moving fast enough to keep those waiting from becoming impatient. Joanna and Deena followed the line, staring up at the arches and their golden mosaics as they moved along.

"Aren't they magnificent?" Joanna said, pointing upward. "The mosaics in that archway tell the story of how two merchants stole Saint Mark's body and brought it here to Venice."

"Even he was stolen goods?" Deena couldn't help but chuckle. "Damn. Someone should have done some hard time over this place."

"You have to appreciate the art history and ignore the criminality of it."

"If you say so." Deena stood in line behind Joanna but her attention was on the sea of young beautiful women milling about the square. "I never realized tourists are such gorgeous people." She winked at a young woman who walked past smiling demurely.

"Come on, Deena. The line is moving." Joanna pulled at her sleeve.

"Do you know what this Francesca person you're supposed to meet looks like?"

"Sort of. I saw a picture of her online. It wasn't very good but at least I know she is fifty-ish, thin, has long dark hair and seems to wear stylish clothes. Francesca DiCarmo."

"Red highlights?"

"I have no idea. I couldn't tell from the picture online. Why?"

"There's a thin woman over there by the door. She's at least fifty. She looks like she is waiting for someone." Deena's keen power of observation had singled out an indeed stylish-looking woman wearing dramatic makeup, stiletto heels and wool coat over a matching dress. She had a thin bony face and was wearing large gold earrings. Her hair was wildly coiffed to the side, looking like a wave breaking against the shore.

"Could be. Let's go see." Joanna stepped out of line and crossed to the woman. "Excuse me. Do you speak English?"

"*Si*. Little bit," the woman said, looking past her as if searching the crowd.

"I'm looking for Francesca DiCarmo."

"*Si*. I am Francesca DiCarmo," she said, making the name sound lyrical. "And you?"

"I am Joanna Lucas from the Straus Center in Boston."

"You?" She looked Joanna up and down. "But you are so young." She smiled warmly then grabbed Joanna and hugged her, kissing both cheeks. "I have been waiting for you."

"How do you do? This is my friend, Deena Garren. She is traveling with me."

"Hello, Ms. DiCarmo," Deena said, extending her hand. Francesca didn't seem to be intimidated by Deena's formality. She ignored her hand and gave her a hug as well, kissing her cheeks.

"Deena, come inside with us. See our basilica," Francesca said, waving extravagantly as if this was her home and she was inviting them in for dinner. "Come, Joanna. I will show you the mosaics you will study."

Francesca's English was broken but the soft lyrical tones made it sound poetic. She locked arms with Joanna on one side and Deena on the other and led them through the door of the basilica.

The floor of the dimly lit narthex was damp with puddles of standing water. They climbed three steps and entered the sanctuary, Francesca chatting away about how glad she was Joanna was there and how honored they were to have her in

Venice. But Joanna's eyes were on the immediate and spectacular grandeur upon entering the church. Every inch of the high, arched ceiling with its celestial domes covered with golden mosaics gleaming down at them. Joanna had read about it and seen hundreds of pictures of the basilica but to stand in its majesty for the first time was breathtaking. Deena, too, seemed mesmerized by the immense size and the overwhelming splendor.

"Wow," Deena said, her eyes moving over the ceiling. "This is really something."

"Are you also a conservator, Ms Garren?"

"No, not me. Joanna is the art aficionado." Deena squinted up at one of the figures in the mosaic overhead.

"She's my traveling companion," Joanna said, pulling her eyes down to the mosaics on the floor.

Francesca unhooked a velvet rope barrier and escorted them into the middle of the sanctuary where rows of folding chairs marked where parishioners sat. Joanna immediately noticed the floor was deeply rippled.

"I didn't realize the floor was so damaged and uneven."

"It can be as much as thirty centimeters," Francesca said, rubbing the toe of her shoe over the marble mosaics.

"That's nearly twelve inches." Joanna squatted and touched the floor, tracing her fingers along the gray mortar.

Twenty minutes of staring at the floor and listening to the damage was enough for Deena. When Francesca offered to show Joanna the restoration being done in other parts of the church, she excused herself and went in search of a police station.

"I'll see you back at the hotel this afternoon, Josie."

"Have fun, honey."

"Oh, I will." Deena had that devilish twinkle in her eye that meant she would be admiring Venetian babes, not Venetian art.

Joanna followed Francesca up steep stone stairs to the second floor and a small corner room marked Private. It was filled with bottles of cleaning fluids, boxes of tools and light bars mounted on tripods. But it was the microscope partially hidden behind a box of rags that brought a smile to her face.

"Boom-mounted articulating microscope," Joanna said, admiring the piece. She snapped on the light under the stage. "This will come in handy."

She draped her coat over a chair and pushed up the sleeves of her sweater. She had instantly changed from an awestruck tourist to a dedicated professional. "Let's see what else we have here."

"Joanna, this is Signor Vittori. He will be in charge of repairing the floor in the baptistery."

Joanna looked up to see a man in an ill-fitting wool sport coat and thick, wavy hair standing in the doorway. His hands were in his jacket pockets and he had a less-than-enthusiastic expression on his face. Francesca said something to him in Italian Joanna assumed was an introduction with a brief history of her qualifications.

"How do you do, Signor Vittori?" Joanna smiled politely and offered her hand.

"Vittori," he said, correcting her pronunciation with an exaggerated roll of the r. His handshake was limp and damp. Joanna noticed a judgmental wrinkle forming at the corner of his mouth after looking her up and down. He said something to Francesca Joanna didn't understand but the tone of his voice told her he was either challenging her age, her qualifications or perhaps merely the fact she was a woman.

Francesca waved him off with a frown. "Come, Joanna. We will look at the floor in the baptistery."

Francesca led the way back downstairs, opened the heavy door on the side of the sanctuary and stepped down into a cavernous side chapel. She snapped on the light, illuminating the altar and large crucifix. A marble baptismal font sat on a raised stage in the middle of the room. It had an ornately decorated metal dome lid. Like the basilica itself, the walls, ceilings and floor of the baptistery chapel were covered with marble, mosaics and granite detailing. The word BAPTISTA was inlaid into the gilded mosaic décor along the far wall. Like the floor in the sanctuary, the surface was uneven and worn, with some of the tessera either cracked or missing.

"Here, Joanna," Francesca said, standing next to the stage. She held out her arms, marking the area to be repaired. "This part of the floor, from the baptismal stage to the back. You can see the damage."

Signor Vittori watched as Joanna circled the area, studying the loose mortar and cracked tesserae. She then circled the stage, examining the floor on the other side for comparison.

"No, no," he grumbled, waving her back. "Here, Signora. This. Only this."

"I know," Joanna said as she continued to study the floor all the way up to the altar.

He said something to Francesca. Joanna didn't need to understand Italian to know he wasn't happy.

"Be patient," Francesca said angrily. "Let her look."

"It's hard to tell much in this light." Joanna crouched down, holding herself on her fingertips as she sighted along the floor, her cheek all but touching the tiles. "We'll have to get some better illumination down here."

"We will supply everything you need," Francesca said reassuringly.

"I'll need more than lights. I'll need a mass spectrometer, your boom arm microscope and perhaps the use of x-ray equipment." She picked at the edge of a loose tile. "I have a list of solutions I'll also need. If you can't get them, I can have them flown in from Boston."

"We can get them, I'm sure."

"Signora, we are ready to begin work," Signor Vittori said, showing no patience. "I have six workers brought here at great expense. It isn't wise to keep them waiting."

"I'm sure not, Signor Vittori." Joanna went to the other end of the damaged area and squatted, again sighting along the floor. "That, along with the expense of bringing me here for analysis, is sufficient justification for me to give as thorough and comprehensive a report as my years of experience can provide. Wouldn't you agree?" She walked past him, smiling. He didn't reply. "And I'm sure I don't have to tell you how time-consuming

46

that process can be when so many factors have to be taken into consideration." If Signor Vittori wanted to be difficult, so could she.

"It is the substrate that is the most troubling, Joanna." Francesca pointed to a small area where the marble tiles were missing altogether, exposing a cracked and crumbling underfloor. "Signor Vittori is concerned it has sustained sufficient damage to compromise the integrity of the floor."

"*Si*," he quickly agreed. "Underneath is no good."

"We don't want to spend so much repairing the mosaic if the floor underneath will only crumble and ruin it," Francesca added.

"So you want my opinion on whether the granite subfloor will support the mosaic restoration, right?"

"*Si*." Francesca nodded in Signor Vittori's direction. "You can see how the tesserae are loosening."

"Then the decision to replace the mosaics has already been made?" Joanna cast a curious look in Signor Vittori's direction. "You've already decided it is not salvageable?"

"*Si*. This is garbage." He hooked the toe of his shoe under the corner of a loose tessera and flipped it out, sending it sliding across the floor.

Joanna retrieved it, examining the edges.

"It will be difficult for me to determine the stability of the subfloor when I can't see it. I'd like to run some tests for pH and calcium content."

"My employees will help with whatever tests you need to conduct," he offered. But it sounded more like he was trying to speed things up than to merely offer assistance.

"Thank you, but that won't be necessary." Joanna didn't need help. And she certainly didn't want his employees gumming up the results. She had a feeling his interest in her analysis ran along economic lines. The more damage she found, the more money he would make. "I'd like to bring down some lights from the lab and a get a closer look," Joanna said, shedding her coat.

"We'll have to wait until after mass," Francesca said, nodding

47

toward the man spreading a cloth across the altar. "Daily mass is said in the baptistery for the local residents at ten o'clock. Yesterday was a special ceremony. That's why it was closed all day but mass is usually said each morning. Would you like to attend mass with me?"

Joanna declined the invitation. She wanted to spend some time upstairs in the workroom familiarizing herself with the equipment.

Like a salmon swimming upstream, Joanna worked her way through the incoming crowd back toward the staircase that led upstairs. As she passed through the double doors from the sanctuary into the narthex, she became sandwiched against the wall by a large man carrying a backpack. The man didn't give even an inch and as he slung the backpack from one shoulder to the other he whacked first Joanna then another woman on the other side. The woman groaned loudly, mumbling what Joanna heard as asshole.

Not in a house of worship, lady. I don't care if he broke your foot. I'm not Catholic but, you don't curse in a church.

Joanna looked through the crowd, trying to see the rude woman. She felt an obligation to at least frown her disapproval for such language. But the instant she made eye-contact with the woman, Joanna felt the blood drain from her head. She leaned back against the door to keep from fainting.

"Hello, Joanna," the woman said, her eyes capturing Joanna's and holding them.

Joanna felt her throat close. She couldn't reply or even move. She could barely breathe as she stared.

"Chandler, come on. I want to get a seat up front before they're all taken." An attractive woman with long chestnut hair tugged at Chandler's sleeve, pulling her along the wall. Chandler let her gaze linger on Joanna for a moment before moving through the door into the baptistery.

As if she had been nothing more than a mirage, Chandler disappeared without another word, leaving Joanna standing in the middle of the entrance.

Joanna followed the crowd back into the church, mindlessly moving toward the baptistery door. She placed her hand on the doorknob. Was that really Chandler? Of course, it was. She wasn't hallucinating. What was Chandler Cardin doing in Venice, Italy? Who was the woman with her? Was she her lover, her new girlfriend? Why did Joanna care?

She hasn't changed a bit. She doesn't look a day older than the last time I saw her two years ago. And she still looks good.

Joanna released the doorknob and stepped back, her heart pounding in her chest. She didn't want another look. That would be too painful. She turned and hurried toward the stairs and the workroom. Venice was a big city. If she was lucky, this one chance meeting would be the last.

CHAPTER 6

Joanna didn't tell Deena about running into Chandler. She didn't want to hear Deena's idea of how she should have handled it. It was a quick five-second chance meeting. Nothing more. Joanna wasn't sure she would ever need tell her.

"Want to try the food at that place we saw down the street?" Deena asked, following Joanna out into the crowded street.

"That's fine with me."

Once inside, they were escorted to the only available table near the front of the café. It was a small table tucked behind a long table of noisy big-eating tourists. From their conversation, Joanna assumed they were from one of the enormous cruise ships anchored in the lagoon.

When Deena went to the restroom, Joanna let her gaze drift around the room, stopping at each piece of art hung on the walls. Most needed a good dusting. As she drew her eyes back, something else caught her eye. Joanna sat staring across the room in disbelief. Was this punishment for her arrogance toward Signor Vittori? Or was fate playing a cruel practical joke at her expense? Whatever it was left her dizzy. Not again, she thought.

Chandler Cardin was sitting at the corner table sipping a glass of wine and staring back at her. Joanna looked away for a moment but curiosity brought her eyes back to Chandler. Chandler lifted her glass as if offering a salute then sipped ever so slowly, her gaze holding Joanna's in soft unspoken communication. As if her brain was stuck on autopilot, Joanna reached for her glass, ready to return the salute.

"Damn, that was a tiny bathroom. You've got to know what you plan to do before you go in because there sure isn't room to change your mind," Deena said, returning to the table. She obviously hadn't seen Chandler but she did see the stunned look on Joanna's face. "Josie, are you okay? You look like you've seen a ghost." She hitched her chair in and finished her last swig of wine. "Joanna?"

Joanna lowered her eyes as her heart began pounding in her chest.

What is she doing here? Why is she disrupting my vacation? And why are her eyes still as soft as velvet?

Joanna knew her face had initially drained of its color but she now felt a flush racing up her body, warming her cheeks. Chandler Cardin was sitting twenty feet away and that alone was enough to ignite a firestorm of emotion.

"Josie, what is it?" Deena turned and scanned the room, searching for whatever had Joanna silent and stupefied. At first she didn't seem to notice anything but then did a double-take. "Fuck!"

Unable to find words, Joanna placed her hand on Deena's leg to quiet the outburst. But Deena was having none of it. "What the hell is *she* doing here? I'm going over there." Deena moved to stand up but Joanna grabbed her sleeve.

"No, Deena. Please. Just ignore her." Joanna kept her gaze down.

"You may have forgiven her but I haven't." Deena perched on the edge of her chair like a fighter waiting for the bell to signal the start of a new round. "What is she doing in Venice?"

"I have no idea."

"Well, I think you're about to find out. She's coming over."

Joanna gasped but didn't look up until a pair of shoes moved into her line of sight.

"Hello, Joanna."

"Hello, Chandler," she replied, barely able to breathe.

Good grief, I sound like a teenager at a sock hop. Snap out of it. Remember, she cheated on you. This woman is nothing more than a piece of my past, like the croissant I had for breakfast.

"Why don't you just keep moving, lady?" Deena snapped.

"I remember you. You're the cop," Chandler said with a quirky grin.

"That's right. And you're the artist who paints naked women, that is after you've slept with them."

Chandler laughed out loud and said, "I see you're still protecting Joanna from evil-doers."

"Damn right, I am."

"Deena, please. You're making a scene," Joanna begged, hoping to diffuse the hostility between the two women. She knew Deena would have no qualms about wrestling this woman to the floor, even if she wasn't on duty in her own jurisdiction. Deena had always said what Chandler needed was a good butt-kicking over what she had done to Joanna.

"I guess this means you won't be inviting me to your hotel for drinks and small talk." Chandler's sarcasm only enraged her more. Deena was on her feet in a microsecond, standing face-to-face with Chandler.

"That's enough," Joanna demanded, pulling Deena back into her chair. "Stop it, both of you."

"She started it," Deena hissed.

"I just came over to say hello and ask what you're doing in Venice."

"We're minding our own business. Why don't you try it sometime?" Deena said.

"Can you call off your guard dog?" Chandler asked.

"Deena, please stop. I can handle this myself. I don't need your help."

"Thank you," Chandler said, smiling down at Joanna. "See, we can be civil. Now, may I ask again? What are you doing in Venice? Vacation?"

"Yes, partially." Joanna couldn't help notice the way Chandler's eyes sparkled when she smiled. And her fingers were still gracefully long and expressive. The most talented fingers in the world, she suddenly found herself thinking.

She's still wearing that silly ring I gave her. Why doesn't she throw it away? Doesn't she know it was cheap costume jewelry?

"Joanna is here for a consult," Deena said arrogantly.

"Consult on what? You're still working for the Straus Center then, right?" Chandler's eyes moved down over Joanna, as if revisiting each and every one of her curves.

"Yes, I'm still working at the Straus Center. What are you doing in Venice?" Joanna asked, feeling Chandler's eyes undressing her.

"I live here. I'm teaching portraiture." She nodded back toward the table where she had been sitting. "Private lessons."

Joanna hadn't noticed whoever was sitting at the table with Chandler. Probably the woman who was with her at the basilica. But at that moment, Joanna didn't care. She was amazed by Chandler's news that she lived here, and the words private lessons dug up an old memory she had no intention of revisiting. But she and Deena both looked in that direction at the same moment.

"Do you want to meet her?" Chandler asked, looking back at the red-haired woman. She was wearing large sunglasses but it was clear she had been watching them closely.

"No," Joanna said instantly. She didn't want to meet the latest notch on Chandler's bedpost.

53

"Sure," Deena said, giving the woman another look.

Please, Deena. Don't say anything rude. Don't make an even bigger spectacle of yourself. We don't know this woman. My past is none of her business.

Before Joanna could say they were just leaving and didn't have time to meet her, Chandler turned and waved the woman over.

"Macy, this is Joanna Lucas," Chandler said, putting her arm around the woman and pulling her closer. "And this is Deena…"

"Garren," Deena supplied when Chandler didn't seem to remember then gave the woman a quick up and down perusal.

"Ladies, this is Macy Whittaker."

"Hello," Macy said cheerfully.

That's a fake smile, Joanna couldn't help thinking. No one smiles that big when they meet strangers. Yep, that's fake.

"Hello," Joanna said with a guarded smile.

"Hi," Deena added, giving her another critical look.

"Are you two art students also?" Macy asked.

"Me?" Deena chuckled.

"No, we're here on vacation." Joanna replied before Deena could say anything crude.

"Joanna is an art conservator. She works for Harvard University's Straus Center for art conservation and restoration," Chandler said.

"Oh, wow. That's sounds very prestigious. Like repairing ripped canvases and stuff?"

"That's a different department. I'm involved with the restoration of art objects and sculpture."

"Like figurines and stuff?"

"Yes, among other things." Joanna allowed herself a quick study of Chandler's face, reacquainting herself with every line and detail.

For heaven's sake, don't stare at the woman. She'll think I approve of this meeting.

"Are you American?" Deena asked.

"Lord, no. I'm Canadian, from Toronto." As Macy pulled off

her sunglasses, revealing a pair of gorgeous big brown eyes, there was a noticeable gasp from Deena. "Where are you from?"

"Bostonian, born and bred," Deena said then gave a throaty moan.

"I've been there. At least at the airport. Lousy customs. By the time I got through the lines I thought I was going to pee my pants. Geez." She rolled her eyes.

Macy Whittaker was an attractive woman, maybe thirty, Joanna guessed as she conducted the dutiful ex-girlfriend appraisal of the new arm candy. A little young for Chandler but who was she to say. Five-feet-six. Size eight skintight jeans. Auburn hair with stunning highlights, probably not a natural color. High cheekbones. Skillful makeup. Stylish dresser. Ample cleavage. Yes, Chandler had done well for herself this time. From the corner of her eye, Joanna could also see Chandler had an unmistakable glow. Macy must be very special indeed.

"So, you're an art student?" Deena asked.

"Is that what Chandler told you? That's a convenient term for it, I guess. What do you do?"

"I'm in law enforcement."

"You're a cop?" She laughed out loud, shaking her head.

"What's wrong with being a cop?"

"Nothing. You just didn't strike me as cop material. You look more like an office manager or a CPA."

"And you are an expert on such things?" Deena asked with a chuckle.

"I'm no expert but yes, I've met my share of police officers," Macy replied confidently.

"You've met lots of police officers?" Deena asked doubtfully.

"Well, not lots but a few. I got a speeding ticket from a cute female officer once. She had zero tolerance though."

"How fast were you going?"

"Sixty-two in a forty-five zone."

"That'll do it." Deena's eyes did one more scan of Macy's trim little body, this time more slowly and deliberately.

"Okay, cop, tell me. What can a person say to get out of a

ticket?" Macy asked, pulling up a nearby chair.

Deena just laughed.

"I mean it. Cops have no sympathy when it comes to women drivers. It's like we are supposed to stay home, tend the young 'uns and leave the driving to men. What's that all about?"

"I think you're generalizing. I don't do that, obviously. How many tickets have you had?" Deena occasionally tossed Chandler a suspicious look as if checking to see if she was still behaving.

"Only four. Two for speeding and two for illegal turns. But one wasn't my fault. I was coerced." Macy turned to Chandler and motioned for her to pull up a chair.

"How can you be coerced into speeding?"

"It wasn't for speeding. I was driving home from the mall. It was late and this car started following me. Around one corner, then the next and the next. Right on my ass for blocks. I couldn't see who it was because they had really dark tinted windows. It was freaking me out so I decided to make an illegal left turn to try and get away from them."

"But a cop saw you do it, right?"

"There wasn't another car anywhere for miles. That's why I did it. The next thing I knew, there was a flashing light on the roof and a siren blasting. It was a freakin' unmarked police car. She was escorting me home for protection."

Deena burst out laughing.

"It's not funny. Cops should have to let you know they are behind you so you don't do something stupid like that. It should be a law."

"Usually people slow down when they see a squad car behind them, that is unless they are trying to hide something, like drugs or a stolen car. Then they floor it and try to get away. The officer must have thought you were fleeing for a reason."

"Yeah, well, she gave me a ticket for an illegal left turn, then asked if I wanted her to follow me home."

"Did you let her?"

"Sure. I'm no dummy."

While Deena was listening to Macy's tale of woe, Joanna sat

quietly, hands in her lap. But she couldn't keep her eyes from drifting up to meet Chandler's. Joanna found herself worried about what she was wearing. Was it clean? Was it good enough? She had no reason to be self-conscious. But she was.

"Where are you staying?" Macy asked, slipping out of her jacket. The bounce of her bosom didn't go unnoticed. Deena's eyes veritably jumped down her cleavage, undressing her all the way down to the tiny nipples making an imprint on her white blouse.

"Hotel Forcola," Deena said, tossing her thumb back over her shoulder. "It's not far."

"I've stayed there. Cute place and they have really unique light fixtures in the breakfast room."

Deena and Joanna looked at each other blankly.

"They're amber frosted glass figurines of a kneeling woman holding up the shade." Macy put one hand on her hip and held the other over her head. "Like this, but naked."

"I have to see these light fixtures." Deena chuckled.

"They remind me of Chandler's paintings," Macy added. "They aren't gross or anything. They have a demure sophistication about them. What is it they call that kind of thing, Chandler? The classic nude." Macy looked at her watch and gasped. "Oh, good grief. I'm going to be late. Got to go. It was nice meeting you, Joanna. You too, Deena." She shook their hands, grabbed her coat and hurried toward the door.

"I'll go with you." Chandler stood but looked down at Joanna. "It was nice seeing you again, Joanna." She took Joanna's hand and held it. "I hope you enjoy your stay in Venice. Deena, nice to see you, too." She dropped a strained though polite nod in Deena's direction then looked back at Joanna, still holding her hand. "Perhaps our paths will cross again." She finally shook Joanna's hand but it was more of an afterthought. She then followed Macy out the door.

"What the heck was that?" Deena declared. "I mean, damn. Did you see her?"

"Yes, I saw her." Joanna meant Chandler but she had a strong

57

feeling Deena meant Macy. They both sat staring at the door. Instead of saying anything, they each reached for their glass and gave a small moan.

CHAPTER 7

Chandler reached over and pushed the alarm clock button before it could shriek. She had been lying in bed staring up at the ceiling for hours. She wasn't even sure she had ever really gone to sleep. Every time she closed her eyes she could see Joanna sitting there with Deena, dressed in an adorable sweater, her figure deliciously perfect, like it had always been. How dare she? Chandler turned onto her side, crumpling the pillow under her head. How dare she still have that look, that delicate sophistication, that tempting sensuality? How dare she still be the most attractive woman she had ever met? Yet the most unapproachable. Joanna obviously hadn't forgotten their past, including the last agonizingly painful moments of it. Chandler turned on her other side and stared out the window at the first golden glimmer of sunrise. She finally kicked the covers back and climbed out of bed.

After a shower, a cup of coffee and a last heel of yesterday's bread she headed for the store. She had let her shopping list grow to an almost unmanageable load, something she rarely did. Like most Venetians, she shopped daily, making the sacks lighter and easy to carry up the two flights of narrow stairs to her apartment. With her three empty tote sacks she headed for the open-air market behind the Rialto Bridge for fresh vegetables, fruit and perhaps some fresh-from-the-sea fish. Even before she stepped off the vaporetto she could smell the pungent stench of the fish stalls. It permeated the air for blocks and hung on like a bad memory even on days the market was closed.

It took some haggling but she secured a nice filet of cuttlefish for three and a half Euros. Her American accent as she fumbled with the language seemed to always give the vendors license to jack up the price or lean a heavy thumb on the scale. She bought a sackful of produce, a loaf of crusty bread, some cheese and sliced meat from a butcher shop and a bag of freshly ground coffee before heading home. As she climbed the stairs she could hear music. She unlocked the door on the second floor that led up a second staircase right into her living room.

"You here already?" she shouted above the music.

Macy came to the top of the stairs and smiled down at her.

"Yes. And where have you been? Shopping, I hope. You don't have anything to eat in this kitchen. I thought my place was sparse. You don't even have crackers." She took one of the sacks Chandler was wrestling up the stairs.

"I didn't know I was feeding you as well as teaching you."

"Of course, you are. Read the fine print in the contract." Macy rummaged in the sacks, looking for something to call breakfast. "I want a croissant. Didn't you buy any?"

"No, I didn't go to the grocery store. I was at the market. And what contract are we talking about?"

"The one that says the student is entitled to partake of the instructor's knowledge and good humor at any hour of the day or night, regardless of weather, health or the instructor's temperament. And what is that smell?" Macy pulled Chandler's coat sleeve up to her nose. "Let me guess. You bought fish."

"Yes, and if you don't like it, go home." Chandler hung her coat on the hook behind the door, but stopped to give the sleeve a sniff, wrinkling her nose at the stench. "I just washed this. I've got to stop wearing a coat to the fish market." She came back into the kitchen to make coffee.

Her apartment was small even by Italian standards. The main space served as living room, dining room and office with one wall dedicated to a kitchen. Two faded upholstered chairs were set diagonally on either side of a stack of antique round wooden boxes Chandler used as an end table. The dining facilities were a tiny table and two rickety wooden chairs. The corner desk was a wire framed affair she had bought in Padua and brought home in parts. It held her laptop computer and telephone, the only things in the room from the modern era. The kitchen had a two-burner stove, a small sink and a refrigerator better suited for a college dorm room. It was mounted on the wall between the only two cabinets. Next to the stove was a combination washer-dryer unit, a small European design housing both in one machine. On top was a wooden cutting board that served as a workstation for anything from cooking to ironing. A doorway led to the bedroom and an oversized twin bed. Chandler hadn't been able to find fitted sheets that fit the odd size mattress, resulting in nightly battles to keep the sheet on the bed. She reminded herself it was just a rental apartment and it would do for now.

At forty-seven, Chandler had a diverse, if not speckled history. She had worked at everything from car-hopping to plucking chickens at a poultry processing plant, all of it to put herself through college to earn a bachelor's degree in secondary education. It took her exactly one semester to realize teaching art to high school students, who would rather flip paint at each other than create works of art, was not her life's calling. She went back to the processing plant while earning her master's degree in fine arts. By the time she was thirty-five, she had taught a year at a junior college in upstate New York, two years at NYU and a year at the prestigious although snobbish Smith College in New England. The jobs paid the rent but did little to satisfy her artistic soul. It wasn't until she'd been snowed-in over Christmas break in Northampton, Massachusetts that Chandler turned to the one thing she had never allowed to flourish, her painting. The long cold days and nights allowed her to find and express herself on canvas.

By Easter she had sold two portraitures and had orders for three more, surprising herself at how easy it was to turn a hobby into a career. A career she loved. So she quit teaching and turned herself to full-time work as a painter. And happily so. There were no tests to grade. No dull faculty meetings to attend. No ambivalent students to motivate. The first few years hadn't been as lucrative as she had hoped, forcing her to turn to occasional stints as private instructor to the avant-garde who fancied themselves artists. Who, with only a little guidance, were positive they could perfect their true artistic flair. Far be it from Chandler to disagree, even though most couldn't tell azure blue from cobalt blue. The money was good. And she had learned to critique without being judgmental. If the client said it was a peony, then it was a peony, never mind it looked like a squashed head of lettuce.

Chandler poured herself a cup of coffee and carried it up the spiral wrought-iron staircase to a glass-enclosed room on the roof, her studio. Originally a rooftop greenhouse, it was small like everything else in her world right now but at least it was a place she could go to teach, to paint and to think.

Macy followed with a cup of tea and stalk of celery. "Did I tell you, I killed off the taxi driver?" she said, looking out at the square below.

"No, you didn't. I thought you liked him." Chandler sipped her coffee while she studied the painting on the easel.

"Nope, he was annoying me. I hate men like that." She turned and gave a smug little grin. "I put a bullet right through his ear while he was chewing on a toothpick."

"Well, I hope he had it coming."

Macy had been an easy student. She had a likable personality and enough talent to keep Chandler amused at her progress. Currently living in Venice, no one would ever guess Macy Whittaker was the author responsible for four in a series of best-selling mysteries set in the European drug-riddled underworld of mob crime and violence. Perpetually inquisitive and energetically charismatic, Macy was the girl next door and the neighborhood sexpot all rolled into one.

"Is this your foreground?" Chandler pointed at the shadows drifting across the canvas.

"No. That's going to be a curtain behind the chair. Why? Doesn't it look like a curtain?"

Chandler looked at her skeptically.

"Okay, it doesn't look like a curtain. It started out to be a stream but I didn't like it. I decided to bring the setting inside instead of doing a landscape." Macy smirked at her work. "I may go back to outside."

"How about go back and look at your light source? Your shadows represent light from both sides. In a natural setting, that wouldn't happen."

Macy studied it, tilting her head one way then the other. She finally pointed her index finger at the canvas as if it were a pistol. "Ka-pow," she said, gurgling the word in her throat. She then blew across the tip of her finger. "You are history." She pushed the canvas to the edge of the easel and let it fall to the floor. "Time to start over."

"It's *your* painting but that's four in a week. You've got more unfinished canvases than I do."

"No, I don't," she said, lifting her chin pretentiously. "I am just experimenting with which type of setting is best suited for me."

"What are you going to try next?" Chandler leaned her hips against a stool while Macy flipped through a stack of unfinished canvases in the corner. "Why not pick something you are actually going to finish?"

"I want to try painting a nude." Macy said it with a coy glance in Chandler's direction.

"No, you don't."

"Yes, I do. I want to paint one of those nudes where the emotions are very understated and subtle. Where the viewer is a voyeur to someone's private world. Like the ones you do."

Chandler wanted to say no, she didn't have time to teach that kind of portraiture. Or maybe Macy wasn't ready to try that kind of work. Anything but to have to teach her that. It wasn't that she couldn't teach her, but Chandler wasn't sure she could survive it. Especially now that she had seen Joanna again. Chandler hadn't painted one of her award-winning nudes in two years, not since she'd packed up and moved out of Boston, leaving her world and her love behind.

"I'd rather we didn't do that right now," Chandler said and started for the staircase.

"What's up with you today? You've been funky since we saw Joanna and Deena at that café last night. What's going on with you?"

"Nothing. Why don't you gesso a canvas so we can get started?"

"I'd rather talk. It's her, isn't it? Your moody behavior has something to do with Joanna, doesn't it?" Macy followed Chandler down the stairs to the kitchen while she refilled her cup.

"No. And I'm not moody. I'm just frustrated with a student who won't concentrate. You're wasting my time and yours."

"But I'm still paying you, aren't I? I think it's time you tell me what that woman means to you."

"She doesn't mean anything to me. She's an art conservator I once knew in Boston. Now can we get to work?"

"No, we can't." Macy leaped over and blocked the stairs, crossing her arms defensively. "There is something you aren't telling me and I want to know what it is."

"Will you drop it? And move," Chandler said, pushing her aside and trotting up the metal steps.

"She's your ex-lover," Macy declared, following her up the steps. "Right?"

"Macy, has anyone ever told you you're a pain in the royal ass?"

"Sure, they have. That's what makes me so lovable and such a good mystery writer. I don't take no for an answer. I ferret out the answers, no matter what. I never give up or give in. I always get my man, or my woman, as it were."

"You also ramble."

"That's the writer in me. I try all the words until I find the ones I need to make my point. Now, who is Joanna Lucas and where does she fit into your past? And it's okay if you embellish a little. I may want to use it in a book sometime."

"There is nothing to embellish. I once knew her. That was years ago. Now she is in Venice on business and we ran into each other. Period. End of story."

"It's the cop. It's Deena you have a history with. Damn, that was good grammar. NOT!" Macy laughed at herself. "But she's the ex-lover, right?"

Chandler couldn't help but laugh. The only thing she and Deena Garren shared was a mutual dislike for each other, at least that's the way Deena would put it.

"It's not the cop?"

"No, definitely not the cop." Chandler set a fresh canvas on the easel and began applying a layer of gesso.

"I didn't think so. She wasn't at all into you. But I was right. It's the blonde. You and Joanna had a fling. It was either brief or protracted, but it was a fling, wasn't it?"

"Okay, yes. We had a short relationship, but that's all you need to know. Grab a brush and help do this."

"You're doing fine," Macy said and went back to her interrogation. "How short? One year? Two? One month? Two?"

Chandler groaned but she knew Macy wasn't going to give up until she had everything she wanted to know. It wasn't worth prolonging the inevitable.

"Two years. We were together two years and that ended two years ago."

"Wow. That's not short. That borders on long and involved.

65

What happened?"

"We drifted apart," Chandler said, keeping her eyes on the canvas so Macy couldn't see that she was lying.

After a moment of silence Macy said, "You are so full of it. But I can accept that you aren't going to tell me, at least not today. That doesn't mean I won't find out."

"I'm sure," Chandler said under her breath. She squatted in front of a box of supplies. "Be right back. I need another jar of gesso. I think I left it on the counter." She hurried down the stairs, as much to get away from Macy's relentless questions as to get away from the memories those questions were raising.

"What do you know about the cop?" Macy called.

"She's a cop and Joanna's friend. That about covers it."

"Do you think they're a couple? After all, they are traveling together and you know what they say. Venice is romantic."

"I doubt it. They've known each other since college. Besides they are so different sometimes it's hard to believe they are even friends. Why?"

"I don't know…"

Chandler heard something strange in Macy's voice. She came to the bottom of the stairs and looked up where Macy was leaning on the railing, gazing into space.

"Macy, what's going on in that twisted little brain of yours?" Chandler said, staring up at her. "You aren't interested in Deena Garren, are you?"

"Huh? Me? No. But I could use a little information from a female officer. Just for research, of course."

"I thought you already had all the cop references you needed." Chandler trotted back up the steps.

"A writer can never have too much background information." Macy tugged at her earlobe as a quirky grin formed.

"And an artist can never have too many completed paintings." Chandler thumped the canvas with her finger. "Why not put that imagination of yours to work on this?"

"Maybe I'll paint a woman in a blue uniform," she said, cocking an eyebrow then chuckling at Chandler's smirk.

"Anything. So long as you actually finish it, I don't care what you paint."

Macy took the brush from Chandler's hand and began applying the gesso but suddenly stopped and glared back at her. "Joanna is the one you recommended for that grant thing, isn't she?"

"Uh-huh," Chandler said, pointing out a spot she missed.

"Now that's very intriguing." Macy closed one eye and gave a witchy cackle.

"And she doesn't need to know. Okay, Macy?" Chandler said emphatically.

"Fine with me."

CHAPTER 8

"Do you have everything you need?" Francesca asked, descending the two steps into the baptistery.

Joanna was sitting on a small stool, peering through the eyepieces of the platform-mounted microscope she had brought down from the workroom. She rotated the focus knob with one hand while she adjusted the light bar with the other.

"Yes, I think so," she replied, her concentration on what she was doing.

"I have to leave for a little while. Meetings. Always meetings. Will you be all right?"

Joanna held her breath, hoping to capture a photograph of the fleeting image before it jumped out of focus.

"Joanna?"

"Yes?" she whispered as it came into clear view. "Right there," she muttered.

"Joanna?"

"Yes, I'll be fine." She finally looked up, letting her eyes refocus. "You go ahead. Take your time."

"If you need something, Adriana will help you." She motioned toward the young woman in a guard's uniform standing by the door.

"Can I send her for coffee?" Joanna joked, not expecting that to be one of Adriana's jobs.

"Sure. Adriana, Caffè Americano for Signora Lucas. *Pronto*," she instructed, waving a hand in her direction. The guard nodded and left.

"She really didn't have to do that." Joanna felt like she had taken the woman away from her official duties as basilica guard.

"Adriana is a nice girl. She will be happy to get whatever you need. Now, I must go. I will be back in one hour, maybe two. *Ciao*."

Francesca reminded Joanna of her aunt in Florida. All flash and glitz, smiling congenially like she never met a stranger. Joanna went back to work, scanning the floor for clues about its age, the extent of the damage and how best to restore it. It was a slow process at best and using unfamiliar equipment in a foreign environment made the work all the more tedious and frustrating.

Adriana brought her coffee in a china cup and saucer. She stood patiently waiting while Joanna took a break to enjoy it and stretch her back. Joanna had just moved the equipment and re-established her field of focus when she heard the door clang open.

"Signora, have you completed your work?" Carlo Vittori asked, an impatient squint in his eyes.

"Good morning, Signor Vittori. Not yet."

"What are you doing there?" he asked as if challenging her competence.

"Contrast analysis of the exposed edge of the mortar. Would you like to see?" She rotated the head of the viewfinder so he could see.

"No, no." He waved her off, giving his full attention to a section of loose tessera. "I will have my worker come remove this for you." He pushed the tiles around with the toe of his shoe. "We will scrape it away so you can see."

"I'd rather you didn't." Joanna wanted badly to tell him he was disrupting her work area. "I'd prefer we don't disturb it any more than we have to until I have finished."

"You must see the under-floor," he insisted. "We must clean away the garbage."

"No, Signor Vittori. I don't need it cleaned away. Please. I'll tell you when it is time to remove it. I want to run some tests on the tessera as well as the subfloor. It shouldn't take long for me to finish what I need to do."

His jaw muscled rippled as he gave Joanna a last look before turning to leave. On his way out the door he grumbled, "*Americano raccomandazioni Americano*. HA!"

Joanna gave a curious look as the door closed behind him.

"Adriana, what does *raccomandazioni* mean?"

"It means…" She thought a moment. "It means recommend."

"Recommend? I wonder what he means by that?" she said and went back to work.

Francesca had been gone precisely two hours when she came hurrying through the door, her face flushed and short of breath.

"I am so sorry, Joanna. I was gone too long. I hurried back as soon as I could."

"Signor Vittori was here," Joanna said, refocusing over a void in the mosaic.

"What did he want? I told him not to be impatient but he doesn't listen to me." She flipped her hair angrily.

"He wanted the same thing he always wants. Am I finished so he can begin the restoration? I wanted to show him an area of mortar erosion but he didn't seem interested."

"He is only interested in one thing." Francesca pursed her fingertips together, pinching the air. "When can the work begin?"

"I thought he'd want to know my findings or at least what I'm working on."

"Ignore him, Joanna. He is *stupido*."

"He said something curious as he was leaving. He said *Americano raccomandazioni Americano*. Do you have any idea what he meant? I assume it has something to do with me and the grant."

"It was probably nothing." Francesca shrugged but something in the way she said it made Joanna think she knew more.

"Did an American recommend me to the Procurator's Council?"

"I'm sure they did. Someone in your office perhaps."

"Perhaps." Joanna let it drop. There was nothing to be gained by quizzing Francesca. She merely worked as a liaison for the proto, the engineering office attached to the basilica's Procurator's Council. She was a very small fish in a large and complex pond of red tape. She was probably right. It could have been Harvey who recommended her for the job and just preferred to remain anonymous.

Joanna packed up the equipment and with Adriana's help, returned it to the lab for the night. As much as she wanted to stay and work late, she was forced to obey her host's rules and regulations. Ceremonies, meetings and mass took precedence over her curiosity-driven work ethic. With a promise to be back in the morning when the basilica opened at nine thirty, she headed for the San Marco vaporetto stop and a ride to the hotel.

"*Buon sera, Signora*," the woman behind the counter said as Joanna claimed her room key from the front desk.

"*Buon sera*," Joanna replied, working on her accent.

"I have message for you." She handed Joanna a folded piece of paper then went back to her telephone call.

"*Grazie*." Joanna started up the steps as she unfolded the note.

71

Hello. I hope it isn't presumptuous of me to ask if I could visit with you for a few minutes. I'm an author. Firsthand information from a female police officer would be extremely helpful. Tavolino? Seven o'clock? Thanks so much. Macy W.

Joanna knocked on Deena's door.

"Come in, Josie," she called.

"How did you know it was me?" she asked, sticking her head through the door.

Deena was stretched out on the bed with her hands folded behind her head. She looked like she had been napping. "How many other people do I know in Venice who would be knocking on my door? Besides, I saw you crossing the square." She nodded toward the window.

"The desk clerk gave this to me but I'm sure it's for you." Joanna handed her the note then waited for her reaction.

"Well, well. Macy is an author." Deena propped herself on one elbow and reread it. "What does she want from me?"

"She probably wants to know if you like being a cop. And do you feel singled out because you are gay? That kind of thing." Joanna went through the bathroom into her own room.

Deena climbed off the bed and followed as far as the bathroom door. "You think so? She didn't strike me as the curious gay type."

"You don't think she's gay?" Joanna looked up with a frown.

"Oh, I'm sure she is. But she didn't seem all that eager to discuss it. She didn't act like she wore it on her sleeve."

"Are you going to meet her?" Joanna dropped her coat on the bed, stepped out of her shoes and pulled her blouse out of the waistband of her slacks.

"I don't know." Deena leaned against the doorjam, rereading the note. "I don't know if I want to discuss my sexuality with a stranger."

"Since when?" Joanna gave a quirky grin.

Deena slowly pulled a cautious smile.

"Yeah, I think I will meet with her. What the hell?" She looked up at Joanna. "Do you mind?"

"Why should I mind? I'm not the cop." Joanna peeled out of her blouse and stood over her suitcase, searching for something comfy to put on.

"You know what I mean, Josie. This puts me, us, very close to Chandler and I know what you think about that." Deena looked worried.

"It doesn't put me anywhere. This is your deal, honey. Keep me out of it."

"That's the trouble. I can't. If I go, you are going with me."

"Oh, no, I'm not." Joanna looked up, scowling decisively. "You are going all by yourself. That note is addressed to you."

"It isn't addressed to anyone. Macy must have told the desk clerk to give it to either one of us." Deena showed her the back of the note. "And she knows we are here together. She probably expects us both to show up."

"Yeah, well, she'll get over it." Joanna went back to rummaging for a top.

"Are you afraid of her?" Deena asked, studying her face intently. "Are you afraid of Macy?"

"Absolutely not. Why would I be afraid of Macy Whittaker?" Joanna scowled indignantly.

"Okay, if you aren't afraid of her, are you jealous of her? Is that it?"

"No," she said, adding a chuckle to make it sound all the more ridiculous.

"I would hope not. Chandler isn't good enough for you. You shouldn't be jealous of anyone she is dating."

"Good, I'm glad you said it. Dating. They are dating. Need I remind you of that fact? They are a couple, as in girlfriends, as in you should keep hands off."

"I'm a cop. She wants to interview a cop. Damn, Joanna. I know better than to lay claim to someone else's property. I'm no letch. I have a few principles. Not a lot, but a few. Now, go with me."

"I'm tired. My feet hurt. My back hurts from crouching over the scanner for four hours and I just want to relax this evening."

"What's wrong, Josie? Are you afraid Chandler will be there?"

"I'm not afraid she'll be there. I assume she will be there. They are a couple, you know."

"Couldn't you come along and just sit there again? After all, Macy said she just needed a few minutes to ask some questions. We could be back in half an hour. Maybe less."

"You don't believe that any more than I do, sergeant Garren. Once you get to talking shop there's no shutting you up."

"Please, Josie? Don't make me do this by myself. I always say dumb stuff and end up sounding like a jerk. Remember that time I was interviewed for the evening news about the new kids' park? I said pubic area instead of public area."

"That was rather funny."

"Please, Josie?"

"Okay," she finally agreed. Joanna wondered how much of her decision came from her inner voice that secretly wanted another look at Chandler.

"Thank you, honey." Deena gave Joanna a kiss on the back of the head as she hurried into her room. "Get dressed. We can have dinner before they get there. I'm starving. By the way, what do you think *Tavolino* means?"

"Little table. I saw it on the napkin."

"Cool. Little table."

Deena, you sound way too giddy about this date. Remember, Macy Whittaker is taken. She is not fair game.

They had just finished their pasta and salad when Macy and Chandler came through the door of the café. Joanna specifically had chosen a round table with a chair backed up to the corner. She wanted to have a clear view of the room and an escape route if she needed one.

"Hi," Macy said, striding up to the table with a wide smile. "I'm so glad you decided to come." Chandler followed.

"We eat here a lot." Deena stood and pulled out a chair for Macy. "It's just a couple blocks from the hotel."

"What kind of books do you write, Macy?" Joanna asked, hoping to get Chandler's eyes off their search of her face.

74

"Romances?" Deena suggested.

Chandler took the remaining seat, bumping her knee against Joanna's as she hitched it in. Joanna's chair was against the wall. She had no room to move out of her way.

"Not quite," Macy said, slipping out of her coat. Deena's eyes went right down Macy's blouse to where the top button was open, exposing her soft cleavage. "I write mysteries."

"Like those cozy mysteries where the chef finds a clue in the pantry and a dead body in the garden?"

"No. Like the crime mysteries where the Russian mob infiltrates the CIA to assassinate the head of the French diplomatic corps and blame it on an American senator's son," Chandler said, chuckling softly.

"Oh," Deena said with surprise. "You write that stuff? Underworld drugs and violence?"

"Yes." Macy blushed a bit. "I'm not smart enough to write romances. I couldn't write two hundred pages worth of anticipation. I'd have the main characters in bed on the second page." She threw her head back and laughed. "In my books, the characters can have sex in the morning, stab someone by noon, shoot someone by dinner and be back in bed again by sunset."

Deena's mouth had dropped.

"Macy's pen name is René Michelle," Chandler said, pouring glasses of wine from the pitcher brought to the table.

"René Michelle, the one who writes the Amber Mysteries?" Deena asked as if it was a revelation.

"That's the one," Chandler said proudly.

"Now, I'm impressed." Deena looked back at Macy. "Very impressed. But you have to tell me, why did you kill off Lieutenant Donovan? I thought she'd make a great police commissioner."

"I thought about it, but I decided she was too wimpy. I wanted a stronger character, one who could scratch her balls and not worry about who was watching, if you know what I mean." Macy passed a glass to Deena, tossing her hair and offering a little grin.

Oh my God, Joanna thought. A hair toss and deep cleavage.

There is no way Deena isn't imagining her hands all over this woman.

"All my books have a gay undertone but I don't smack my fans with it. I want straight readers buying my books, too."

"Then why did you want to meet with me? You must have all the law enforcement expertise you need."

"Oh, I don't know. I thought maybe you had some tidbit of knowledge I might need." Macy took a sip from her glass then propped her elbow on the table and rested her chin in her hand, staring straight into Deena's eyes. "So, sergeant Garren. What's new in copland I ought to know? Who's sleeping with who?"

"You're pretty young to be writing hard-core mysteries like that. It usually takes a pretty cynical mind to hack someone's guts out with a meat cleaver."

"Young?" Macy snickered. "How young do you think I am?"

"Gosh, I don't know. Twenty-eight. Twenty-nine." Deena shrugged, obviously not wanting to embarrass herself or Macy.

"Very good. Very polite answer. Now, try again and be honest this time. How old?"

Deena looked over at Joanna, her eyes seeking help.

"Thirty-one?" Joanna offered.

"Okay. You're not being honest either. Come on. One more time. How old?" She leaned back in her chair and straightened her posture, her perky breasts assuming the position.

"Okay," Deena said, scrunching her mouth in contemplation. "Thirty-six. Best and last guess."

"When I guessed," Chandler said. "I said thirty-six. I was wrong by ten years. Macy is forty-six." She held up her glass as a salute.

"Naw," Deena said, laughing it off. "How old are you, really?"

"I'll be forty-seven next month."

"No, you aren't," Joanna said with a chuckle. "You can't be forty-anything."

"Why does no one believe me when I say how old I am?"

"Because you don't look it, that's why," Chandler said, casually

76

draping her arm over the back of Joanna's chair. The gesture made Joanna stiffen.

"Okay, so I help the gray hair a little."

"That isn't your real hair color?" Deena asked, touching one of Macy's luscious curls.

"It was, almost. The highlights are a little fibbie, but I'm a natural redhead."

Deena's eyebrows raised skeptically before taking a sip of wine.

"I know what you're thinking," Macy sang, bumping Deena's arm. "And yes, the carpet matches the drapes." Deena immediately sprayed her mouthful of wine. Macy laughed at her. "What? You've never heard that expression before?"

"Yes, but not as a confession from a stranger in a restaurant."

"I'm not a stranger. And you sure blush easily, Officer Garren."

"It's sergeant Garren."

"Oops, sorry, sergeant Garren." Macy snapped a silly salute. "So, how many pair of handcuffs do you carry?" Macy seamlessly launched into her interrogation.

As Macy and Deena's conversation drifted into the nitty-gritty of police procedure, Joanna became more conscious of Chandler's arm across the back of her chair. It could have been completely innocent but Joanna couldn't help remember a time when she was comforted, even reassured to have Chandler's strong arm so close.

"How's your work going?" Joanna asked, trying to find innocuous conversation.

"I haven't done much serious painting lately but I keep busy. How about you?" She plucked a piece of lint from Joanna's shoulder then used the back of her hand to gently sweep it clean. The feel of Chandler's hand against her shoulder sent a tingle through Joanna.

"I keep busy, too," Joanna said, her voice tightening as Chandler's eyes captured hers and held them.

Why are you staring at me like that? Couldn't you look at the floor or how about look at your girlfriend. In case you haven't noticed, she's flirting with Deena like a two-dollar hooker on the Navy pier. Or is this the way you prefer your relationships? Open and casually noncommittal? Is that what you expected from me? Was I supposed to ignore and accept that you couldn't be faithful?

Macy giggled and leaned into Deena's arm. "Now that's what I call undercover police work," she said, blushing.

You used to blush like that, Chandler. And so did I.

"I'm glad we got to meet again, Joanna. You look good," Chandler said softly.

"Thank you. You haven't changed in two years. You still look the same."

"I hope that's good," she said, pouring them each more wine.

"Yes, you still look good."

Joanna felt her defenses softening. Chandler's easy conversation and her soft eyes had done it. There was no denying. The attraction was still there. Joanna wanted to think she had suppressed it but it was still there, intact, vibrant and throbbing. And she hated herself for that weakness.

"I wasn't sure I should come with Macy this evening. I wasn't sure you'd want to see me again. But you're okay with it?"

"Sure. We're both adults. We're both in Venice. Our paths happen to cross. I can live with that coincidence. It's not as if we had planned some clandestine rendezvous after two years."

"Good. I'm glad. Besides, Macy seemed to think Deena could offer some background information for her book."

"And you came along because she didn't want to come alone, right?"

"Something like that." Chandler smiled, her face lighting up. "How is the appraisal at San Marco coming? Any decision on the mosaic yet?"

Joanna looked over at Chandler curiously. "How did you know about that?"

"You said you were here doing a consult at the basilica."

"No, I didn't. In fact, I made a point not to say anything about it."

"I don't know." Chandler chuckled. "Maybe Deena mentioned it."

"I doubt it."

"Sure she did. She said you were here on business."

"But she didn't say where or doing what. How did you know?" Joanna had a suspicious feeling in the pit of her stomach. She had been very careful not to tell Chandler what she was doing in Venice. But she seemed to know anyway.

"I might have heard about it somewhere. I go to a lot of museums and galleries."

"From who? Where?"

"What difference does it make?"

"Yeah, what difference does it make?" Macy added, having overheard their conversation.

"Where, Chandler?" Joanna continued to challenge her, determined to find out how she knew.

"My God, Chandler. Tell her before she has a conniption."

"Macy," Chandler snapped angrily.

"What are we discussing here?" Deena asked curiously. "Did I miss something?"

"Chandler was about to tell me how she knows why I'm in Venice."

"How the hell does she know?" Deena joined Joanna in scowling at Chandler. "She shouldn't know anything about your business."

"She should if she's the one who got her the job," Macy said, as if coming to Chandler's rescue. As soon as she said it, all three of the women looked at her, the harshest stare coming from Chandler. "Oops."

"Chandler got me what job?" Joanna asked carefully. She instantly remembered Carlo Vittori's comment about an American recommending an American. Chandler was that American?

"Chandler couldn't find her way out of a bathtub without a map," Deena sniped. "What makes you think she could do that?"

"Please, Deena. You aren't helping," Joanna said, holding up a hand.

"Chandler recommended Joanna to the Procurator's Council," Macy said in her defense. "She knew they were looking for someone to evaluate the floor in the baptistery before it was repaired. She told them Joanna was the best person they could find. She got her the job. You're here because she recommended you." Chandler's jaw muscles rippled and her face turned crimson red. "I'm sorry, Chandler. But why not just go ahead and tell her?"

"I think you just did," Chandler replied, staring daggers at her.

"What do you mean *you* recommended me? How could you do that? You don't work for the basilica or the Ministry of Culture."

"Don't believe her, Josie. She's just trying to take credit for it. That's nothing more than a crock of BS."

"You give me such a pain in the butt," Chandler said, turning her stare to Deena. "Yes, I recommended Joanna for the grant. I happen to know members of the council. They needed an independent authority to give an unbiased opinion on a potential million-dollar piece of restoration. They needed someone with the expertise to evaluate the mosaics accurately. Joanna has that expertise." Chandler's eyes moved to Joanna. "So I recommended you."

"Why me?"

"Because I don't know any other art conservators who specialize in mosaics."

Joanna didn't know whether to thank her or be angry with her. Her first instinct was to be furious Chandler had manipulated her without her knowledge.

"Don't you think you should have asked me first?"

"I'm sure they did. You could have turned down the grant and they would have found someone else."

"That's not what I meant."

"Are you mad it was me who recommended you? Would it have been all right if someone else did it?"

Joanna had to admit that was exactly the problem. She didn't want Chandler Cardin involved in her life, ever. And to be summoned to Venice on her whim was unforgiveable. Yes, she was honored to be invited to give an opinion on such a prestigious project but having Chandler involved in it, even in passing, somehow tainted it.

"You could have had the decency to let me know you were involved. The other night when I saw you, you might have said something."

"Would you have accepted the grant if you knew I recommended you?"

"Maybe," Joanna said, sitting up straighter.

"Maybe, my ass. I know you, Joanna," Chandler declared. "You would have let your stubborn pride keep you from accepting just because it came from me. That's exactly why I didn't tell you. And before you make any foolish assumptions, I didn't do it for personal reasons. I did it so the work to be done at the basilica can have a fair and honest appraisal. Nothing else. I did it for Saint Mark's Basilica. I would have recommended Jack the Ripper if he was the right person for the job. Look, if you don't want the job, tell them. Tell Francesca you want to go home. They can find someone else. You can go back to Boston and forget it. Forget you had an opportunity of a lifetime, an opportunity to make a real difference. Go ahead, Joanna. Quit. Run home."

"You're an ass," Joanna said coldly then stood up, pulled on her coat and strode out of the café.

She was halfway back to the hotel by the time Deena caught up to her.

"Wait, Josie." She trotted up alongside and fell into lockstep with her. "Are you okay?"

"Just dandy," Joanna snapped and quickened her stride.

Deena seemed to know better than to say anything else, at least not tonight.

CHAPTER 9

"Where are you off to so early?" Deena stood in the bathroom doorway and stretched. Her hair was matted to one side and her boxer shorts were askew.

"I have an errand to run before I meet Francesca at nine thirty at the basilica. They finally got the mass spectrometer calibrated for me."

"I'm thrilled for you." She went back into the bathroom to use the toilet but didn't close the door. "Think you'll be free for a late lunch?"

"I don't know. I wouldn't count on it. You know how it is once I get started. I'm sorry, hon." She checked her tote bag for her map and umbrella.

"What's your errand? I've got Pepto if you need it." Deena washed her hands, looked in the mirror and smirked. "Something died in my hair. I can see the nest."

"I need a bra, remember? The one I'm wearing is heaving its last dying breath. I'm afraid it'll be down at my waist any minute. If I wash it one more time there won't be any threads left."

"Maybe I should go with you," Deena said.

"I'm not a child. I don't need you to hold my hand. I can find a bra store without police intervention."

"I worry about you, Josie."

"I'm on an island. How lost can I get?" She pulled on her coat and headed for the door. "See you later, honey."

Chandler rounded the corner and headed for Joanna's hotel. About to open the door, she noticed Deena sitting at a table outside the café across the way, sipping coffee and reading.

"Is Joanna here?" Chandler asked, striding up to the table.

"She's at San Marco working," Deena replied coldly, exactly the kind of greeting Chandler expected from her.

"She was due at the basilica hours ago. Do you know where she went?"

"I told you, she's at San Marco." Deena looked up at her with a frown. "What do you mean she hasn't been there?"

"Which way did she go? On foot or on the vaporetto?" Chandler didn't have time to banter with Deena.

"I have no idea. She left before breakfast. She had shopping to do then she was going to meet Francesca at nine thirty. Maybe she's meeting with the officials at their offices."

"She isn't." Chandler turned and squinted across the square. She gave an exasperated groan. "Where was she going shopping?

"I don't remember the name of the place. Some lingerie shop north of the Rialto Bridge. Someplace by a bronze statue."

"What did she need at a lingerie shop by the Rialto Bridge?"

"A bra, if it's any of your business." Deena's tone was caustic.

Give it a rest, cop. I'm not here to argue with you. Just tell me where she is and I'll leave you to your picture book.

"Why is she shopping for a bra all the way over there? There are closer places. I bet she's lost."

"How can she be lost? She told me Venice is an island. When you get to the edge, you just turn around and go the other way."

"You obviously haven't gone very far on foot since you got here. Venice is over a hundred islands and over four hundred bridges. It's a maze of hidden sidewalks and alleys out there. She *can* get lost and Joanna's stubborn streak is exactly the kind of thing to encourage that. If you're as good a friend as you think you are, you'd know that about her. She'll be halfway to Rome before she asks for directions."

Deena laughed for a moment before her expression changed to concern.

"As much as I hate to agree with you about anything, you could be right. Joanna can be a little headstrong."

"A little?"

"I guess I better go look for her." Deena stood up.

"Oh, that's a good idea. Let's send a blind woman to find a blind woman. You'd be lost before you got to the end of the street."

"I would not." Deena glared at her.

"The hell you wouldn't. You may know your way around Boston but you are in my neighborhood now. And I don't have the time or the desire to find two women lost in Venice. I'll go find Joanna. You stay here. I'll call the hotel later and check if she's shown up."

"One question. Given the fact I don't give a crap about you or what you do, why should I listen to anything you say?" Deena demanded.

"You don't have to. Go ahead and get lost. Just don't expect me to come rescue you."

"Rest assured you are the last person I'd ask for guidance," Deena retorted.

Chandler headed back across the square, muttering to herself, "And I thought Joanna was stubborn."

She didn't need a map to know what happened to Joanna. She probably rode the vaporetto to the Rialto Bridge then headed out on foot in search of a square with a statue. Unfortunately, that described dozens of Venetian squares. The maze of streets and bridges, some ending in nothing more than someone's front door, could have easily swallowed Joanna up, leaving her winding her way hopelessly further and further from her destination. Knowing Joanna's stubborn pride and limited Italian vocabulary, she might not ask for help until midnight. One wrong turn and she could be miles from her hotel or anything familiar. Chandler had probably crossed every one of the 410 bridges at least once since she came to Venice. She knew all too well how easy it was to get turned around and become disoriented. She wouldn't bet against Joanna having turned one too many corners and ending up on the back side of the city, looking out at the lagoon without a prayer of knowing how to get back.

Chandler headed for the Rialto Bridge then began a methodical search, weaving her way through the maze of streets, sticking her head in every shop that had lingerie in the window, asking if a five-foot-six-inch blond American had been in shopping for a thirty-six C bra. She remembered that about Joanna. Even though she had never been able to convince Joanna of it, her figure was flawless and perfectly proportioned. Her skin was as soft as velvet. It still was. She was perfect as always. Still ravishingly sensual.

Chandler meandered north and east, fanning her search. The sun had set behind gray skies and a fine mist had begun to fall as the city darkened. Twice she telephoned Joanna's hotel but she hadn't been seen. Just Deena, pacing the lobby and wringing her hands.

It was dinnertime but Chandler ignored her grumbling stomach and the fact that she hadn't eaten lunch. She had one thing and one thing only on her mind. The endless grid of look-alike streets was beginning to confuse even Chandler. She could just imagine Joanna stubbornly crisscrossing the back streets of Venice alone, determined to find her own way back to the hotel without benefit of directions or aid.

As she stood on a small stone bridge, deciding which way to try next, she wished she had her trusty map with her, the one speckled with notes and landmarks so she too wouldn't end up lost in the bowels of Venice.

"*Mi scusi, Signora*," she said as a woman climbed the bridge toward her. "*Campo?*" Chandler had learned locating a square, even a small one, was a good way to keep track of where she was. Most squares had signs posted giving directions to the nearest tourist attraction. Signs for such things as San Marco, Rialto Bridge and the train station were meant to keep tourists from doing just what Joanna did.

"*Campo Santa Ternita.*" The woman nodded over her shoulder as she continued on down the street.

"*Grazie.*" Chandler replied. Campo Santa Ternita. The Holy Trinity. No wonder nothing looked familiar. She was nearly to the Arsenale and the back side of the city, deep in a residential district. "I hope Joanna hasn't drifted this far east," she muttered as she sat down on the step of the bridge to catch her breath. Her feet hurt. She was hungry and she was mad. Mad at Joanna for getting lost in Venice and mad at herself for not being able to find her.

"*Signorina?*"a woman called from an upstairs window. "*Ti sei perso?*"

"I don't understand. *Non capisco. Perso?*"

"Lost. Are you lost also?"

"No. *Non perso. Riposo.* Resting," Chandler replied.

"*Si. Riposo.*"

"Was there someone else lost? *Perso?*"

"*Si.* Always people lost." She laughed.

"Today?"

"*Si.* Two, three hours ago," she said, holding up fingers.

"Her hair. *Capelli.* What color was it? *Colore?*" Chandler tugged at a lock of her own hair.

"Blond, I think. Pretty woman in a blue coat."

Joanna had on a blue coat at Tavolino yesterday.

"How do you know she was lost?"

"She go over the bridge that way." The woman leaned out and pointed. "Then she go over the bridge that way." She pointed in the other direction. "Then that way again. Three times she change her mind. Maybe four."

"Which way did she go? Do you remember?" Chandler climbed to her feet, rejuvenated that she might be on the right track after all.

The woman leaned both elbows on the windowsill. "I think she go that way. But who knows?" She shrugged.

"*Grazie, grazie,*" Chandler said and started in that direction.

According to the woman's time schedule, Joanna should have reached the northern shore of the city with nothing but a view of the Cemetery on San Michelle Island and begun making her way back by now. Perhaps she would pass her.

But Chandler made it all the way to the wharf without any sign of her, or any blonde, for that matter.

"Where do I look for you now, Joanna?" she said, leaning on the railing that looked out over the lagoon.

She turned and started back. She rounded the corner onto a narrow street where a small chapel was wedged between two apartment buildings. The chapel door was open. The only light inside came from a few flickering candles. Chandler stood in the doorway, her eyes becoming accustomed to the light. She hoped against hope that someone inside had seen Joanna and noticed which way she had gone. Somewhere in the darkness she heard what sounded like quiet weeping.

"Hello?" she said into the dim light. "Is anyone there? *Mi scusi.*" There was a silence then a bat flew past her head. "Shit," she screamed, waving at it.

"You shouldn't talk like that in a church," a voice said faintly.

Chandler stared at the silhouette of a woman sitting on the step at the bottom of the altar. "Joanna, is that you?"

"Yes," she replied stoically.

87

Chandler had never been so relieved to hear someone's voice in her life. But she doubted Joanna shared that opinion.

"What are you doing sitting in a dark church in the backwaters of Venice? Francesca expected you at San Marco hours ago." She started up the aisle, determined to hide her relief at finding her.

"I know. I'm sorry." Joanna looked up at her curiously. "How did you know that?"

"I went by the basilica. She told me you hadn't been there yet today. She was worried you might be sick or something. Then I went by your hotel. Deena said you had shopping to do but you were on your way. You got lost, didn't you?"

"Wait, wait, wait. You went to Saint Mark's and Francesca told you I hadn't been there? Then you went to my hotel and Deena told you I had shopping to do?"

"Yes."

"What business is it of yours if I'm at work or not?"

"None."

"Then why are you here? Do you think just because you recommended me for the grant you have a right to know what I'm doing every minute I'm in Venice? If that's the case, you're dead wrong, Chandler. You may have recommended me, and you already know what I think about that, but my comings and goings are none of your business."

"You haven't answered my question. What are you doing here?"

"I'm drinking in the art and culture of Venice. I'm here to appreciate the historical importance of this little church. It shouldn't be missed."

Chandler looked up at the wooden crucifix suspended on the wall behind the altar. "Even when you're lost?"

"Oh, are you lost?" Joanna asked innocuously.

"No, I'm not lost. But I think you are."

"I'm not lost. I'm sitting in this chapel, admiring its simple beauty."

"It smells like dead fish in here."

"It smells like seawater and the decaying organic matter deposition by the tides." Joanna touched the mortar between the

88

stones on the floor by her feet and drew back damp fingers. "It's wicking up through the subfloor. Probably a sand and pebble base. These smaller churches couldn't afford granite or marble footings."

"Admit it. You were lost."

"I was not lost. I was sightseeing. And even if I was, you make it sound like I did it just to inconvenience you. I might ask you the same thing. What are you doing out here in the backwaters of Venice, as you call it? I think you're the one who is lost."

"I've been searching for you. I know how easy it is to get lost in this city. The locals do it all the time."

"Like you?"

"I am not lost," Chandler shouted, then sat down next to her on the step and took a deep breath. "Look, Joanna, there is nothing wrong with admitting you took a wrong turn. I did it when I first got here."

"I did not take a wrong turn," Joanna insisted then stared down at her mud-splattered shoes. "I took dozens of them," she added softly. "All day. Every turn I made just got me more lost. I've walked every back alley and dead end in this city, many of them twice." She looked over at Chandler. "I've been here for hours. I was too tired to go on. I've walked miles. I was hoping someone would come in for mass or at least to blow out the candles so I could ask for directions."

"What were you going to do? Sleep in the church?"

Joanna shrugged and hugged her knees. "I don't know. I lost my map. It fell out of my bag somewhere."

"Why didn't you ask for help?"

"I did but I can't speak the language. One man was trying to help but he couldn't speak English and I didn't understand him. He kept saying *perso*. I don't know what *perso* means. I said no *perso*. He finally gave up and went away."

"He asked if you were lost. *Perso* means lost." Chandler wrapped her arm around Joanna, hoping to ward off the look of imminent tears. "I'm sorry. Did you at least find the store you were looking for to buy a bra?"

Joanna looked at her curiously.

"How did you know I was shopping for a bra?"

"Deena told me. Of course, she also told me it was none of my business."

"Well, I didn't find it. I couldn't make out Claudia's directions. That's what got me lost."

"Does it have to be that particular shop?"

"Not necessarily. I just need someplace that sells..." Joanna hesitated.

"Underwire thirty-six C," Chandler said with a smile. "Preferably beige."

Joanna immediately blushed. "Yes."

"I'm not so demented that I don't remember that." She rubbed Joanna's back reassuringly. "Come on. Let's find someplace on this side of town." She tried to keep herself from remembering how soft and round her breasts were and how much she had loved to touch them.

"That's okay. I'll shop tomorrow." Joanna stood up and headed for the door.

"I'm sure we'll pass several shops that sell lingerie between here and the vaporetto stop." Chandler followed her out into the street.

"It's too late to do any shopping tonight."

"No, it isn't. That's the great thing about Venice. The stores stay open late." Chandler pointed for them to turn left.

"I'm not sure that's the right direction." Joanna looked both ways.

"I am." Chandler took her arm and guided her down the narrow street.

Joanna walked along quietly until they rounded the next corner. She stopped and looked over at Chandler.

"I'm not sure I want you shopping for a bra with me."

"Because of our past? Because you and I have seen each other in a bra before, and even less? Or because you hate my guts?"

"There is no you and I anymore. That is all history."

"I didn't say there was. I'm just protecting my reputation."

"YOUR reputation?" Joanna scowled deeply.

"I'm the one who recommended you for the grant. How will it look if you go traipsing off on a shopping expedition and get yourself lost again? The proto's office is expecting you to evaluate the mosaic and give an educated appraisal. You can't do that if you are sitting on the floor of an abandoned chapel feeling sorry for yourself. So swallow your pride, forget our past and let's find you a bra or whatever it is you need so you can get back to work at the basilica."

Joanna stared at her in silence, her resentment obviously bubbling just below the surface. She finally heaved a disgruntled groan and continued down the street. "Okay, this once. But we are NOT making a habit of this."

"It's probably none of my business but why didn't you bring an extra bra with you?"

"I forgot an extra one. I forgot any of my decent bras. I'm wearing one that is being held together by four safety pins that have been poking me all day. My good bras are washed and hanging over the shower pole in my bathroom back in Boston and I forgot to pack them. There. Are you happy you now have the rest of the story?" She turned and continued down the street with purposeful strides.

"Yes, thank you. More than I needed to know but thank you. Turn here," she said, grabbing her arm and steering her around the corner.

The closer they got to the Rialto Bridge, the heavier the foot traffic became. The streets were clogged with tourists.

"How about a bite of dinner? You're probably starved." Chandler asked, her stomach grumbling so loud she was sure Joanna could hear it.

"No. I just want to buy a bra then go back to the hotel. Deena will be worried."

"Maybe you should call her and let her know you've been found?"

"Yes, perhaps I should," Joanna said.

They found a pay phone and left a message with the desk clerk.

"Look, Joanna. Over there," Chandler said, pointing across the street at a store window. The mannequin was dressed in a bright red lace bra, panties and garter belt holding up red and black fishnet stockings.

"That's not really what I had in mind."

"But at least they sell lingerie. Let's go see." Chandler led the way down the aisle between the men's pajamas and the panty hose. "*Scusi, Signora*. Do you speak English?"

"*Si*. May I help you?" The sales clerk's English wasn't good but it was better than Chandler's Italian.

"Bras?"

"*Si. Reggiseno*." She nodded with a pleasant smile.

"Do you have underwire?" Joanna added.

"*Non capisco*," the clerk said. "Underwire?"

"Under wire," Joanna said, drawing a smile with her finger under her breast.

"What size?" the woman asked.

"Thirty-six C," Chandler replied just as Joanna was about to answer.

"Ah, size four, maybe three. We see," the woman said, turning to a stack of boxes.

"How did you remember what size?" Joanna asked behind her hand.

"It hasn't been *that* long. Some things you just remember." Chandler winked.

The woman spread several choices across the counter. Joanna rejected the see-through lace one and the one with push-up padding.

"How about this one?" Chandler held up a plunge cut beige one with lace detailing. "I like the lace. It reminds me of Burano."

"I don't know about the back. There's only one hook. I prefer something with a little more security."

"You mean like a straight jacket?" Chandler teased.

"No. I'd just feel more confident if I knew there was more than one tiny little loop of wire between me and disaster."

"I didn't know having a bra come off was a disaster." She chuckled. She couldn't help remember two years ago when Joanna eagerly welcomed the release of her bra and Chandler's gentle caress.

"More hooks." Joanna pointed to the closure.

The woman raised her eyebrows as if questioning the need for more hooks but went back to the stack of boxes. "This one?" she said, pulling out a wide-backed support bra. Chandler burst out laughing. "See. More hooks," the clerk said.

"No kidding," Chandler said, continuing to giggle. "Six of them. You'd need a pair of wire cutters to get that thing off."

The sales clerk pulled out the bottom box. "This is our new style." She took out a beige lace-trimmed underwire with a tiny lace butterfly sewn where the cups met. "Very nice for you."

Joanna first checked the closure. Two hooks.

"Nice," Chandler said, feeling the fabric. "Soft. I like this one."

"What size is this one?" Joanna asked, holding it up.

"Size four."

"And that's the same as a thirty-six C?"

"*Si.*" The woman sounded confident but when she waggled her hand, Joanna seemed skeptical.

"Try it on," Chandler suggested.

"*Si.* Try it on, Signora." The clerk pointed to the back of the store.

The clerk showed Joanna to the dressing room in the back of the store then went about her work. Joanna was only gone a minute when she came hurrying up the aisle and grabbed Chandler's arm.

"Come with me," she demanded. "Don't ask. Just come."

"Okay," Chandler said, following close behind.

"There is no curtain on the dressing room." Joanna stood in the open cubical, waving her arms. "I can't undress without a curtain. And certainly not with that man standing up there. He could walk back here any second."

"So? Do it really fast."

"I am not trying on a bra in an open dressing room," Joanna said in an angry whisper.

Chandler looked around for something she could hold up as a curtain but there was nothing but a mop and a bucket in the corner.

"Just turn around and do it really fast. You don't know these people and you'll probably never see them again in your entire life."

"Here," she said, taking off her coat and handing it to Chandler. "Hold my coat open." She adjusted Chandler's arms to cover as much of the opening as possible. "Hold it right there." She peeked over the coat to see if anyone was looking then stripped out of her blouse, covering herself with it as she glared up at Chandler. "Not one wisecrack, you hear me?"

"Not a word." Chandler held the coat high enough so Joanna couldn't see her grin.

Joanna draped the blouse over Chandler's outstretched arm. She quickly peeled off her old bra and slipped on the new one. She struggled with the hooks then leaned over, wobbling her breasts to fill the cups.

"Looks good." Chandler looked her up and down while Joanna checked her look in the mirror. "Cups seem right. Nice and full. Good separation."

"Oh, hush."

"I'm helping. You asked me to help so I am."

"I didn't want an opinion on how it fit. I just wanted you to hold my coat."

"Coat held," Chandler said, smiling behind it. "Nice nipple projection, by the way."

"Chandler!" Joanna said sternly.

"What?" Chandler raised her eyebrows innocently. "Are you going to buy it?"

"The lady told me to take my time."

"Yes, but in about one minute I'm going to drop this coat. My arms are getting really tired." Chandler bit down on her lip, struggling against shoulder fatigue.

"Okay, one more second," Joanna said, taking one last look. "I guess it fits. I think I'll buy it."

She paid for the bra and allowed the sales clerk to discard the old one. Joanna started up the street toward the vaporetto stop, Chandler following her through the crowd.

"I'm going back to the hotel. You don't have to escort me any further. I can manage from here."

"That's okay. I want to make sure you get there all right."

"Yes, yes. I know. You're protecting your reputation."

"And your safety."

Chandler accompanied Joanna as far as the lobby to the hotel.

"Thank you for your assistance, Chandler. I'm sorry I was so much trouble." Joanna shook Chandler's hand.

"My pleasure, Joanna," she said, squeezing her hand gently. "Are you sure you don't need some dinner? It's getting late. The restaurants will close soon."

"No, I'm fine. Good night." She claimed her room key from the desk clerk before starting up the stairs.

Chandler waited until Joanna disappeared up the stairwell before opening the door and stepping out onto the street. She hadn't noticed it before but the evening had turned chilly. She buttoned her coat and pulled the collar up around her chin then looked up at the hotel windows. A light came on in the second-floor corner window and the silhouette of a woman appeared through the curtains. Chandler wondered if it was Joanna. She also wondered how long Joanna was going to stay mad at her. Forever?

CHAPTER 10

"Knocky, knocky," Macy said, opening the door and shouting up the stairs. "Are you having passionate sex with some hot Italian babe? Do I need to come back in three minutes?"

"What makes you think three minutes is enough time if I did have some hot Italian babe up here?" Chandler was standing at the counter, spreading jam on a pancake.

"Sorry. Five minutes." Macy giggled. She let herself in and climbed the stairs. "Good morning."

"Again, the question that begs to be asked is why only five minutes?" Chandler rolled up the pancake and took a bite.

"Because I know you. You haven't had a date in months. Probably years."

"Have too," she said, taking another bite. She hadn't but she wasn't going to admit it.

"You have not. In fact, it has been so long if you did get some innocent waif up here, it would only take you twelve seconds to reach orgasm. The rest of the five minutes would be you apologizing for not being able to wait for her."

"It's called self-control."

"It's called a vibrator."

"I don't date indiscriminately, unlike some people," she said, raising her eyebrows.

"I do not date indiscriminately. I have wells of self-control." Macy turned her nose up as if aloof and innocent. "But you never know. Things might change. I may widen my horizons."

"What are you going to do? Put an ad in the singles column or join a dating Web site?" Chandler washed her hands and started up the spiral staircase to the studio.

"Nope. I may not have to do any of that." Macy dropped her coat in a chair and followed. "Tell me what you know about Deena Garren that would preclude me from going out with her?"

Chandler glared back at her, almost losing her footing on the stairs. "You mean to interview, right? Not as a date?"

"Not necessarily."

"You're kidding, of course."

"No, I'm not kidding. I find her very interesting for a cop."

"I can't believe you're serious. You'd really consider going out with her?"

Macy hesitated a moment then said, "Actually, I already did. Last night. We had dinner. But that's all. Only dinner," she was quick to add. Chandler stared at her with her mouth open. "I know, you don't like her. But you aren't the one having dinner with her. She was very cordial and polite. And don't say anything but she seemed into me."

"Macy, Deena Garren dates women by the dozens. She doesn't have a little black book. She has a little black library."

"I know. She told me."

"She actually told you she picks up girls like some people

97

pick flowers? Grab a bunch, smell them all and toss them out as they begin to droop."

"It's nothing serious. I went by their hotel and she told me about Joanna. How you were out looking for her. We decided to have dinner. That's all. People have to eat. She gave me some great ideas for the book. I may introduce a new character, one with a little crust to her."

"So you were out with Deena when we got back to the hotel?"

"Probably. We got to talking and the time got away from us. She's very intelligent. She has a master's degree in criminal justice."

"And she's going to chew you up and spit you out before you can say Kevlar."

"Not if I do that to her first. Maybe all I'm after is what she can do for my book."

Chandler heaved a sigh and shook her head. "You're a big girl. You know what you're doing, I hope."

"I am. Now, can we get to work? You were going to show me how to sketch a nude. Notice, I didn't say paint a nude." Macy grinned.

"How about we work on establishing depth perception first?" Chandler opened a window to air out the stuffy studio. "Baby steps, Macy. Baby steps."

"By the way, how did it go with Joanna? Was she as lost as Deena said?"

"She was north of the Arsenale."

"In Castello?" Macy made a face. "How did you find her?"

"Divine guidance," she said and pointed to the canvas. "Let's see you get a little more depth behind the table. Try burnt umber with a dab of deep ochre. You need to push the curtain back but bring the pleats forward."

"Was she happy to see you?"

"She was probably happy to be rescued but I wasn't the person she most wanted doing that."

"Is she still pissed about the grant thing?" Macy lazily pinched out a dab of paint on a board.

"Yes. Can we concentrate on art?"

98

"Is it true? What Deena said about you and Joanna. Did you really cheat on her?"

"Is this conversation really necessary?"

"I was just wondering how anyone could cheat on that gorgeous bouquet of womanhood. I mean, she isn't my type. But God, she is one hot-looking babe, for an art conservator. Don't you think?" Macy looked at Chandler curiously.

"That's too much ochre," she said, frowning at the glob of paint. It seemed like an easy way to ignore Macy's question.

"Well, don't you and did you?"

"Don't I and did I what?" Chandler snapped.

"Don't you think she is hot looking and did you cheat on her?"

Chandler plucked a brush from the jar and began mixing the paint, finding it hard to hide her frustration with Macy's insistence.

"Yes, she is a hot-looking woman."

"And the other?" Macy hadn't taken her eyes off Chandler. "Did you cheat on her?"

"She saw it that way. And before you ask anything else, as Deena would say, the rest is none of your business."

"Aren't we Miss Grumpy today?" Macy said sarcastically. "I was just asking."

"Well, ask less. Paint more."

Macy was silent for a minute then said, "One more teensy little question, okay?"

"What?" Chandler knew she wasn't going to give up until she asked it, whatever it was.

"Do you still love her?"

Chandler glanced over at Macy. She had never considered that a question she might ask. In fact, she had never considered having to explain that part of her life to anyone ever again.

"I thought so," Macy said, pulling a sympathetic smile.

"I didn't say anything," Chandler argued.

"You didn't have to. You still love her."

"I don't know where you get this stuff. No wonder you're a fiction writer."

"You love her. Always have. Always will. Hence, no dating. Not even me. You are living with the heartache you caused by cheating on her. You have donned the veil of martyrdom as punishment for your transgressions."

"What is this? Fiction psychology? You make it up as you go along?"

"The only thing we don't know, the one key piece of information necessary to complete this plot progression, is does Joanna still love you."

"I can assure you the answer to that is no. Now, the inquisition is over. The end. Period."

Macy opened her mouth to say something else but Chandler held up her hand. "Unless this has something to do with paint, don't say it. I mean it. I'm the teacher. You're the student. The social hour is over."

"I was only going to ask if that is your phone ringing," Macy said.

"Oh." Chandler turned and trotted down the stairs to answer it. "*Buon giorno.*"

"*Buon giorno.* This is Francesca." She sounded frantic.

"Hello, Francesca. What's up? You sound upset."

"*Si.* I am," she said dramatically. "Is Joanna coming to the basilica today?"

"I think so. Why? Is something wrong?" Chandler checked her watch. "She should be there any time now?"

"Did you talk to her yesterday?"

"Yes." Chandler didn't want to admit Joanna got herself lost. She owed her that much, not to completely destroy her dignity. "Something important came up. It was unavoidable. But I'm sure she'll be there today."

"Good. It is most important she come today. I have to go." Francesca hung up before Chandler could ask why or if there was a problem.

"Macy?" Chandler called from the bottom of the stairs. "Can you work awhile on your own? I need to run an errand."

"Sure."

Chandler made it to San Marco in record time, partly because the traffic on the vaporetto was light and partly because she practically ran the last hundred yards up the piazza. She impatiently waited her turn in the line to get inside then pushed her way through the crowd toward the baptistery. Francesca was standing just inside the door, talking on her cell phone.

"Did she make it?" Chandler asked.

Francesca pointed to the back of the baptistery where Joanna was flipping through a stack of photographs. It took a moment before Joanna noticed her and looked up. For a split second Chandler thought she saw a twinkle in her eye before her expression turned serious.

"What are you doing here?" Joanna asked as Chandler strode up to her.

"Did you get lost again?"

"I beg your pardon. I did NOT get lost." She went back to her photographs.

"Francesca called me. She said you hadn't showed up yet."

"Well, I'm here. Your reputation is secure." Joanna kept her eyes on what she was studying.

"Was there a problem here this morning?" Chandler insisted, anxious to hear what had happened. "Francesca called at nine forty-five. I thought you began work at nine thirty."

"Why did she call you? She knows where I'm staying."

"She was worried."

"Oh, that's right. Chandler Cardin is protecting her reputation because she recommended me for the grant. I have news for you, Chandler. I can make it to work without you checking up on me."

"Signora DiCarmo?" Adriana called from the baptistery door. "Father Aldo is ready to say mass."

Chandler could see a tiny worry wrinkle form over Joanna's nose. That was her frustration wrinkle, the one that cropped up when she was exasperated with someone or something beyond her control.

Joanna heaved a sigh then turned to Chandler. "I need to talk with you for a minute," she said sternly.

"Now?"

"Yes, now. I'll be upstairs in the lab, Francesca. Let me know when Father Aldo is finished."

Chandler followed Joanna out into the narthex and up the stairs to the workroom and the tiny adjoining laboratory.

"Is this the laboratory for all the basilica's restoration?" Chandler asked as Joanna unlocked the door and let them in.

"There's another larger one in the building across the street but this is the one being made available to me." She snapped on the light in the lab and set the photographs on the table. "I can do some things here. Some tests have to be run across the street."

"What did you need to talk to me about?" Chandler roamed around the room, looking at the odd pieces of marble, granite and ornamental detailing, most of them broken and fragile. "What's this?" She picked up a sliver of something dark. "Part of a crucifix? Some ancient saint's bone?"

"Neither. It's the guide from the top drawer of the desk." Joanna took it and slipped it in the drawer. "What I want to discuss with you is us. Would you like to sit down?" Joanna pointed to a wooden stool.

"No, thank you," Chandler said then gave a coy smile. "Us? I thought you said there was no us."

"There isn't. And that's the way I want to leave it. I don't want our personal life to interfere with my professional life. I don't want another situation like what just happened. That is very unprofessional and I can't have Francesca knowing there is anything in our past that is going to become a problem."

"There is no problem. I was just checking to see if you made it work. She called me, Joanna. She was worried, that's all. I came to see if I was needed."

"And why did you come to the basilica yesterday? Did she call you when I didn't show up?"

"No. I came by and she told me you hadn't come in to work."

"But why were you here at all?"

"Couldn't we just say I came by to see how the work was going?"

"Is that the reason?" Joanna didn't sound like she believed her.

"Yes. Partially," she finally added. "Okay, I had another reason. I wanted to apologize."

"For recommending me without asking first?"

"That and I wanted to apologize for being an ass, as you put it. Our first meeting at Tavolino didn't go very well. And the second one went even worse. I'm sorry. I wanted you to know it was all my fault. And yesterday, I was a little judgmental. I didn't mean to make it sound like you couldn't have found your way home without help." Chandler diverted her gaze. "I was worried," she added quietly.

"Apology accepted. I understand you have a vested interest in my work. But that's where I want to draw the line. I don't want a repeat of what just happened. I don't want to have to explain our past to anyone, especially Francesca."

"She wouldn't say anything. I've known her since I moved to Venice. She's trustworthy. Your grant money is secure."

"This has nothing to do with the grant. It has to do with privacy. No one needs to know we were once in a relationship. That might invite suspicions of nepotism. I'm having enough trouble with Signor Vittori without fueling that fire."

"Carlo is a jerk," Chandler said disgustedly. "I'm sorry if you are having trouble with him."

"I can handle him if you and I can agree to a truce, Chandler."

"I didn't know we were at war. But yes, I should probably have asked before recommending you. I was afraid you'd say no just because it came from me. I wanted this project to have the very best."

"Thank you but I'm not the best. I'm just one of many qualified to do the job."

"So you have forgiven me?"

"Yes, I forgive you. You only had Saint Mark's best interest at heart," Joanna said softly.

"I meant have you forgiven me for what happened two years ago," Chandler asked solemnly.

Joanna seemed surprised she would even ask that, too surprised to answer. She turned away.

"Maybe I shouldn't have asked that. I'm sorry, Joanna. I had no right," she said, touching Joanna's arm.

"I need to apologize as well. I wasn't very appreciative of your help yesterday. I was so mad at myself I couldn't think straight. I let my stubborn pride get in the way."

"That's okay. I came on a little strong."

"Chandler, we have to work together here." She looked back at Chandler plaintively. "We have to at least pretend to get along."

"Pretend we're friends."

"Yes. All I'm asking is you not say anything. Act natural. You know, as if nothing happened. It shouldn't be difficult. We're adults."

Chandler studied Joanna, trying to read her motives.

"What? You can't do this one little thing for me?" Joanna asked. "I'm not asking you to lie. We can get along. People do it all the time. I'm perfectly capable of ignoring our past. It is just history. Nothing more."

In the middle of Joanna's explanation, Chandler couldn't stop herself. Something in her eyes, her voice, was screaming at her, beckoning her closer. In that one moment, Chandler needed to know the answer to Macy's question. Did Joanna still love her? Was there any spark of affection still left? There was only one way to find out.

Chandler leaned over and kissed Joanna, taking her completely by surprise.

"What are you doing?" Joanna gave a stunned gasp and backed away.

"Getting along." Chandler moved closer. "Isn't that what you wanted?"

"That is NOT what I meant and you know it. I just meant—"

Before Joanna could finish, Chandler kissed her again, this

time parting her lips and pressing her tongue against Joanna's clenched teeth.

"Nut-uh. Nut-uh," Joanna muttered as Chandler continued to kiss her.

"Uh-huh," Chandler moaned, leaning her back against the counter.

"Nut-uh." Joanna unclenched her jaw just enough for Chandler's tongue to slip inside. Chandler could feel Joanna's hand slide around her waist.

"Uhhh-huhhhh," she sighed, her arm pulling Joanna closer.

Joanna didn't seem to be able to catch her breath. The shock of Chandler's kiss had rendered her speechless, something that didn't happen very often. For Chandler, the exhilaration at having Joanna back in her arms was enough to make her weak in the knees.

"See. We can get along," Chandler whispered softly, her arm still holding Joanna against her.

The door opened and Francesca rushed in, her face red and flustered. Joanna quickly stepped away from Chandler, wiping her hand across her mouth to repair her smudged lipstick.

Francesca didn't seem to notice anything unusual. "There you are. I am so angry." She shook her head and waved her arms in the air as if dispelling a curse.

"What's wrong?" Joanna asked.

"Carlo is going to drive me insane."

"Signor Vittori?"

"*Si*, but today, he is just Carlo, the idiot."

"Why?" Chandler asked, her eyes falling softly on Joanna before turning her attention to Francesca.

"He has petitioned the Procurator's Council." She folded her arms over her head like she was protecting herself from falling plaster. "I will kill him for this."

"Petitioned them for what?" Joanna asked cautiously.

"He has petitioned them for a replacement."

"To replace him?" Chandler asked.

"No. To replace Joanna."

"Why? I haven't even turned in my report yet. For all he knows, I may agree with him."

"He is trying to convince the council it was a mistake to bring in an outside opinion to decide the fate of the baptistery floor. He is suggesting only Italians can appreciate the true importance of the restoration. He said you don't have the emotional attachment to make the correct decision."

"That's ridiculous." Chandler scowled. "Joanna is the most professional person I know."

"I know exactly why he is doing this," Joanna declared. "He wants to strip off the tessera. He is pushing to have the entire underlayment replaced. He thinks just repairing the mosaic is like smoothing unstable frosting on a rotting cake."

"Did the council agree with him?" Chandler asked.

"They haven't decided yet. They are meeting to discuss it. Carlo is suggesting they honor the grant to you but put him in charge of the restoration. According to him, hundreds of thousands of euros are being wasted while they wait to begin the work."

"How much time do I have? Do you know when they're meeting?"

"I don't know."

"I need a day. One day," Joanna said.

"What can you do in one day?"

"I want to look at other sections of floor in the basilica. Not just the baptistery."

"It covers thousands of square meters. That will take more than one day, Joanna," Francesca said with exasperation.

"I don't need to examine the entire floor. Just a few key sections."

"What are you looking for, Joanna?" Chandler asked.

"I want to compare the sections of mosaic we know have been replaced with the ones in question. I also want to look at the mortar. Sea salt penetrates the mortar and causes salt explosions under the tessera, pushing them up."

"*Si*, we know this. The Adriatic Sea has saturated the basilica for centuries," Francesca said.

"But it can be a way to determine age. The mosaic shouldn't be removed until I can establish a comparison."

"But don't you think you should spend your time testing the granite under the mosaics? That is what Carlo is most unhappy about."

"If I only have one day, I'd rather spend that time analyzing the mosaic."

Francesca stared at Joanna curiously, as if she wasn't sure she trusted her judgment.

"You hired me to give an appraisal of the floor in the baptistery. If Carlo Vittori has his way, it will all be ripped up anyway. What have you got to lose?"

"A very valuable section of our beloved basilica," Francesca replied.

"And I want to protect that piece of Venetian heritage as much as you do. This is what I do. This is my life's work." She took one of the tessera rescued from the baptistery floor and placed it in Francesca's hand. "Do you really want me to just look at the subfloor?"

"What do I tell my boss in the proto's office?" Francesca asked, looking at the tiny marble tile.

"Tell them I am doing what I was hired to do."

Francesca set the tile back in the box and gave Joanna a nod. "I will talk with you in one day," she said, patting Joanna's cheek. "One day. Carlo will not bother you for one day. Now, come show me what you want to examine." She opened the door and waved for Joanna to follow.

"First I want a closer look at the area behind the altar. I'll need the magni-scanner and the light bar."

Joanna stopped at the door and looked back at Chandler, their eyes meeting for a brief moment. Joanna had said there was no *us* left in their relationship. But the look in her eyes made Chandler think otherwise. Or was this just another desperate plea for silence? Chandler took a business card from her wallet and wrote a message on the back.

Call me if you need anything, anything at all. Chandler.

She set it on top of Joanna's tote bag before pulling the door closed behind her.

CHAPTER 11

Joanna spent four hours photographing the mosaic floor and collecting data. With Adriana's help lugging the cumbersome equipment, she was able to compile several dozen magnified images. The more she thought about it, the angrier she was with herself for not insisting they do this first. Carlo Vittori had almost succeeded in intimidating and distracting her from her primary assignment, that of appraising the mosaic floor in the baptistery. That is what the grant was designed to accomplish and she had nearly overlooked it. Or maybe it was Chandler who had distracted her. Whatever it was, she knew better than to let anything get in the way of her work. She was a professional, paid to put personal matters aside and do what was asked of her.

Saint Mark's Basilica might be larger than anything she had worked on before but the principles were still the same. And her determination to complete the task meant no one and nothing should interfere with her concentration. Not Carlo Vittori. Not Chandler Cardin. And certainly not her kiss, even if it did make her weak in the knees and sent her heart racing. And if Chandler had stayed around until after Francesca left, she would have told her that.

Joanna had collected her coat, purse and tote bag and was reading Chandler's business card when Francesca came in the workroom.

"I'm so glad I found you before you left. I have some bad news." Francesca's face drooped.

"What is it? The Procurator's Council agreed with Carlo and are going to let him rip up the mosaic?" Joanna braced herself for the worse.

"No, no. I haven't heard from them. But you will think this is just as bad. The weather is going to be very bad tomorrow. Rain. Lots of rain. And high tides. They are calling for *acqua alta*."

"*Acqua alta*? That's when the streets flood, right?"

"Yes. The sirens will sound before dawn, alerting the city to prepare for flooding. And the basilica will flood. Not all of it. But some."

"The baptistery? Will it be underwater?" Joanna asked fearfully.

Francesca nodded. "Sometimes, not so much. But this one, probably yes."

Joanna had wanted to see and experience Venice's *acqua alta* up close but not tomorrow and not where she needed to complete her work.

"Maybe it won't be very bad. I can finish my work if it's just a little damp."

"Maybe yes. Maybe no," Francesca replied, shrugging.

"What time is it projected to happen?"

"It will begin to come over the seawall and into the piazza by eight o'clock tomorrow morning. The piazza will be flooded by ten. Twenty-five to thirty centimeters."

"Ten to twelve inches?"

"*Si*. Some places in the city will have less. Along the canal will be more."

Joanna checked her watch then looked back at the worktable and the computer where she hadn't yet examined the photographs she needed.

"No, no, Joanna," Francesca said, wagging a finger at her. "I know what you are thinking. You have done enough for today. Go back to your hotel. Have some *vino*. Relax. Enjoy dinner in Venice. There is nothing more you can do tonight." She seemed to know leaving work unfinished was bothering Joanna.

"I wish I had known. I would have worked through lunch. I could have gotten more done."

"And hurried your work?" She took Joanna's hands in hers and said, "That's why I did not tell you this morning, when I heard the report."

"You knew this morning and didn't tell me?" Joanna asked, both surprised and disappointed at Francesca. "Why, for heaven's sake?"

"I have seen you work. You are very dedicated. You work hard enough. I didn't want you to be distracted thinking you only had a few hours to complete your work."

"But you said I had one day. I thought I'd have tomorrow morning to finish."

"We will have to see what the Adriatic Sea has to say about that. Now, go. Don't worry about the mosaic or marble or anything." She hugged Joanna warmly. "Relax and enjoy."

"I will be here when the basilica opens at nine thirty. Maybe it won't be too bad."

"Maybe." Francesca didn't sound hopeful.

She walked Joanna down the stairs and out the front door of the basilica into the piazza where a light rain had begun to fall.

"And so it begins," Francesca said, folding her collar closed as she stood staring up at the dark clouds.

Joanna popped her umbrella and hurried toward the vaporetto

stop. She now had a new and more pressing issue, more pressing than Chandler's surprising kiss. The time constraints on her appraisal, stiff enough already, had just been reduced even more. In fact, it seemed her work had just come to a screeching halt. Why hadn't Francesca told her high tide was going to flood the basilica? Why hadn't she herself considered the possibility and checked the forecast? She knew this was the season the tides and the rain most often joined forces to wreak havoc on Venice. She blamed herself. And curiously, she blamed the breathless thrill of Chandler's lips against her own. If only she had found it repulsive, even distasteful she would have thrown herself into her work. Instead, there were moments during the day when all she could think of was how soft Chandler's lips still were and how unmistakably attracted she still was to her.

Joanna scanned her travel card in front of the machine and stepped onto the vaporetto clogged with passengers on their way up the Grand Canal. The rain increased and by the time she stepped off at the San Marcuola landing it was a full-fledged downpour. As she rounded the corner and headed for the hotel she heard a sharp whistle, one she instantly recognized as Deena's. She was standing in the doorway of the café across the street, waving her over.

Joanna was soaked to the knees from walking through puddles along the cobblestone streets and would have preferred a hot bath and dry clothes but she hurried to join her.

"Are you drowned?" Deena said, holding the door for her as she collapsed her umbrella and stood it in the holder.

"Almost." She unbuttoned her coat and shook off the rain. "What are you doing over here?"

"Waiting for you. How did your day go?" Deena gave her a kiss on the cheek.

"You don't want to know." Joanna heaved a sigh, ready to put the bad news out of her head but it was hard to do with a monsoon outside the door.

"Sounds bad. Come sit and have a glass of *vino rosso*." Deena escorted her to the table where her coat, book and a half-filled carafe of wine were waiting. "Tell me what happened."

Joanna filled her in, leaving out the part about Chandler.

She concluded, "It makes me mad the fate of this historic piece of art isn't important enough to wait a few days while I analyze the damage." Joanna took a long drink of wine, hoping to quell her anger, at least for tonight. "What did you do today, honey? Did you go anywhere I'm going to be jealous of?" She forced a smile, ready to find a different subject.

"Yes, I did." Deena refilled Joanna's glass, grinning as if her news was exciting. "I went to Mickey D's." She held up her glass, toasting her revelation.

"You went to McDonald's?" Joanna couldn't help but laugh. "You came all the way to Venice to eat at McDonald's?"

"I didn't plan on it. But I couldn't help myself. I had to see what it was like to eat a Big Mac in Venice."

"Well, how was it?"

"It was okay. Not exactly the same but pretty close. The pickle was a little funky. The really good thing is the girls behind the counter." Deena grinned wickedly. "Way sexy."

"I can't believe you are picking up girls in McDonalds."

"I didn't pick up anyone. But it never hurts to look."

"My pant legs and socks are soaking wet and I'm cold. I'm going to my room to change. You stay here. Finish your wine. I'll talk with you later about what we're going to do about dinner."

"About dinner," Deena said hesitantly. "I've already made plans. I hope you don't mind."

"Who are you going to dinner with, as if I couldn't guess."

"Macy, and you can say whatever you want. I'll let you. Go ahead."

"I don't want to say a thing, Deena. If you are comfortable having dinner with Macy, fine. You're a big girl. You think you know what you are doing. Fine. I have nothing to say."

"But you want to say something, right?"

"Nope."

"Josie, you know I hate it when you act all smug and righteous. Go ahead. Say I'm stupid. Say I'm going out with Chandler's

113

girlfriend. Say I'm making a mistake."

"I'm not saying anything. You can have that conversation with yourself. You don't need me."

"Damn it, Josie, I like her," Deena called after her. "You're supposed to yell at me. Tell me I'm being a horse's rear."

Joanna shook her head without turning around. She plucked her umbrella from the stand and went out into the downpour, leaving Deena to her date. She had enough troubles of her own without trying to fix Deena's misguided attractions.

She had just stepped out of her wet slacks and hung them over the shower pole to dry when there was a knock at the door.

"One second," she said, pulling on her robe. "What did you do? Change your mind?" she said as she opened the door. It was Chandler, leaning against the doorjamb.

"Change my mind about what?"

"Oh, it's you," Joanna said with surprise.

"Who were you expecting?"

"Deena." Joanna looked out into the hall but there was no one else there.

"Deena is with Macy. They are probably discussing how to murder a spy without leaving a trace of evidence." Chandler picked up a package she had left in the hall and handed it to Joanna. "You're going to need these."

"What is it?"

"Open it." She stepped in the room and closed the door then leaned on it. "I hope they fit."

Joanna removed the lid to the box and folded back the tissue paper.

"Boots?" Joanna held up one of the green rubber knee-high waders.

"Didn't you hear? Tomorrow is going to be high tide. You'll need those to get around."

"Thank you but I was going to buy some tomorrow."

"You'll be sloshing through six inches of water before you can get to the store. Try them on. Let's see if they fit." Chandler took the other boot from the box and removed the tissue stuffing.

114

Joanna sat down on the bed and slipped her foot into one of the boots.

"Too tight? Too big?" Chandler said, kneeling in front of her and pressing her thumb down on the toe of the boot.

"I think it's okay," she said, wiggling her foot.

"Let's try the other one just to make sure," Chandler said, holding the boot and cupping her hand behind Joanna's calf.

"Your hand is cold," she gasped, flinching and jerking her foot.

"Sorry." Chandler quickly rubbed it up and down on her thigh to warm it. "How's that?"

Joanna slipped into the boot, stomping it down snug. But her eyes were on Chandler, kneeling in front of her. It took a moment before Joanna realized her robe was open and Chandler had an unobstructed view all the way up to her panties. She quickly closed the robe over her lap.

"They fit fine. Thank you. How much do I owe you for them?" Joanna stood up, moving away from Chandler as she tried out the boots.

"Nothing."

"Oh, no. I'm not taking these boots from you without paying for them." Joanna dug in her purse for her wallet.

"Can't they be a gift?" Chandler asked, still down on one knee.

"No, they can't. I pay for them or I give them back." She held out two twenty-euro bills. "Is it more?" She took out another one.

"Why don't you wear them for a day and make sure they fit before you pay me?"

"Why don't you take my money before I take the boots off and put them back in the box?" Joanna insisted, waving the money at her.

"Okay," Chandler groaned and climbed to her feet. "But they were cheap. Real cheap. I got them at one of the kiosks by Rialto Bridge."

"How cheap?" Joanna asked suspiciously.

"Twelve euros," Chandler said but didn't make eye contact.

"I don't believe you. Take twenty."

"It was twelve, Joanna." Chandler took one of the twenties and counted out change. "Here. Eight for you. Twelve for me."

"Thank you. I appreciate your getting them for me." Joanna looked down at the boots, wondering if she would be the only person in Venice wearing ugly green ones.

Chandler joined her in studying them. "I assume you know the basilica will probably be at least partially flooded."

"Yes, Francesca told me. I wish I had known sooner. I'll just have to wait a day to finish."

"Or two."

"What do you mean two?"

"The high tide flooding is forecast for tomorrow and the day after. Didn't she tell you?"

Joanna couldn't keep from groaning at the news. "No, she didn't. Will the water remain in the streets and in the basilica all that time?"

"No, it will recede tomorrow evening but come back up again the next day with the next high tide. It might not be as deep but it will be enough to flood the low-lying areas, like San Marco square."

"And the baptistery."

"Probably. The way it was built, that room is like a bathtub. You step down into it."

"It's amazing to me the entire mosaic floor hasn't bubbled up and floated away from all the years of flooding."

"The artisans who created those masterpieces must have known what they were doing. Which is why you are here," Chandler said, smiling softly. "You are here to protect it."

"I'm not so sure. Time is not on my side."

"I have confidence you'll find a way."

Chandler's confidence made Joanna blush. She tried to hide it by staring at her boots.

"Did you know high water was expected when you came by the basilica this morning?"

116

Just mentioning her being at the basilica that morning brought a small smile to Chandler's face.

"I don't know. Probably."

"Why didn't you tell me? Didn't you think water covering the mosaic I was analyzing might be an important piece of information?"

"I assumed you knew. And if you remember, I believe you informed me your comings and goings were none of my business."

"You're right, I did. I'm sorry. Which brings me to another subject."

"What's that?" Chandler was doing her best to look innocent.

"You kissing me."

"I wondered how long it would take for you to bring that up." Chandler unbuttoned her coat.

Why are you unbuttoning? You certainly don't expect a repeat of this morning's kiss.

"Should I apologize for that, too?"

"Yes." Joanna gave an emphatic nod.

"Okay. I apologize. I'm not sorry I did it but I apologize," she added with a chuckle. "You're still a good kisser, Joanna."

Joanna wasn't sure it made any difference but she asked anyway. "Why in heaven's name did you do it?"

"Why? That's hard to explain." Chandler went to the window and looked out at the street below.

"We're finished, Chandler. We aren't dating anymore. I've moved on and so have you. And that means we don't kiss."

"Who are you dating?"

"That has nothing to do with it."

"Why didn't she come with you to Venice? Oh, crap, it isn't Deena, is it?"

"No. It isn't Deena." Joanna couldn't hide a chuckle. Joanna quickly assessed Chandler's need to know and found no reason to lie. "Actually, I'm not seeing anyone right now."

The news brought an even wider smile to Chandler's face.

"Then I wasn't stepping on anyone's toes when I kissed you."

"Yes, you were. Mine." Joanna scowled. "And you still haven't told me why you did it."

"For the hell of it," Chandler replied with a shrug.

Her flippant answer was insufficient and only served to aggravate Joanna. She had decided two years ago it wasn't worth the heartache to rake up their past but before she could stop herself she said, "You sure have trouble keeping all your eggs in one basket."

"What does that mean?"

"It means you don't seem to be able to restrict yourself to one woman at a time."

Chandler didn't answer. She only stared, her jaw muscles tightening.

"Or do you and Macy have an open relationship? That may be your idea of acceptable, but it certainly isn't mine."

Chandler suddenly looked surprised then burst out laughing. "You think Macy and I are a couple?"

"Of course. It's not hard to notice."

"Then you think Deena is out with my girlfriend, right?" Chandler continued to chuckle.

"I don't think it is all that funny."

"I do. Wait until I tell Macy we are suspected of being a couple."

"You aren't?"

"No," she said, shaking her head.

"But you have been," Joanna suggested.

"Nope. Never have. She'd like to claim that but no. I'm just her teacher and she is nothing more than a student. And a friend. So you see, my eggs are all in one neat little basket," Chandler said, pulling the top of Joanna's robe closed all the way up to the neck.

"Macy and I are not sleeping together. I reserve that pleasure for special people," Chandler whispered as she looked deep into Joanna's eyes. "Very special people."

Joanna couldn't move. She could barely breathe with

Chandler so close and the memory of this morning's kiss swirling in her mind. The fact Chandler had cheated on her was being dimmed by the fact she wasn't in relationship with Macy. She was available. God, help her, Chandler was available. She tried to put that thought out of her mind but it was undeniable. Chandler could still make Joanna moist by just touching her hand.

"But why, Chandler? Why did you kiss me this morning?" Joanna said, barely above a whisper herself.

"Because I had to know." With that Chandler kissed her again, softly, tenderly, her lips moist against Joanna's.

This is wrong. I know this is wrong. I shouldn't be doing this. Remember what she did two years ago. Wrong, wrong, wrong...

"Chandler, I can't. I can't do this," she said, finally able to come to her senses and push Chandler away. She opened the door, holding it while she clutched at her robe. "The fact that you and Macy aren't dating doesn't change our past. I want you to go, please."

"Okay, I'll leave." Chandler stopped in the open doorway and looked back at Joanna. "But you should know I'm reading a lot into that kiss, Joanna. I hope I'm right to do that."

"No, you aren't." Joanna diverted her gaze.

"I think I am," she said, gently lifting Joanna's chin. "And you don't need to hold your robe closed so tight. You are safe with me."

Chandler pulled the door shut, her steps fading down the hall.

Joanna leaned her forehead against the door. She smiled to herself, touching her lips where Chandler had kissed them, then she frowned, mad at herself for having let her do it. She closed her eyes and heaved a deep sigh as a tiny smile reappeared.

She spent an hour with the bed pillows propped behind her head, reading, or at least her eyes were scanning the words. She hadn't assimilated a thing. Her brain was totally consumed with Chandler and their kiss.

She heard Deena come back to her room. She climbed out of bed and went through the bathroom to her door.

"I hope you aren't asleep yet. I need to talk to you," Joanna said, opening the door to Deena's room.

But Deena wasn't alone. She and Macy were on the bed, naked, Macy sitting astride Deena. Both of them looked up in shock.

"Oh, my, I'm sorry." Joanna gasped and quickly closed the door. She could hear giggling.

"Come in, Josie. We're decent."

"No, no, I won't bother you. You go ahead." She knew that sounded stupid but she had never walked in on anyone having sex before.

"Open the door, Josie," Deena said with a chuckle. "You might as well. You killed the mood."

"I'm sorry, Deena. I should have knocked."

"That would have killed it, anyway," Macy said, giggling wildly. "Deena says you're probably blushing. Open the door. I want to see."

"Come on, Josie. Show your face."

Joanna slowly opened the door, peeking inside shamefaced.

"I'm so, so sorry, Macy. I never just walk in without knocking. I'm so embarrassed."

They were sitting up leaning against the headboard with the blankets pulled up over their breasts.

"Don't be. It was cute. It shows how good a friendship you have with Deena."

"Come on in and sit on the bed. Tell us why you're wearing green rubber boots at ten o'clock at night."

The boots were comfortable enough Joanna hadn't taken them off and she had no idea why. Was it because Chandler gave them to her? Whatever it was, she was wearing boots and a robe and feeling silly.

"Are those the ones Chandler gave you?" Macy asked then snuggled closer to Deena.

"Yes. I guess I'll need them to even get to the vaporetto stop tomorrow."

"Deena has no artistic flair. She picked out black ones."

"I've got big feet. The only ones that fit were black." Deena pinched Macy's nose playfully.

"I'll talk with you in the morning, Deena," Joanna said, backing out the door.

"No, no, Josie. What's up? You must have wanted something."

"It's nothing, really."

"She wants to ask if we should be sleeping together since she thinks Chandler is my girlfriend." Macy slipped her hand under the covers and was obviously flirting with Deena's nipple. Deena gave her a seductive wink.

"No, I wasn't."

"Sure you were."

"No, I wasn't because Chandler already told me you two weren't dating."

Macy said, "It's not that I didn't try. But as they say, she just wasn't that into me. And Joanna, I want you to know I would never have done this if I thought you and Deena were a couple." Macy smiled big. "But Chandler is certainly into you."

"No, she isn't." Joanna knew better. It was obvious Chandler did still have feelings for her or she wouldn't have kissed her, twice.

"Oh, yes she is. She may not admit it but she is. She wouldn't have hiked all over Venice searching for you if she wasn't. After she saw you at San Marco, she found out what hotel you were staying at then found the most obvious café and staked it out until you came in."

"She did that?" Joanna had considered their first meeting at Tavolino nothing more than a coincidence.

Deena scowled but before she could say anything Macy put her hand over her mouth.

"I know. Deena hates her. But you really should give her another chance, Joanna. She is such a kind person. At least don't completely close the door on the idea."

The blanket had slid down, revealing Macy's breasts and her dark erect nipples, serving to remind Joanna she had interrupted their lovemaking. This was neither the time nor the place to mention Chandler had kissed her.

"I'm going to bed. You two have fun," she said, smiling and pulling the door shut. "Good night."

"Good night, Josie."

Joanna had no sooner returned to her room than she heard giggling followed by moaning. Like she always seemed to do, Deena had found someone to keep her company. If that was the way she wanted it, good for her. But all Joanna had found was confusion.

CHAPTER 12

The siren that Francesca said would remind Venetians of the impending high water sounded just after dawn and repeated every thirty minutes. Joanna was dressed and standing at the window, watching the rain-soaked pedestrians scurry past.

Deena opened the door between their rooms, yawning and scratching.

"Good morning," Deena said and gazed at her through sleepy eyes.

"Good morning, honey. Is Macy still here?"

"Yep. She's still sleeping." Deena went back into the bathroom to brush her teeth. "So Chandler came over last night?"

"Yes."

"How did it go? Was she still being a pompous horse's rear?"

"No, actually she was very pleasant." Joanna saw no need to chastise Deena for her remark. She wouldn't listen anyway.

"I find that hard to believe," Deena said, standing in the doorway as she brushed her teeth.

"Suit yourself. But I'm telling you she was very pleasant, even kind." Joanna looked over at Deena to see how she reacted.

Deena went back to the sink. "She must have ulterior motives. What does she want? You to forgive her for screwing up?"

"No, she doesn't want anything. She is just being nice to me."

Deena glared at Joanna as she sloshed her mouthwash. She spit it in the sink and immediately asked, "And you don't think that's strange?"

Joanna went back to the window and looked out before quietly admitting, "I kissed her, Deena. Or rather, she kissed me."

There was a long moment of silence. When Joanna looked back, Deena was staring back at her with her mouth open.

"YOU WHAT?"

"Twice. Once yesterday morning at the basilica. Again last night when she brought me the boots."

"She brought you boots so you kissed her? Damn. And I thought the girls I dated were easy."

"That's all we did. Just kiss."

"That's enough, Josie. Do I need to remind you of two years ago?"

"No, no, you don't." She traced a raindrop down the windowpane with her finger. "I have no idea why I let her do it. It just seemed like the right thing at the moment. And yes, I know. Her track record isn't exactly exemplary."

"Exemplary? Hell, it isn't even average." Deena came closer. "Josie, it's none of my business but I don't want you to get hurt again. She's nothing but another heartache waiting to happen."

"I appreciate your concern. " Joanna patted Deena's cheek. "I think you've got enough to worry about with Macy."

"I don't have anything to worry about. Macy is a sweet, kind woman."

"My point exactly."

"We're not setting up house, Josie. We're just having fun."

"Okay." Joanna knew Deena's reputation and what she expected from her girlfriends. It sounded like she had found exactly what she was looking for from her trip to Venice. A casual, consenting and attractive bed buddy. Joanna wondered why she had never found casual sex thrilling like Deena did. The hollowness of it wasn't what she wanted, not then, not now, not ever. If that meant she was doomed to sleep alone, so be it. Sometimes the logic of that philosophy was a bit obscure. Especially on a cold, rainy night after the love of her life had just wandered back in and planted a kiss on her lips that curled her toes. Her pillow was a poor substitute for Chandler's warm body.

Joanna ate breakfast in the dining room before riding the vaporetto to San Marco. As soon as she stepped off the water bus she saw the devastating effects of *acqua alta*. The tides and rain had joined forces to bring the lagoon over the seawall and into the piazza, washing the cobblestones with a layer of dirty seawater. It was hard to tell where the sidewalk ended and the lagoon began. The vast square in front of the basilica was awash beneath several inches of water, some low spots even deeper. And from what Francesca and Chandler had told her, it would get even deeper before receding. But the flooding hadn't deterred the tourists, out by the hundreds to take pictures of it, walk in it—with or without boots, and participate in part of Venice's charm and culture. The city had provided raised platforms set end to end for pedestrians to traverse the square without having to wade through the water. They reminded Joanna of high school choir risers, providing pathways for those who were patient enough to follow the single-file line from the dock to the front door of the basilica and other buildings around the square.

Thankful for Chandler's thoughtfulness in providing her boots, Joanna angled her umbrella toward the driving rain as she made her way up to the front of the basilica. Even before she was inside she could see the standing water covering the marble mosaics in the atrium. It was greenish brown and smelled disgusting. The art conservator in her could just imagine the organic material being left by the seawater to decay and fester beneath the aging and cracked mortar. The art lover in her still saw the beauty in the intricate designs arranged by hand hundreds of years ago. The tourist in her wanted to take a picture of it to show she too had experienced a Venetian flood.

"You're here early," she heard a voice call as she entered the cathedral.

It was Chandler, standing against a pillar with her arms crossed. She was wearing faded jeans tucked into a pair of boots identical to Joanna's but with bright orange flames shooting up the sides. The hood of her tan rain jacket was bunched up at the back of her head and her hair was matted to her forehead. Her face looked fresh and eager and like always, free of makeup.

"Hello." Joanna couldn't help but smile. "Nice boots."

"Do you like these?" Chandler looked down, tapping her toes together. "I was bored one night and got a little carried away. I was watching a rerun of *Grease* on TV, dubbed in Italian. The flames are like the ones on John Travolta's car. Now they just look stupid."

"I like them. They're unique. But what are you doing here? Protecting your reputation?" Joanna chuckled, hoping Chandler would think that was funny. She did, blushing bright enough to be seen in even the basilica's dim light.

"I'm probably here for the same reason you are. To see how bad it is." She fell in line behind Joanna as they followed the velvet rope barricade to the baptistery door.

"I was hoping it wouldn't be that deep and I could finish my work."

The door had a Do Not Enter sign on it.

"Shall we take a look?" Chandler said, reaching around her and opening the door.

Joanna held her breath as the door swung open. She was immediately struck by the noxious smell. The seawater had indeed invaded the baptistery, depositing a layer of green slimy water over the pink and white marble mosaic. She stood on the top step, shaking her head as she looked out over the heartbreaking mess.

Chandler stepped down into it. "You know it's going to get worse before it goes down."

"I feel so helpless. It's such a tragedy." Joanna stepped into it, walking carefully so not to splash.

"The floor isn't very even, is it?" Chandler squatted, studying a sunken area several inches deep.

"Not at all. Look over there by the wall. It isn't even wet. It slopes up."

"And this is the area you're analyzing, right?"

"Yes, this whole center section." She pointed out the perimeter.

"Pretty, isn't it?" Chandler reached down through the water, running her finger over the tiles.

"Yes. Gorgeous workmanship. And to think this was all done before electricity or running water or central heat. Each tiny tile was cut and set by hand with only the simplest tools."

"Yep. And no computer printout to show them what the grand scheme was." Chandler smiled up at her. "How would you like to see some of Venice's other sites instead of spending the day depressed about this?" She brushed off her hands and climbed the steps.

"If you mean the Rialto Bridge, I've seen that. And when I was lost, I must have crossed every square and bridge on this side of the Grand Canal."

"That's my point. You're only seeing half the city if you don't venture to the other side. There's a whole list of things to see away from San Marco and the Rialto Bridge."

"I know. And before I leave I hope to see them. I just haven't had time yet."

"Then, shall we?" Chandler opened the door and held it, bowing deeply. "Your tour guide is at your complete disposal, Madame."

"I thought you gave art lessons during the day."

"Normally I do but I told Macy we were taking the day off. I think she had other plans anyway." She gave a coy smile.

Joanna couldn't say no. As hard as she tried and regardless of what had happened in the past, she couldn't bring herself to decline Chandler's offer. She looked back at the flooded mosaic, resigning herself to the fact there would be no work done today. She then looked up at Chandler. Why not, she thought. Why not act like an adult and accept her offer?

"If you're sure you don't mind showing me around, I'd love to see more of Venice."

"My pleasure, Joanna." Chandler's smile lit her face, twinkling in her eyes. She held out her hand to Joanna and waited for her to take it.

Joanna felt a flutter deep down in her stomach, the same flutter she used to feel when she would see Chandler coming down the street and run to meet her. She hesitated a moment, her eyes searching Chandler's for even a hint of trust. Had Chandler changed? Could Joanna trust her enough to spend the day with her and not regret it? Even though it would be completely innocent, Joanna wanted that assurance this wasn't a mistake. Chandler stood with her hand out, patiently waiting for Joanna's decision. Something in her eyes told Joanna it would be all right and she placed her hand in Chandler's, accepting her help up the steps.

It had stopped raining, or at least it had stopped dumping on the city. A fine mist was falling, just enough to dampen hair but not require an umbrella.

"Don't you have an umbrella?" Joanna asked, holding hers over her head.

"I don't use one. Just a hood." Chandler left her hood back, grinning up at the sky. "I like the rain."

They rode the vaporetto to the San Toma stop then followed the crowd up a narrow street and around the corner to the left. As was custom, they walked single-file to allow unobstructed passage for oncoming pedestrians, Chandler leading the way. Many of the shops had a two- to three-foot-tall metal plate blocking the doorway and acting as a dam to keep out the rising waters. Joanna fell behind. Managing her umbrella so she didn't poke anyone with it and avoiding the deeper puddles left her well back as Chandler rounded the corner.

"Chandler, wait," she called, trotting to catch up but as she came around the corner Chandler was nowhere in sight. "Oh, pickles and poodles!" she grumbled. "Have I done it again?" She scanned the crowd looking for a tall brunette in a tan rain jacket and feeling foolish for not keeping up with her. "Chandler?"

"In here, Joanna." Chandler was standing in a darkened doorway. It was the side entrance to a huge brick building that seemed to fill the entire square and was the object of dozens of curious tourists.

"There you are," Joanna said, heaving a sigh of relief and crossing to her. "I thought I was lost again."

"Don't worry. I won't let that happen." Chandler took her hand and led her inside. Joanna had meant it jokingly but Chandler seemed to be dead serious. And that fact gave Joanna a surprising sense of security.

"What is this? Whatever it is, it's huge. Is this the Frari Church?"

"Yes. My favorite collection of art in all of Venice. I want to share it with you. I've already got your ticket." She waved the tickets, grinning like an eager child.

Chandler guided Joanna through the admission gate and into the cavernous cathedral. The ancient building was cold and musty smelling. The pieces of art and sculpture were sparsely lit, most of them accented by a single spotlight. Tourists roamed the sanctuary, their voices echoing up to the vaulted ceiling. Chandler led Joanna around the room, pointing out works by Titian, Donatello, Bellini and others. They discussed color, depth, religious interpretation and relevance to the Renaissance. Their personal relationship and all the painful memories were forgotten as they studied the exquisite pieces of art and sculpture. For that moment in time, it was their appreciation and understanding of art that bonded them. They spent two hours studying and admiring the works before stepping back out into the street.

"Good, it's stopped raining," Chandler said, steering Joanna down the street. "I've got something else I want you to see."

"What's that?"

"You'll see." She gave a cheeky grin and hooked her arm through Joanna's as they walked along. "It isn't as old as the Frari but it's a Venetian must-see."

"Aren't you going to tell me what it is?"

"Ponte de le Tette."

"Okay. Now can you tell me in English? All I understood was *ponte* which means bridge, right?"

"That's right."

"Is it a big bridge?"

"No. A little one. Off the beaten track but important to the cultural history of Venice." She continued to grin, seeming to enjoy that she had piqued Joanna's curiosity. "Watch the puddle."

Joanna allowed Chandler to guide her around corners, across squares and down back alleys until she was sure she couldn't possibly find her way back without help.

"And you're sure you know where we're going?"

"I'm sure. But in case I'm wrong, have you been dropping bread crumbs?"

"Should I start now?"

"Never mind. We're probably already too far off the canal to be rescued anyway."

She laughed, squeezing Joanna's arm.

"At least this time it won't be my fault if we're lost." Joanna returned a playful bump.

Chandler led her through a passageway and around a corner then stopped, pointing at a small stone bridge that arched over a narrow canal. "There it is."

"That's what we came to see? I suppose you are going to tell me why this is a significant piece of Venetian culture."

"Absolutely. But you have to climb up on the bridge first."

Joanna followed her to the apex of the bridge and looked down into the canal. It too had risen and was lapping at the sidewalk that ran alongside. The surrounding buildings were covered in well-worn and cracked plaster. The windows were small and simple. Joanna scanned the neighborhood, the art conservator in her analyzing and dating the buildings. A tarp-covered gondola was tied to a landing a few dozen yards down the canal but there was no one else in sight and the silence was eerie.

"Okay, what's the story behind Ponte de le Tette?" Joanna asked, leaning back against the stone railing and smiling.

"You are looking at one of the more unique historic bridges in Venice. Ponte de le Tette. The bridge of tits."

Joanna couldn't help but burst out laughing.

"The bridge of tits? You have to be joking."

"Ponte de le Tette." Chandler pointed to the sign on the adjacent building. "It's no joke. This happens to be a very important bridge. Or so the Serenissima decreed. This used to be the heart of the red-light district. Behind these humble walls, many a Madame plied her trade. By the fifteenth century, Venice was thought to have about ten thousand prostitutes and many of them worked this part of town. Sex was pretty much everywhere. Men and women, men and men, women and women, you name it. Unfortunately, the nobles and the city council were more than just a wee bit homophobic. First they tried to stop homosexuality by passing a law against it. Any man caught having sex with another man was publicly decapitated in San Marco square." Chandler sliced her hand across her throat.

"Really? Chopped their heads off?"

"Yep. But just men. Three hundred years ago women were pretty much ignored. They were only good for cooking, cleaning, spitting out kids and being sex slaves. The nobles figured women having sex with other women was because the men weren't doing their job. But when lopping off heads didn't discourage homosexuality, the council decided that the ladies of the night needed to do a better job of attracting the men. It was thought that if the prostitutes were more readily available then men wouldn't go looking for other men. So it was decreed that the

131

ladies of the evening should bare their breasts, and anything else they felt necessary, to attract the men."

"So women stood on this bridge topless?"

"You got it. The city council told them to flaunt them big time." Chandler opened her jacket and pranced back and forth. "Come and get it, big boys." She laughed.

"I assume it didn't work to eliminate homosexuality," Joanna said, chuckling at Chandler's antics.

"Nope. Probably made for some very wealthy pros, though. I bet you never thought you'd visit a site dedicated to eradicating being gay."

"No. I can't say I did. I have to take a picture." Joanna pulled out her camera. "You stand up here in the middle. I want to get a shot of this. No one is going to believe me when I say there is a bridge in Venice dedicated to tits." She climbed down and backed along the sidewalk to get a shot of Chandler holding her coat open. "That's good. Let me get another one with the sign in the background," she said, taking one more step backward. "I want the entire bridge in the picture." But that one step was one too many. She lost her balance and stepped back into the canal.

"Joanna!" Chandler screamed and ran down the bridge. "Oh shit!"

Joanna was both shocked and stunned at the cold water. She wasn't submerged for more than a moment but it was enough to turn her into a thrashing maniac. In one adrenaline-driven grasp, Chandler reached down and hoisted her up onto the sidewalk by the lapels of her coat.

"Are you okay?" Chandler didn't let go of Joanna's coat, her white knuckles holding tight to her. "No, you're not, are you?"

Joanna was too stunned to do anything but gasp. She was soaked to the skin and frightened. She never thought the seawater would be that cold.

"Take off your coat," Chandler demanded, pulling at the sleeves. She quickly took off her own coat and wrestled Joanna into it, zipping it up to the neck. Surprisingly Joanna's tote bag was still over her shoulder and her camera was still in her hand.

Chandler dropped the camera in the tote, slung it over her own shoulder and collected Joanna's coat. "Come on. We need to hurry and get you out of those wet clothes."

"I can't believe I fell in," Joanna said.

"I know. You're in shock. The longer you're in those wet clothes, the colder you're going to be." Chandler wrapped an arm around her, hustling her down the street.

"Are you sure this is the right way?" Joanna asked with a quiver in her voice. She assumed Chandler was taking her to her hotel where she could get out of the cold, wet clothes but she was too cold to make sense of it.

"Yes, I'm sure." She hurried Joanna along, hugging her close. "Come on, Joanna. Walk faster." They finally rounded a corner and stopped in front of a green door. Chandler already had her keys out and unlocked it.

"Where are we?" Joanna wondered why she even asked. She was too cold and too wet to care.

"My apartment. Come on, Joanna. We've got to go upstairs."

Nothing made sense to her. She knew she should object but at that moment all she could think about was how cold she was. Chandler trotted ahead, yelling encouragement for her to hurry. When Joanna reached the hall at the top of the stairs and saw Chandler pointing up another staircase, she felt her legs growing weak and each breath torture. It was all she could do to climb the stairs.

"In here, Joanna," Chandler called from the bedroom. "Get out of your wet clothes." She set a pink sweater, black spandex pants and a clean towel on the bed. Joanna stood watching her, shivering, her mind too numb to think. "Joanna, take your clothes off," Chandler demanded. "You're white as a sheet. We've got to get you warm before hypothermia sets in."

"I'm so cold," Joanna mumbled, unable to move or even blink.

"I know, baby. I know. We're going to get you warm."

"What?" she heard herself say mindlessly.

"Shit. Don't you pass out on me." Chandler grabbed Joanna around the waist to hold her up.

"Joanna? Joanna?" She heard Chandler's voice coming toward her through a fog. When she opened her eyes she was in bed, covered to the neck with a heavy comforter. "Joanna, can you hear me?"

"Yes," she managed feebly. "What happened? Where am I?"

"You fainted. You're in my bed. How are you feeling?"

Joanna looked over at Chandler lying next to her under the covers. She could feel Chandler's arms wrapped around her. It was all suddenly coming back to her in an embarrassing rush of emotion.

"What are you doing in bed with me?"

"Trying to warm you up. You were so cold you passed out before I could get you into the dry clothes." Chandler rubbed her hand up and down on Joanna's leg as if she still needed warming. "Are you feeling warmer?"

"Chandler, are you naked, too?"

"How else was I going to warm you up? I used the old principle of shared body heat."

"You could have just covered me up. You didn't need to rub up against me. Stop that. We're not dating anymore. We broke up. Remember? Get out of this bed, right now."

"Okay. I'm going." Chandler tossed back the covers and stood up, her body just as toned and sleek as Joanna remembered. "By the way, even limp, white as a ghost and passed out, your body is still incredible." She seemed to know exactly where Joanna's eyes would go and they did. As much as Joanna tried to fight it, she couldn't help staring at Chandler's dark nipples and the thick patch of curly hair. "I left a towel and some clean clothes for you in the bathroom so you can shower off the canal water." She finally stepped into her clothes and left Joanna to her privacy.

Joanna got up and showered, allowing herself an extra few minutes under the warm water. Even the brutal New England winters had never left her as cold as she felt wearing clothes soaked in frigid October seawater. And once again, she had Chandler to thank for coming to her rescue.

She washed her hair, towel dried it and replaced the band

holding the ponytail. She pulled on the pink sweater and spandex pants Chandler had set out for her. The sweater wasn't as loose as she'd like considering she wasn't wearing a bra. She tugged at the hem and sides to loosen them but her nipples were still clearly visible.

"Chandler, where are my wet clothes?" she asked, coming out of the bedroom. "I want to take them back to the hotel and wash them out before they start to smell like dead fish."

Chandler was pouring hot water into a teapot. She nodded toward the washing machine. "After a soak in the canal they need to be machine washed. Sugar in your tea, right?"

"Yes, thank you. But I don't want to be a bother."

"You aren't, Joanna. Believe me, you aren't a bother at all." There was something joyful in the way she said it as if Chandler had just been given a present. "I stuffed your boots with towels. It won't dry them completely but good enough for tonight."

"Chandler, I really appreciate the shower and the dry clothes, but—" Joanna started, but Chandler thrust a cup of tea in her hand and smiled.

"Here, drink this. It's herbal tea. You need it to regain your strength. That sweater looks good on you by the way. Pink is still your color."

"Yes, well, it's a little revealing." She crossed her arm over her chest.

"Don't do that." Chandler pulled her hand down. "You look sexy. Don't hide it and don't be so self-conscious."

"Judging by the way this fits me, I have to ask. Have you ever worn this sweater?" Joanna looked down, tugging at the hem. "It seems like it would be a little…"

"A little too small for me? Yes. I'm sure it is. I've never worn it. It was a gift."

"I like the color but maybe I shouldn't be wearing it if someone gave it to you. Have you got an old sweatshirt or something?"

"Nope. I want you to wear it. And it wasn't a gift to me." Chandler adjusted the neck, flipping Joanna's ponytail out of the way.

135

"If this wasn't a gift to you, oh, good grief. Is this a gift you were going to give someone? Chandler, you shouldn't have me wear it if you are going to give it to someone else."

"I want you to."

"No. I insist. Find me something else to wear before I get it all stretched out of shape." Joanna set her cup on the counter and headed back into the bedroom.

"Joanna, it was a gift for you," Chandler said then sipped her tea, looking for Joanna's reaction.

"Me? I don't understand. Why would you be giving me a gift?"

"I bought it at Filenes in Boston but by the time it was your birthday we weren't still together." Chandler's eyes had gone soft. "I never got a chance to give it to you."

"You mean my birthday two years ago?"

"Yes." She handed Joanna her cup. "Drink your tea."

"Why didn't you just take it back?"

"I didn't want to." She smiled over the rim of her cup then took another sip. "I was hoping someday I'd see you again and could give it to you. And here you are." Chandler looked her up and down as if she were scrutinizing a painting. "I visualized painting you like that. But your hair was different."

Joanna unconsciously ran her hand over her ponytail, smoothing it into place.

"What's upstairs?" Joanna asked, hoping to change the subject. She stood at the bottom of the spiral staircase, looking up at the light streaming in from the wall of glass tiles.

"My studio. Want to see it?"

"No, that's okay." Joanna didn't hold fond memories of the last time she was in Chandler's studio in Boston.

"Come on up. I've got a great view." Chandler started up the stairs.

Maybe a quick look at the view would be all right, Joanna decided and followed.

"You've been busy," she said, noticing the stacks of canvases.

"Those two piles are Macy's. She's really good at starting projects. Not so much at finishing."

136

"Still lifes and landscapes?"

"Pretty much."

"Or as you used to call them, still-scapes," Joanna said with a chuckle.

"And land-lifes," Chandler added, laughing along.

"As I remember, you hated them both."

"Still do. I hate to paint bowls of anything or wide open spaces."

"Just portraiture, right?"

"Mostly. What do you think of my view of Venice?"

"Impressive," Joanna said, standing at the windows. "The domes of San Marco—you must spend a lot of time up here painting. With a view like this, it would be hard not to." Chandler stood beside her but Joanna could feel her eyes not on the city but on her. "What did you mean my hair was different?"

"The way I visualized it?"

"Yes. How was it different? Not that I'm going to change it but I was just curious."

"It wasn't so much different as just combed differently. The way you used to wear it. Down and soft, flowing over your shoulders."

"I don't wear it that way anymore. It gets in the way of my work." Joanna knew she sounded defensive. She never knew why she changed her hairstyle after she and Chandler broke up. It was just easier to say it got in the way and not think about it.

"Do you mind if I see what it would look like down?" Chandler reached for the ponytail holder and slipped it out, releasing Joanna's hair to fall freely.

Joanna didn't stop her and the look in Chandler's eyes made her glad she didn't. No one had ever looked at her with such devotion. Even though they weren't still together it was nice to know someone still did.

"Yes, that's much better." Chandler ran her hand through it. "That's the way I visualized it on canvas."

"Why aren't you painting?" Joanna asked, looking around the studio. "You should. You're too good to just teach."

She shrugged. "I haven't had the time."

"How long has it been since you did some serious work? How many months?"

"Two years."

"Why? For heaven's sake, why?" Joanna pleaded.

"I haven't been in the mood." Chandler tossed it off nonchalantly but something in the way she said it made Joanna doubt that was all there was to it.

"Chandler, you should. If there is one thing I do know, it's that you should be painting. Not teaching."

"Maybe one of these days I'll get back to it." She picked up one of Macy's half-finished paintings and studied it. "You were going to pose for me. Remember?"

"Yes, I remember," Joanna replied quietly.

"I've always been sorry you never did that."

"Things happen." Joanna didn't want to relive that time or the fact her own insecurities kept her from posing for Chandler. She had always been self-conscious. She never felt secure enough in her body to be an exhibitionist. She blamed it on a case of extreme modesty. Somewhere in her memories was an awkward little girl growing up with skinny legs and stringy long hair. From the time she first started school, she remembered hearing how unattractive and homely she was. How she would forever be simple and plain. By the time she was a teenager the damage was done. The cruel and heartless words from a cruel and heartless mother had left her with no self-esteem. It didn't matter that her figure had ripened and her face had matured into attractiveness. Joanna was an intelligent woman, college-educated, world-traveled and sophisticated. But she still couldn't look in a mirror without hearing her mother's words of warning.

Get yourself a good job, Joanna. You're going to need it. No one will give you a second glance. We Lucas women aren't blessed with good looks.

But her mother had been an attractive woman, even stunning. Joanna always wondered if her mother had been told she was unattractive and felt the need to pass on that legacy to her daughter. Chandler had used all her cunning to convince Joanna to pose for her. If they had done it that very afternoon two years ago, that very moment, maybe with one more glass of wine Joanna might have agreed. But a day to think about it was enough for Joanna's modesty and fear to take hold.

"That was a long time ago," Joanna said reflectively.

"Not so long." Chandler turned to Joanna and stared deep into her eyes. "Would you sit for me? Would you reconsider and pose for me?"

Joanna was surprised Chandler would even ask. She chuckled and turned away, making light of it. "No, I don't think so."

"Why not?"

"I'm not going to pose nude for you, Chandler. I told you no two years ago and I'm telling you no again."

"For God's sake, Joanna. I've seen you naked. You've seen me naked. Many times. We've made love. You're a gorgeous woman. I want to capture that."

"Absolutely not."

"I don't paint porn. You've seen my work. No one will ever know who it is. It's the essence of you I want to capture. The power and fragility of you."

"No." Joanna started down the stairs. "I'm not posing naked for you, Chandler. You can stop asking. The answer is no, now and forever. No."

"You know, I can understand you saying no now. But back then? That I don't understand."

"I'm sorry. All I can say is I had my reasons. And the buzzer on the dryer is going off. I better check it."

Chandler leaned her elbows on the railing and looked down at her. "I'm not giving up, you know. Someday I'll get you to pose for me."

"I don't think so." But Joanna hid a smile at Chandler's persistence.

Joanna's clothes needed five more minutes in the dryer.

"How about something to eat?" Chandler said, making up two plates. "It's four o'clock and I'm starved. All we had was that cup of coffee and a half a sandwich by the Frari."

"No, I'm fine. Thank you, though. Do you think the water has gone down in the basilica by now?"

"It's hard to say. Maybe. It depends on how much rain we had and how high the tide was. Let me guess. You want to squeeze in an hour's worth of work this afternoon."

"Yes, I was hoping I could."

"By the time you got there it would be closing time."

"I feel under such a time crunch over this. I thought I'd have two weeks to complete a thorough assessment and file my report. Here it is Saturday and I have to give my opinion in twenty-four hours or risk surrendering my grant."

"But Francesca said they wouldn't take away the grant money."

"I know. But if I'm not able to do the job I was hired to do, I won't keep it."

Joanna went to the window and stared out at the city. The more she thought about it, the more frustrated she became. She doubted she would have accepted the job had she known the time frame would be cut so short. She didn't like being rushed into giving an appraisal. Carlo and the council didn't intimidate her. Being denied ample time to do her job to the best of her ability did. She stood at the window, arms crossed and a worried scowl on her face.

"Here. Eat this." Chandler handed her a plate of cheese, salami, olives and a slice of crusty bread. "You need something in your stomach before you give yourself an ulcer worrying about the mosaic."

"Thank you, Chandler. I appreciate that." She took the plate and ate an olive. There was a key rattle in the door at the bottom of the staircase then it opened.

"Hello. Anyone here?" Macy called.

"Yes. We're here." Chandler called. "I thought I told you we weren't having a lesson today."

They heard two sets of footsteps climbing the stairs.

"I told you they'd be here," Macy said, looking back at Deena. "Chandler is a hermit. She hangs out in her hovel and broods, pining over lost love and missed opportunities to paint gorgeous women." She tossed a wicked grin at Chandler.

"What are you two doing here? I figured you'd be on some far-off island in the lagoon admiring the view over a glass of lust," Chandler teased.

"What a terrible thing to say, Chandler. Shame on you," Macy replied, feigning outrage. "We are not in lust with one another. Are we, Deena?" She pinched Deena's bottom. "Or are we?" She winked then laughed wildly while Deena blushed.

"Where did you get that sweater, Josie?" Deena asked.

The buzzer sounded on the dryer.

"I'll get that," Joanna said, taking her plate to the kitchen.

"I've got it." Chandler opened the door and pulled out Joanna's bra.

"Okay, I need clarification here," Macy announced loudly. "Why are Joanna's clothes in your dryer? Nice bra, by the way."

"I think I'd like to hear this as well," Deena added, scowling at Joanna.

"I can assure you it is nothing like what your naughty little minds are thinking," Joanna said, grabbing her clothes and heading for the bedroom to change.

"Oh, yeah?" Deena chuckled.

"Yeah!" Joanna closed the bedroom door.

When she was dressed and reopened it, Macy and Deena were waiting for her with wide grins.

"You fell in the canal?" Deena said, barely able to keep from laughing.

"You told them?" Joanna frowned at Chandler.

"They forced it out of me."

"You can't be trusted." Joanna shoved the sweater and pants she had been wearing into Chandler's stomach.

"And I thought I was clumsy," Macy snickered.

"Did you fall in the canal, too?" Deena asked Macy.

"No. But I fell off the raised sidewalk during high water last month. Landed on my rear right in front of a big crowd of people. Very embarrassing. I had a skirt on."

"At least no one was around when Joanna fell in," Chandler offered, as if trying to help the situation.

"If you hadn't told them it could have remained a secret."

"You looked good in that sweater and tight pants, Josie."

"They weren't that tight, were they?"

"Your butt looked like it had a coat of black paint on it." Macy giggled. "Besides, it was cute."

"Hey, I'm innocent," Chandler protested as Joanna frowned at her. "I didn't do anything. I just warmed you up and washed your clothes."

"How did you warm her up, Chandler?" Macy asked with a fiendish little grin.

"I covered her with a blanket, of course. How else do you warm someone up when they're cold?" Chandler looked over at Joanna, their eyes meeting.

"Oh," Macy said, seemingly disappointed there wasn't more to tease about. "We came by to see if you want to go with us this evening."

"Where to?" Joanna asked.

"For a gondola ride."

"In the rain?"

"It's not raining. The forecast is for clearing skies until after midnight then more rain tomorrow. Probably more high water."

Joanna drew an exasperated breath then groaned.

"Sorry, Joanna," Chandler said. "Maybe it won't be as high. It's possible the baptistery will remain dry."

"This isn't your fault, Joanna," Macy said. "Don't stress over something you can't control. I think you and Chandler should go with us this evening. We'll have fun and you can forget all about mosaics and flooding and your falling in the canal. What do you say?"

"I think she's right, Josie," Deena said. "You can't control the weather. Don't sit and stew over it. Go with us. We'll ride down the Grand Canal and forget our troubles."

"We'll ride the gondola then have a late dinner. I know just the place," Macy said, taking charge. She leaned into Deena and kissed her cheek. "You're going to love riding in a gondola. The gondoliers sing. They are like operatic tour guides. I know the best place to get one. There is a landing behind San Marco. You can pick whichever guy you want."

"Aren't there any women gondoliers?" Deena asked.

"I wish."

"The council in charge of licensing the gondoliers hasn't allowed any women yet. But times are changing. Maybe someday," Chandler said.

"That's discrimination," Deena said with a frown.

"Yes, but we're talking traditions passed down from father to son to grandson here. The Italians hold on to their heritage with a death grip."

"Anyway, I'm glad there will be a guy gondolier," Macy said, grinning up at Deena. "That way I know you'll be looking at me instead of some cute Italian hottie driving the boat."

"Can we stop by the hotel so I can change my boots for shoes?" Joanna asked, trying to ignore the goo-goo eyes Macy was giving Deena.

It was dark by the time they crossed under an archway where several gondoliers stood visiting and waiting for customers.

"Look at that gondola over there with the red fringe on the seat cushions," Macy said, looking like a kid in a toy store. "It looks like the inside of a cheap hooker's flophouse. How about that one?"

"It doesn't matter to me. Pick one," Deena said, following like a doting spouse. "How about you, Joanna? Is that one okay with you?"

"They all look pretty much the same. Long, black, shiny and a little tippy."

Chandler said, "Don't worry. Gondolas are very stable in the water. You'd be surprised how easily they glide along."

"You'll love it," Macy said. "It's relaxing. And very romantic." She slipped a look at Deena.

"How much does it cost and who do I pay?" Deena asked, scanning the dock.

"You pay the gondolier and you ask him what he charges. The gondoliers own their gondolas so they set the prices and it's pretty much whatever the market will bear. During high season it can be eighty to a hundred euros for an hour's ride."

"How about now? Mid-October can't be high season."

"No. Prices aren't as low as they will be in January when it's snowing but you can still haggle a little."

"Did you know you can be gay and be a gondolier but you can't be a woman," Macy said covertly.

"That's still a load of BS," Chandler muttered, shoving her hands in her pockets.

"I agree," Joanna said. "The gondola trade is kept alive by tourism. They should acknowledge the changing times and allow women to be gondoliers."

"Signoras? Would you like to ride my gondola?" a man asked. He was dressed in the traditional gondolier's wardrobe, black-and-white striped shirt, black pants and flat-brimmed straw hat with red hatband and ribbon. He displayed a congenial smile.

"How much? *Quanto costo?*" Chandler asked.

"For you, special price. Eighty euros." He flashed a big toothy grin as if he was doing them a favor.

"That's a special price?" Deena scoffed.

"Come on. Let's go over to the Rialto Bridge," Chandler said, taking Joanna by the arm. "It's only forty-five over there. The Grand Canal is spectacular at night."

"Signora, wait. I go out into the Grand Canal as well," he said, following them down the sidewalk. "For tonight, I have extra special price for you. Sixty-five euros."

"I'll pay you fifty," Chandler said over her shoulder, but kept walking.

"Okay. *Si.* Fifty euros," he finally agreed, heaving a resigned sigh.

"Deal." Chandler turned and led them back to the loading platform.

Chandler took a seat next to Joanna, across from Macy and Deena.

"Signora, blanket?" He handed each couple a plaid afghan. Macy unfolded hers and draped it across her lap and Deena's, tucking and folding it neatly. Deena leaned back and draped her arm around Macy, watching while she built their nest.

"Warm enough?" Macy asked Deena, looking like she'd give up her share of the blanket if Deena wanted it.

"Plenty," she replied with a wink.

"You want a lap robe?" Chandler asked, unfolding theirs.

"No, I'm fine. You go ahead."

"Let me know if you need part of it. It's only forty-something degrees."

"I'll let you know." Joanna could hear the little voice in her head saying use the blanket. It's cold. But she had spent enough time under the covers with Chandler for one day. So she locked her knees together, buttoned her coat to the neck and slipped her hands in her pockets. She could hear a soft chuckle from Chandler.

The gondolier pushed the boat away from the loading platform and headed them down the narrow canal past returning gondolas and on toward the Grand Canal. "What's your name?" Macy asked him.

"Marcello," he said with a rich Italian accent and a sparkling smile.

"So, Marcello, tell us something romantic about gondolas."

He laughed as he kept a steady stroke of his oar against the *forcola*. "No one ever asked me that before. They ask me many things but not that."

"What kind of things do tourists ask you?" Joanna was eager to know all about these ancient crafts and the allure attached to them.

"Number one question is do I ever fall in the water."

Joanna instantly blushed.

"Number two question, do people kiss on my gondola."

"And do they?" Macy asked, obviously curious to know his answer.

"*Si*. Many people kiss on my gondola. This is the most

romantic place in all of Venice."

"Even women?" Macy asked coyly.

"*Si*. Even women." He seemed to understand what she meant and gave a cocky little grin.

"Good." Macy turned to Deena and planted one on her before she saw it coming. Although Deena loved to chase women, Joanna had never known her to show that kind of affection in public so she too blushed. But joined in with enthusiasm.

"Look at that." Joanna wanted to find something else to discuss before Chandler decided she should demonstrate her kissing ability. "There's a garden behind that iron gate."

"Many of the palaces in Venice have their main entrances facing side canals." Chandler nonchalantly draped the blanket over Joanna's lap. "The only way to see them is from a gondola."

"I've heard the gondoliers singing. Do you sing, Marcello?" Macy asked.

He waggled his hand back and forth. "*Si*, a little." He sounded shy.

"You have to pay extra for him to sing," Chandler said softly.

"Oh." Macy looked up at him curiously. "Joanna, did Chandler show you my paintings?" Her hand was clearly on Deena's knee beneath the blanket.

"Yes." Joanna didn't know how to tactfully give an opinion on her work since nothing she saw was even half-finished. "I like your color palette."

"Thanks. Chandler thinks I lack artistic discipline."

"You do," Chandler chided. "You've started twenty-five paintings and finished two."

"At least I've started something, unlike my teacher who only pretends to paint. Don't tell me those postcard-size paintings and notecard sets are art."

"Notecard sets?" Joanna asked, staring over at Chandler.

"She does these cutzie watercolors of the Rialto Bridge, gondolas and Carnivale masks for the tourists instead of doing real paintings. That's the kind of stuff sidewalk painters do. Not true artists. You are wasting your time. Tell her, Joanna. You know what she can do. Tell her she should be creating breathtaking compositions, not fodder for refrigerator magnets."

Joanna could tell Chandler was uncomfortable with Macy's assessment.

"I bet you could get her back to serious painting, Joanna. Why don't you pose for her?" Macy asked innocently.

Joanna saw the shocked look on Deena's face and quickly said, "No."

"Why not?"

"Because she isn't going to pose naked for Chandler, that's why," Deena declared, once again being the protector. "She is here to analyze a mosaic. Not pose naked."

"I asked her but she said no," Chandler offered, and Deena looked relieved—and gratified.

"I've known Chandler for six months and I've yet to see her paint anything decent. She needs to get back to real artistry."

Macy leaned over Deena, staring up at a canal-side café. "Oh, look. There's that place I was telling you about."

"The one with the chocolate coffee?"

"Yes. It's so good it should be illegal," she said dreamily.

"It looks like those are steps over there that go right down into the water. Can we get off?" Deena asked.

"This isn't like a taxi," Chandler said. "He won't stop and wait while you have coffee."

"Sure it is. I don't want him to wait but I paid for the ride. I can get off anytime I want."

"You don't mind, do you, Josie?" Deena grabbed the railing as they eased up to the stone steps. She helped Macy up the steps then followed.

"We'll meet you later." Macy looked back and smiled.

"Where? When?" Joanna called as they hurried into the café.

"Are you getting off, too?" Marcello asked, resting his foot against the sidewalk to steady the boat.

"No, we're not getting off, too," Chandler replied.

"I don't think we were invited." Joanna gave a last surprised look in their direction.

"Not to worry, Signora. A gondola ride with Marcello is better than coffee. I show you." He steered down the narrow canal and under a bridge. "I show you my beautiful city."

"Yes, it is beautiful." Joanna's eyes couldn't stop darting from one piece of architectural wonder to the next. "It's like stepping back in time."

"*Si*. Venice, she never changes. We have no skyscrapers, no streep stores."

"Streep stores?" Joanna asked curiously. All she could think of was Meryl Streep.

"*Si*. Many stores together in one."

"Ah, strip mall."

"*Si*. Strip mall. My English is not so good."

"Your English is wonderful."

"Yes. I wish my Italian was as good as your English," Chandler said. "Tell your mother she should be very proud of her son, Marcello."

"*Si*?"

"*Si*." Chandler smiled up at him. "*Molto buono*."

The compliment seemed to please him, so much so that, although they hadn't paid for it, he began to sing, his voice rich and melodic, sounding like an operatic aria. His voice echoed off the buildings like an opera house with fine acoustics.

"That was wonderful, Marcello. Thank you," Chandler said, discreetly passing him a folded bill. "*Grazie*."

"*Si, grazie, Signora*," he said, slipping it in his pocket. But he seemed happier with the compliment for his mother than the money.

"Would you tell me something honestly, Chandler?" Joanna asked.

"Sure, if I can." Chandler draped her arm over the back of the bench and looked over at her.

"Why did you recommend me to the Procurator's Council?"

"I told you. I thought the job required an expert."

Joanna narrowed her eyes and studied Chandler. "I believe you think restoring the mosaics is important but I don't believe that was your only motive and I want to know what was."

"What do you think my motive was?" Chandler captured Joanna's eyes and held them with a softened smile.

"I don't know but I have a feeling it runs deeper than just mosaics on a floor."

"Okay, yes. I confess I had ulterior motives. I wanted you to come pose for me," she said, grinning, apparently making light of it. "The only way I could possibly capture you on canvas was to have another look at your fabulous body."

"Like a writer's block, eh?"

"Yes, exactly."

"Uh-huh. Well, nice try but I don't believe a word of it."

Chandler looked down, weaving the fringe on the blanket between her fingers. "It's true. Well, maybe not the nude part. But I do want to paint you someday. And I wanted you to be able to come here and be part of Venice's artistic culture."

"And?" Joanna asked softly.

"And I wanted to see you again. I know you didn't want to see me. But I had to see you one more time. You didn't answer my phone calls. You ignored my e-mails. It was the only way I knew how to reach you. When I heard they were looking for an independent art conservator to take a look at the baptistery floor I knew it was my chance. I already knew Francesca through the Ministry of Cultures Web site for the restoration and conservation of Venetian antiquities. I'm a dues-paying member so I contacted her. I told her she couldn't find a better person for the job. And in case you didn't know it, Francesca is gay." Chandler said it so only Joanna could hear. "I know what you're thinking. But yes, she is. Her last girlfriend was a professional women's soccer player from Germany."

"I would have never guessed." Francesca DiCarmo was as feminine a woman as she had ever met.

"She prefers it that way. She likes to come across as a femme fatale."

"I wonder if she has said anything to Carlo, you know, about me."

"I doubt it. He isn't her favorite person."

"I'm not sure I trust him. He has already discounted the tessera as unsalvageable. He insists they are nineteenth century slipshod repairs and wants them all removed."

"What do you think?"

"I'm not sure yet. I've spent most of my time examining the subfloor, like he suggested I do. I've just begun a closer look at the individual tiles."

"Then deep down in your gut you're not totally convinced the mosaic is not repairable?"

"No, not entirely. And I'd never make that decision until I had ruled out everything else. That would be my last option."

"You ask me why I recommended you for the grant. Yes, I was being selfish, wanting to see you again. But there was something else, Joanna. And you just hit the nail on the head. This is exactly why I recommended you. Since Francesca works for the proto's office and their engineer, she is bound by secrecy and can't tell you but I can. There are seven members on the council, supposedly one for each district in Venice. Carlo Vittori's brother-in-law is one of the council members. He is the one who convinced the proto's office to hire Carlo for the repairs to the baptistery floor. The council has always had a strict policy against nepotism but somehow this got overlooked. We are talking hundreds of thousands of euros to be made off of this."

"If he gets his way and replaces the entire floor, underlayment and all, I'm sure it would be much more than that."

"That's why Francesca is doing her best to keep him off your back and buy you some time. But he is using every trick he can come up with to sidetrack you."

"Thus the subfloor diversion?"

"I'd say so. I'm not saying he's wrong. And Francesca can't prove he is doing anything unethical. She just wants to be sure."

"I'm not ready to sign my name to it, but I'd bet the mosaic won't need to be ripped out. I've seen much worse. And I'd bet the granite underlayment doesn't need replacing either. And if it hadn't flooded today, I might have been able to prove it. I'll be there waiting for the doors to open tomorrow morning. Flood or no flood, I'm going to complete my work."

"How can you examine the tiles if there is an inch of water on them?"

"I remember reading about some repairs done on the church in Ravenna. They constructed a sandbag moat around the area they were working on and had a small pump running to keep it dry."

"And that's what you plan to do?"

"If I have to, yes."

A smile grew across Chandler's face. "I like that you're so dedicated. That's exactly why you are the right person for the job."

"So, let me review what we have. Reasons you recommended me for the grant. I'm dedicated, you were being selfish, Carlo may be plotting something unethical and you want only what's best for the basilica. Anything else?"

"I wanted you to pose for me."

"Oh, yes. I forgot that. Posing." Joanna shook her head and smiled. "Anything else?"

"No, I think that covers it for now. Here we are, back where we started," Chandler said as they floated up to the loading platform. "Thank you, Marcello."

"Yes, thank you, Marcello. It was fun. You are a wonderful tour guide," Joanna said, accepting Chandler's hand as she stepped out of the gondola.

"*Grazie, Signora.* You come ride with me again." He grinned and tipped his hat, steadying the boat with his foot.

"I promised you dinner after the gondola ride. What are you hungry for?" Chandler asked.

"Pizza," Joanna said without hesitation. "I've seen all these cafés selling pizza but I've yet to try one."

"I know just the place." Chandler took her arm as they weaved their way through the evening crowd.

Joanna was busy window-shopping and didn't pay much attention to how they got there but after rounding a series of corners they found themselves walking along the Grand Canal in the shadow of the Rialto Bridge. They crossed the bridge and entered a café, some of its tables under a canopy along the canal.

"*Tavolo esterno*," Chandler said to the maître d'.

"*Si. Tavolo per due.*" He escorted them through the doorway onto the patio. He was ready to seat them at a table near the side of the building but Chandler pointed to one at the railing next to the water. "*Si.*" He smiled, agreeing with her choice.

Chandler held Joanna's chair for her before taking a seat across from her.

"Is this okay?" she asked.

"This is beautiful," Joanna said. "It's like dining on Main Street at Christmas."

"The Grand Canal *is* Main Street." Chandler gazed over at Joanna, the twinkle lights shining in her eyes. "And you look gorgeous tonight." She ordered a bottle of wine then flipped to the pizza page in the menu. "What would you like on your pizza?"

CHAPTER 13

"Dinner was wonderful, thank you." Joanna buttoned her coat as they headed back over the Rialto Bridge.

"I'm glad you suggested pizza. I haven't eaten at that place in months. I seldom pick a place for the view if I'm eating alone." She stopped at the top and looked out over the Grand Canal.

Another couple, young women in their twenties, were leaning against the stone railing, their eyes locked in a lovers' gaze. Joanna couldn't help notice and remember that there was a time when that couple could have been her and Chandler, lost in the romance of the moment.

"I bet they kiss," Chandler whispered, also noticing the women.

"Think so?"

"Yep. Venice will do that to you. It brings out the romance in even the stiffest collar."

"That's what my boss, Dr. Finch, said."

"It's true. Whether you're just starting a relationship or trying to rekindle a stale one, Venice is the perfect place for it." She pulled a frisky grin. "Want to try it? Don't you want to say you kissed on the Rialto Bridge?"

"I don't think so," Joanna said, pushing against Chandler's chest as she tried to step closer.

As much as Joanna said no to the kiss, something inside was dying to say yes and feel that incredible thrill of Chandler's lips against her own. Joanna knew the only way to avoid this was to keep moving so she started down the other side of the bridge.

Vendors with their rolling kiosks of tourist curios filled the street at the bottom of the bridge. The chilly evening temperatures and threat of rain hadn't discouraged the crowds that milled around.

"I like the little gondola," Joanna said, admiring a plastic toy. "Look. It even has a tiny Marcello standing on the back."

"Only ten euros, Signora," the young man said.

"Thank you, but no." She put it back and moved on. "It was plastic and made in China," she whispered.

"All this stuff is."

"I want a souvenir but not that. I could probably find one of those in the Italian North End of Boston."

"If you want authentic Venetian souvenirs you have to look at Burano lace, Murano glass or one of those handmade Carnivale masks."

"Or," Joanna said, smiling at a rack of notecards. "You can buy hand-painted notecards of San Marco." She plucked a card from the rack and held it in front of her face so Chandler could see.

"Oh, crap. You're not going to buy that, are you?"

"Yes, I am. It's an original Chandler Cardin. See the way she interlocks the c's. She makes them look like a little heart."

"Don't buy that, Joanna." Chandler had a pained expression. "It's junk art."

"It's cute. Pastel watercolors. Simple composition. I love it."

"I wish I had some already made up. I'd give them to you so you don't have to waste your money."

"I want to buy it, right here on the Rialto Bridge, the merchant center of Venice." She grinned happily.

"How much is it?" Chandler asked as she dug in her pocket and pulled out a money clip.

"You are NOT buying my card. Don't even think about it. This is *my* souvenir. I'm buying it."

Chandler grumbled something as she moved to the other side of the kiosk.

"How much is this?" Joanna asked the vendor.

"Three euros. Two cards for five euros."

Joanna pulled out a ten-euro bill, checked to see if Chandler was watching then plucked the last three cards from the rack.

"Did you buy it?" Chandler asked as Joanna roamed around the display.

"Yes, I did. And don't you dare say anything. I like it."

"At least they only had that one of my cards."

"How many different scenes are there?"

"Eight or nine. I can't remember. I distribute them through the tourist bureau."

"Does someone around here carry them all?" Joanna moved to the next vendor and scanned the cart.

"I hope not," Chandler muttered.

"Did you do one of Ponte de le Tette?"

"No. I paint things tourists recognize. Most people have never heard of that."

"I think you should include it. Narrow street, pink and white stone bridge. Perfect."

Stop that! Stop visualizing Chandler's firm round breasts every time you hear Ponte de le Tette. And for heaven's sake stop staring at the way her jacket drapes over them.

"If I do I'll send you a copy."

155

"I want a full set of your cards. All of them."

"Joanna," Chandler whined.

"I do."

"If you want to take something home from Venice buy some Venetian pasta or a bottle of olive oil."

"I may take those, too. But I want something that represents the art and culture of Venice. And I want you to stop trying to talk me out of it. You know you can't."

"No, I definitely can't do that. When you set your mind to something, you're pretty much an immoveable object. A blond-haired blue-eyed boulder." Chandler sounded angry but she smiled.

"So you'll help me look for more of your cards?" Joanna pulled Chandler's sleeve as she moved to the next kiosk.

"Do I have to?" Chandler played the complaining child.

"Yes, you do."

They roamed the dozen or so vendors' carts but didn't find any more of Chandler's watercolors, to her relief and Joanna's frustration. It was after nine when their window-shopping ended back at Joanna's hotel. For dessert, they purchased a decadent looking chocolate-covered canoli at the bakery across the street and carried it to her room to share, giggling over the calories it surely contained. Joanna unlocked the door and snapped on the light, hurrying inside to snatch down the clothes she had drying around the room.

"Chinese laundry?" Chandler teased.

"Yes. Sorry."

"I don't mind."

"I do." Joanna cleared the chair but Chandler sat on the edge of the bed, watching Joanna divide the pastry and use tissues as napkins. "Sorry I don't have plates and forks."

"I like it this way. Kind of like a picnic." Chandler took a bite and moaned softly. "Oh, my. Yum!"

Joanna tried a taste and agreed, sighing mournfully.

"I haven't had one of these in years." Chandler consumed hers in three big bites.

"We had canolis at that little bakery on the corner near my apartment. Remember?"

"In the North End, corner of Prince and something. Martinelli's Bakery?"

"Marchiano's."

"They had the best pastry in Boston. I miss that place." Chandler smiled, seeming to enjoy watching Joanna lick the filling out of her pastry shell. "Do you still go there?"

"Yes," Joanna said then grimaced. "I shouldn't though."

"Why shouldn't you?"

"I gain ten pounds every time I walk through the door."

"No, you don't. You've got a gorgeous shape." Chandler gave her a disparaging smirk.

"Thank you but I need to keep at least a mile between me and pastry. I shouldn't have eaten any of this."

"Let me see." Chandler stood up and reached for Joanna's waist.

"Stop that. It tickles," Joanna said, wiggling away.

"Hold still. I'm checking for love handles."

"Take my word for it. I've got them." She backed against the dresser as she ate the last bite.

"Where? In your suitcase? I certainly don't remember any." Chandler moved in for another feel.

"Stop," Joanna giggled, twisting and turning as Chandler tried to pinch-an-inch.

"Consider me the pastry police." She laughed and moved closer, pinning Joanna against the wall. "Left side, no handle. Right side, no handle."

Joanna couldn't help herself. Even the slightest touch to her side sent her into a screaming frenzy and Chandler knew it. Joanna braced her forehead against Chandler's chest as she laughed and fought against being tickled. The more Chandler picked and pinched at her sides the more she stomped and twisted.

"Quit, Chandler. You're going to make me pee my pants," she squealed.

"I'm the pastry patrol. I'm frisking you for concealed

weapons." She chuckled. "I can't feel anything but I know they're here somewhere. How about back here?"

Joanna's sweater had come up, exposing her midriff. Chandler's fingers worked their way around her waist to the back, igniting a new and more intense frenzy. As if jolted by an electrical charge, Joanna jerked her leg, kneeing Chandler squarely in the crotch. Chandler immediately gasped and doubled over, clutching her hands over her mound. It took Joanna only a moment to recover from being tickled and realize what she had done.

"Oh, my God. Sweetheart!" Joanna grabbed for her, kissing the top of her head repeatedly. "I'm sorry. I'm so sorry. I didn't mean it. It was an accident."

Chandler groaned.

"I didn't mean it. I'm so sorry." She placed another healing kiss on Chandler's head. "Do I need to look at it?"

"Damn," Chandler finally managed, sucking air between her teeth. "That'll get your attention." She rubbed herself vigorously as if stimulating the circulation.

"Are you all right?"

"That was worse than the time I rode my brother's bike and sat down on the bar." She took another deep breath, sat back on her heels and braced her hands on her thighs. "Next time, babe, just tell me not to tickle you."

"I didn't mean to do it, Chandler. I swear. It was just a bad knee-jerk reaction." Joanna helped her up so she could sit on the bed. "And I think I did tell you. You know I'm ticklish."

"Yes, I know. I'm going to have to learn not to do that. The last time I tickled you I got elbowed in the nose."

"I remember. I've never seen a nose bleed so much," Joanna said, grimacing. "But I can't help it. I'm just ticklish. I can't stop myself."

"You become like a wild woman, possessed by the devil. By the way, did I hear you call me sweetheart?" She looked up at her curiously.

"Me? No, I don't think so." Joanna couldn't honestly remember what she said. In the panic of the moment she could have said almost anything.

"I think you did. And you also offered to look at my boo-boo. Does that offer still stand?" Chandler grinned and began unzipping her jeans.

"Here, hold this over it. It'll be fine." Joanna tossed her a bed pillow.

"Speaking of kisses."

"We weren't."

"Then why did you kiss me?"

"I didn't."

Oh, geez. Yes, I did. Lots of them. And she may have been in pain but I bet she felt every single one of them.

"How about just one more." Chandler caught Joanna off guard and pulled her down on her lap. "One more for old time's sake and for the sake on my bruised twat."

"Chandler?"

Before Joanna could object, Chandler kissed her. For a moment Joanna relented, that powerful magic in Chandler's lips too much for her to resist.

Oh, please. Don't do that. Don't send your kiss directly to my nipples. I hate it when you do that. How can I stay mad at you when my body wants you to ravage me right here, right now?

"God, I've waited so long for this," Chandler whispered then placed another kiss on Joanna's lips, devouring her with her tongue.

"Chandler, please. I can't do this," Joanna said, struggling to free herself and scramble off her lap.

"Why?" There was a look of complete surprise on Chandler's face.

"We're not dating anymore." She backed away, putting as much distance between herself and Chandler's kiss as possible. There was something tempting in Chandler's eyes and Joanna wasn't sure she had the strength to resist.

"But we could be."

"No, we couldn't." Joanna was mad, at herself for letting the evening get this far and at Chandler for assuming what she did two years ago didn't matter. The more Joanna thought about it, the more tightly she crossed her arms over her chest. "Why, Chandler? Why didn't you find me enough? I swore I'd never ask but I have to know." Joanna felt tears welling up in her eyes. "I'm not blaming you. It had to be me, I know that."

"It had nothing to do with you, Joanna. Nothing."

"Then why? Please. I have to know."

"I loved you," Chandler confessed, coming to Joanna.

"I think I'd rather hear that you didn't." One tear spilled out and ran down Joanna's face. Before she could wipe it away, Chandler pulled her into her arms, the sound of desperation in her sigh.

"I'm sorry, Joanna. I'm so very, very sorry if I hurt you," she whispered. "That wasn't what I meant to do." Joanna tried to pull away but Chandler held tight to her. "I still love you." With that, Joanna couldn't hold back any longer and began to cry, burying her face into Chandler's shoulder. "Shh, don't cry." Chandler's voice cracked and Joanna could feel her tears against her forehead. "I didn't cheat on you," she managed to say.

Her words made no sense at all. How could she even say them? Whatever Joanna's definition of cheating was, it sounded like Chandler's was very different.

"Let me go," Joanna said through her sobs, pushing back on Chandler's chest.

"I didn't cheat on you, Joanna. I made a mistake, a terrible mistake but I never had sex with anyone else," Chandler said, holding Joanna by the shoulders. "I'd never do that."

Joanna stared daggers at her.

"How can you say that? You admitted it to me. You admitted you had sex with Tracey, that model."

"I didn't say I had sex with her. You said that."

"And you didn't disagree with me," Joanna shot back. "You as much as admitted it. You just stood there with a dejected look on your face and kept saying I'm sorry, I'm sorry."

"I know. I was a fool to let you think I did that but I didn't."

"You let me think you cheated. If you didn't do it, why didn't you say so? I would have believed you. But you just hung your head and said I'm sorry."

"I know, I was wrong. I should have said something right then. But you have to believe me when I say I never ever cheated on you."

"Yeah, right. You never cheated like you never look at those naked women you paint."

"That's my work, you know that, just like you look at marble statues of naked women. Yes, I look at them and yes, I admire their bodies and try to capture their beauty on canvas. But that doesn't mean I have sex with them."

Joanna pulled away, too confused to comprehend why she had done it.

"I still don't believe you."

"I know it sounds like I'm lying but I swear to you, I never had sex with Tracey or any other model. Ever."

"If that's true, I don't understand why you'd let me think that. You know that's what ended our relationship." Joanna gasped. "Oh, God. I know why you did it. You wanted out because I wouldn't pose for you. That's it, isn't it? You wanted to get back at me because I wouldn't pose nude for you?"

"No. That had nothing to do with it," Chandler exclaimed.

"Then why didn't you defend yourself?"

"I was afraid."

"Of what?" Joanna demanded, glaring at her.

"Of disappointing you. Joanna, I had never been in a committed relationship before. I was like Deena. I dated someone different every week." Chandler's eyes softened. "Then I met you. I fell in love so fast and so deep I didn't know how to handle it." She shrugged. "I thought I could step back and figure things out but I let it go too far. I read your body language when you came to my studio that last day. You had gone cold. You no longer wanted me in your life. I messed things up bad and I didn't know how to fix them. I just hoped someday, somehow, our paths would cross again and I could explain."

"So you recommended me for the grant?"

161

"Yes."

"What if they hadn't needed me? What if I never came to Venice? You were willing to let me go on believing you cheated?"

"It isn't exactly an accident you're here. I spent the first few months after we broke up hating myself. Then I decided to do something about it. That's why I came to Venice. It was the most romantic place I could think of where your work might bring you. When I met Francesca at the artist's guild reception and heard her talk about the restoration projects in the basilica, I knew fate had dealt me another chance. And here you are." Chandler took Joanna's hand. "I am begging you, Joanna. Pleading with you to believe me. I love you. I made a mistake. A bad one. I admit it. I'm a colossal fool. But please understand I did *not* cheat on you. My God, I could barely figure out how to be in one relationship. How could I be in two or three?" She managed a smile. "I'm monogamous. I sometimes have trouble showing it, but I am monogamous. From the first moment I met you there has never been another woman in my life or in my bed. And when I saw you sitting at Tavolino that first time, I'd be lying if I said that wasn't what I dreamed might happen again."

"Why didn't you trust me enough to tell me this before?"

"You don't know how many times I tried. I drove down your street, praying for the courage to knock on your door. I was afraid you'd slam the door in my face and I'd never get a chance to explain. I can tell you aren't sure how to accept it even now. You're still skeptical."

"Don't you think I have a right to be skeptical? You wait two years then tell me I should forgive you for pretending you cheated on me because you were afraid."

Chandler took Joanna in her arms, pulling her close as if she expected a kiss in forgiveness.

"No, Chandler," Joanna said, placing her hand on Chandler's mouth. "I can't do this."

"I thought you believed me."

"I'm not ready to pretend nothing happened. I don't know if

I can ever do that."

"Tell me what I can do, what I can say."

"Explain why I should trust you now. How do I know you won't find things too tough to deal with and bail on me again? I can't go through that again."

"You're right," Chandler said and stepped away. "You're not ready to trust me and I don't blame you. You need some time to think and I understand that."

"Yes, I do. I've got so much on my mind with Carlo breathing down my neck and high water putting me behind schedule, I can't concentrate on anything but my work right now. I came to Venice to do a job. Now you come in here and tell me you were just joking, all the pain and heartache should just be forgotten. I'm sorry, Chandler. My emotions don't work like that. I need more than a few minutes to process this."

Chandler picked up her coat, opened the door and looked back, forcing a stoic smile. "I understand completely, Joanna. Whatever you decide, I'll accept. But I want you to know I love you."

She closed the door behind her, her footsteps hurrying down the hall.

For a brief moment Joanna wanted to run after her, beg her to come back. Instead, she squeezed the doorknob until her fingers hurt. It was the only way she could keep from calling out to Chandler. She leaned her forehead against the door as she came to grips with what had happened. All the details and the questions paled to the one overriding fact. Chandler had never cheated. But what now? Of course she wanted Chandler. She had always wanted Chandler. But could she live with the fear that one day her worst nightmare might come true and Chandler's demons would return and she would disappear again?

She stood at the door, arguing with herself. The choices were muddied by the job she had to do at the basilica and the fact that her trip to Venice ended in less than a week. She had spent two years adjusting to what she thought Chandler had done. Was she ready to forgive and forget? And what if she did? Joanna wasn't ready to move to Venice, Italy. And it sounded like Chandler had found a new home she wasn't ready to give up either. Yes, she was relieved to know the truth but it wasn't that easy. Her memories couldn't be washed clean by Chandler's kiss or the touch of her hand. She gave a little moan as she turned, smiling as she relived that kiss.

Deena was leaning against the bathroom doorjamb, her arms crossed and a cold stare on her face. She had a white handkerchief wrapped around her hand.

"I didn't hear you come in." She wondered how long Deena had been standing there.

"I heard *you* come in."

"How long have you been here?" She looked past Deena through the open door into her room. The bed was neatly made and there was no sign of Macy.

"A couple hours."

"What's wrong with your hand?"

"I scraped it."

"I thought you'd be with Macy. What happened?"

"Nothing happened with me. The question seems to be what happened here."

"What makes you think anything happened? Chandler and I had dinner, did a little shopping and ended up back here to share a pastry for dessert. They have the best pastry here. Three hundred calories per bite, at least." She sighed dreamily.

"These old buildings may look thick and substantial from the outside but the walls between the rooms are thin, Josie." Deena gave her a long look. "You don't believe what she told you, do you?"

"You heard?"

"Yep. If it had been me, I would have kneed her again. And again. My experience as a cop has taught me once a liar, always a liar."

"Chandler isn't one of your criminals who lie about buying drugs. You weren't there. You don't understand the nuances." Joanna spun on her heels and went to her suitcase to find pajamas.

"I know you don't trust her but this is my decision, Deena. Mine and mine alone. Please don't interfere."

"I just don't want you to get hurt again. But if that's the way you want it, okay." Deena held up her hands in surrender but it was plain she wasn't happy about it.

"How about you? Why aren't you with Macy?"

"She went home after dinner."

"How come? I thought you two were getting along pretty well," Joanna said. Before Joanna could question the odd look on her face, there was a knock at Deena's door. But she pretended not to notice. "There's someone at your door."

"It's nothing. Forget it." There was a second louder knock.

"Deena?" Joanna was surprised at her indifference.

"Just ignore it, Josie. They'll go away."

The knock got louder and a voice called, "Deena? Deena, let me in." It was Macy and she sounded desperate.

Joanna made a move to answer it but Deena stopped her, shaking her head adamantly.

"Deena, please. We need to talk," Macy called through the door.

Deena held a finger to her lips, staring Joanna into silence.

"Why?" Joanna whispered. Deena shook her head.

"Deena?" Macy sounded like she was about to cry. She finally gave up, her footsteps fading down the hall.

"Why, Deena?" Joanna insisted. "What happened?"

"Nothing."

"Don't give me that. A few hours ago you and Macy were practically having sex under the blanket on the gondola. Now you won't open the door for her."

"Look, Josie. I need you to stay out of it, okay? Macy and I aren't joined at the hip. I don't have to be with her every second." She went to the bathroom door and held it as if waiting for Joanna to return to her own room and take her questions with her. "Good night, Josie. I'm tired. I'm going to bed."

"Honey, what's wrong with you?" Joanna studied her face, wondering what happened to make such a drastic change in

Deena's happy-go-lucky attitude.

"For the last time, nothing is wrong."

"I want to help."

"As you most recently and succinctly said, I'll make my own decisions. Please, Joanna."

When she used that name, Joanna knew better than to interfere even though they were best friends. She reluctantly headed through the door, then looked back at Deena. "At least tell me you're all right, honey."

"I'm fine."

Her voice wasn't convincing nor was her face but Joanna didn't argue with her. She squeezed Deena's hand and offered a supportive smile.

"Good night, Josie." Deena closed the door as soon as she was through it.

CHAPTER 14

Joanna was up, dressed and knocking on Deena's door by seven but she didn't answer. Joanna assumed either she had a restless night and was sleeping in or she still didn't want to talk and wasn't answering the door. Joanna went down to breakfast, anxious to get to the basilica. She had stuffed her boots in her tote bag just in case, although the forecast had been revised, suggesting only a slight chance of high water and limited to only along the water's edge. With a little luck and determination, she was going to complete her work today. Yes, it was Sunday but the basilica was open and she wasn't going to be denied. One quick cup of coffee, a croissant and she would be ready to meet the day. Just as she was finishing her last swig of the strong stuff she heard a voice behind her.

"Good morning, Joanna." It was Macy.

Joanna had a brain full of questions for her but the anguished look on Macy's face kept her from asking any of them. "Do you want a cup of coffee? I'm sure they won't mind." Joanna motioned for her to join her at the table.

"No, thank you. I don't want anything. I thought maybe you'd know where Deena was going?"

"Deena? I don't think she's going anywhere. She's not up yet."

"Yes, she is. The lady at the front desk said she left about an hour ago. Her key is hanging on the peg."

Macy sat down as if she expected Joanna to confess what she knew. "Didn't she tell you where she was going?"

"I didn't know she left."

"I have a note I was going to leave under her door." Macy fingered the edges of a small envelope with Deena's name on it. "But if she has already gone, I don't know if I should leave it. I don't want the housekeeper to find it and read it." She looked up at Joanna plaintively. "I feel like I can trust you, Joanna. Would you give it to her?"

"I think you should do that, Macy. I don't want to interfere." *Not to mention Deena told me in no uncertain terms to stay out of it.* "I'm sure she'll be back later. Remember, it's an island. How far can she go?" Joanna chuckled, trying to brighten Macy's face. But Joanna now had a new worry. It wasn't like Deena to run away from her troubles. Treat them with silence or even anger, yes. Run away from them, no.

"I don't mean you should read it and give an opinion. Just give it to her." Macy placed it in front of Joanna.

Joanna looked down at the envelope. She was dying to know what it said and even more, what Deena would think in return. But she couldn't go against Deena's wishes. She slid the envelope back to Macy.

"Whatever is in this note, I think you need to give it to her yourself. You haven't known Deena very long. If I can offer one piece of advice, she is a very private person about some things. I think she'd prefer to get this from you."

"How can I give it to her? She won't talk to me."

Joanna felt the words bubbling up in her throat even though she knew she shouldn't utter them. Just one quick question, she thought. Just one.

"Is everything all right with the two of you, Macy?"

That sounded lame. Of course they weren't all right. Deena didn't answer Macy's knock at the door and now she was wandering the streets of Venice at dawn. Something was definitely wrong.

Macy lowered her eyes and said quietly, "She hates me." Her voice wavered just enough for Joanna to think she was on the verge of tears and placed a hand on hers.

"I don't think she hates you."

Macy only nodded.

"What makes you think so?" If there was one thing Joanna knew about Deena, under that gruff exterior she was a tender, gentle person. She would never knowingly hurt anyone, at least not anyone she was in a relationship with, regardless how short a time it was. "No, wait." Joanna wiped her mouth with her napkin and shook her head, remembering her promise to Deena. "She asked me to stay out of this. Deena is my oldest and dearest friend and I have to respect that. I've probably said too much already."

"That's why I'm here. You and Deena go way back. I thought you'd be able to tell me something."

"I don't know that I can." Joanna ate her last tidbit of croissant then couldn't help herself. "What?"

"Is Deena in a relationship back home?"

"No."

"Are you sure?"

"Yes, I'm sure." Oops. Did she say something she shouldn't have? "At least I don't think she is," she added.

"I didn't think so."

"Macy, I may get myself into *really* hot water for telling you this, but I think you need to know. Deena isn't looking for a long-term relationship with anyone. That just isn't her style. For some reason she has trouble making that kind of commitment."

"I know. It isn't mine, either. But I get the feeling she has some baggage she isn't sharing and that's what friends do. They share. They share and offer support."

"What do you mean by baggage?"

"Deena keeps me at a distance. I know. We've only just met. But there is something she isn't telling me. Something she prefers to keep a secret. She won't or can't share it. And that isn't fair. I'm not exactly sure what it is but it has something to do with her work. But the more I ask, the more closed she becomes. I told her she owed it to me to be truthful. That's what lovers do. They share. And believe me, we have shared a lot of secrets the past few days." She gave a little blush. "But whatever this is, she is unapproachable about it." Macy looked up at Joanna fearfully. "I didn't think she'd react like she did. I just wanted to be supportive. I've asked her a million questions about being a cop for my book. And she's answered every one of them. She's my walking police encyclopedia. But when I ask about her work, her own experiences, she changes the subject."

"She's like that when she is on vacation."

"It's more than that. On the way back to my apartment last night she told me to stop asking. To just forget it. But you know me. Ms. Blabbermouth. I can't stop from asking questions. When I didn't stop, she got this angry look on her face. That's when she hurt her hand."

"She told me she scraped it."

"Scraped it, my ass. She punched a stone wall. She told me to f-off and left me there, standing on a bridge like an idiot. She didn't even wait for me to apologize." Macy straightened her posture. "I don't expect anything from her. I know this is just one of those vacation flings. But I care for her, Joanna. I only want to help."

Joanna placed her elbow on the table and leaned her chin in her hand, watching Macy closely. This was a perceptive woman. She had read Deena like a book. Yes, she had some baggage and yes, it had to do with her work. And most of all, yes, she needed to share her pain with someone.

"Macy, I can't tell you anymore. I promised her. But I can tell you, if you are as good a friend as you think, don't give up."

"What is it? What should I know?"

Joanna stood up and put on her coat. She gave Macy a long look, wrestling with the urge to tell her about the shooting but knowing she shouldn't. She finally headed out the door.

Macy followed like a puppy. "Tell me. I promise she'll never know you told me," Macy pleaded, matching Joanna stride for stride.

"Macy, I just can't." She turned the corner and headed for the vaporetto.

"Joanna. Please. I want to help her," Macy said, pulling at Joanna's arm. "How else am I going to understand why she wants to quit the police force?"

Joanna stopped and glared over at her. "Quit the police force? Deena isn't going to quit. She's a good cop. In fact, she's a great one. She has compassion. She cares about the people she is sworn to defend. She'll never quit. They'll have to take away her badge and lock her out."

"That's not what she told me."

"What did you say?" Joanna couldn't imagine Macy knew more about Deena in a week than she knew in fifteen years.

"She said she wasn't sure it was worth the effort. That's when I asked what happened to change her mind. She said lots of things but then her forehead got all wrinkled and she got this faraway look in her eyes. I knew it had to be something specific. But the more I pressured her to tell me the angrier she got. She finally told me it was none of my business and to just forget it."

"What were you talking about right before that?"

Macy frowned in thought.

"We talked about a lot of things. The long hours. The round-the-clock awareness they have to keep. Oh, and the fact they have to carry a gun all the time, even off-duty. She didn't bring her gun with her, did she?"

"No." Bingo! Deena's gun. Macy said it but did she realize it?

"That's a relief to know she isn't packing a weapon," Macy

said then stopped and rolled her eyes up to Joanna's. "Is that it? Does this have something to do with her carrying a gun?"

Joanna met her gaze with silent agreement.

"Either she shot someone or someone shot her. Is that it?"

Joanna tilted her head and cocked an eyebrow.

"She shot someone?" Macy gasped then whispered, "Did she kill someone?" She immediately raised her hands to stop Joanna before she answered. "Don't tell me. I don't want to know. If she shot and killed someone, I want her to tell me. Not you. Now I understand why she was so mad at me." Macy kissed Joanna on the cheek and turned to leave. "Don't worry, Joanna. She'll never know we talked." She smiled and waved then hurried up the street.

Joanna didn't know if Macy could get Deena to talk about those guilt feelings she had harbored for so long but she hoped so. She applauded Macy's intentions. But would Deena? Probably not. And Joanna would have hell to pay if Deena thought she put Macy up to it. It's a good thing there's a bathroom between us, she thought. Time to run when I hear her coming.

Joanna stepped onto the vaporetto and braced her foot against the side like she did when she rode the MTA through Boston. She rode down the canal like a veteran Venetian, watching the people and the other boats go by, flexing her body with each lurch and sway of the boat.

Once inside the basilica she went right to work. She had only a few more pictures to take for comparison before beginning her report. And to her pleasant surprise, no one came to bother her. She had the laboratory and workroom all to herself. In spite of the revised forecast a gentle rain left puddles around the piazza. The square never completely flooded but it was enough to put several inches in the atrium of the church. Joanna hurried back and forth from the baptistery to the workroom, choosing pictures for magnification and saving them to her file. She skipped lunch, determined to finish the job today before water covered the mosaics.

"I knew it," she muttered, peering into the microscope. "You

172

are wrong, Carlo. Wrong, wrong, wrong." She pressed the button to save the view to the computer.

It was five minutes before closing time when Adriana, dressed in her guard's uniform knocked on the workroom door and let herself in.

"Signora Lucas, the basilica will be closing soon."

Joanna continued to type at the keyboard. With her eyes riveted on the screen, she only nodded. She quickly scanned the text, making corrections as she read.

"Signora?"

"One moment, Adriana," she said, her words garbled by the pen she held between her teeth. She typed a last sentence then took a deep breath as she saved it. "All done," she said, sending the e-mails on their way.

"It is five o'clock, Signora. The basilica is closing."

"I'm finished." Joanna pressed the buttons to shut down the computer and stood up, stretching as the computer screen went black and the lights went out. "I'm sorry I made you wait." Joanna collected her things and followed Adriana down the stairs.

"Will you be coming back, Signora?"

"To see the basilica, yes. To work, no. I want to thank you for bringing me coffee every day and for helping me carry the equipment up and down the stairs. I don't think I could have done it without you. *Grazie*. By the way, I haven't seen Francesca today. Has she been in the basilica?"

"No, she is sick." Adriana patted her chest. "With a cold."

"Tell her I'm sorry she is sick. Perhaps I'll see her before I leave Venice. I hope she is better very soon."

"*Si*. I will tell her." Adriana waved as Joanna stepped out into the piazza.

The fickle Venice weather was showing a new side. Instead of gray rainy skies the evening air had turned cold. A thick fog hung low over the square obscuring all but the ground floor of the campanile. Joanna hurried along to the vaporetto stop wishing she had brought her gloves and scarf. The fog was so low she could barely see the boat until it was practically bumping against the dock. She stepped on, finding a seat in the enclosed back section. No one seemed to be worried as they chugged up the Grand Canal, plowing deeper and deeper into the fog, no one except Joanna. She pulled her guidebook from her tote and began reading about Renaissance influence on Venetian architecture and prayed nothing crossed their path or if it did, it was a soft target. When they pulled up to the San Marcuola stop without ramming anything she heaved a sigh of relief and stepped onto the platform.

"*Grazie*," she said when the uniformed woman attendant offered her a hand up.

"*Benvenuto*," she replied, squeezing Joanna's hand and offering a sultry little smile. Oh, yes. She's gay, Joanna thought.

It was six thirty when she unlocked the door to her room. She dropped her purse and tote on the bed and turned up the thermostat then went to knock on Deena's door.

"Are you there?" She knocked again. She put her ear to the door, listening for sounds she was entertaining company. "Deena, are you sleeping or are you still mad at me?" she called as she turned the knob and opened the door enough to see inside. The room was empty. "I bet you're still mad at me. That or you are out prowling." Wherever Deena was, Joanna hoped she was safe.

Joanna undressed and spent a few minutes sponge bathing the basilica's dust and musty smell from her body. Wrapped in her robe she was sorry she hadn't brought something back for dinner. All she had was a baggie of trail mix and a half bottle of strawberry-flavored water. And without lunch to quiet her hunger pangs, she needed food. She dropped the robe on the bed and stood at her suitcase, deciding which pair of slacks and sweater would be the warmest.

In the bathroom, she looked at herself in the mirror. Her body was just there, plain and simple as her mother had told her. Nothing remarkable. Ample breasts but so many other women had better ones. Pale skin, absent of tan lines or rigid abs. A triangle of thin pubic hair, disappearing into slender thighs. She lacked muscle tone or athleticism of any kind. Even her bottom was shapeless and unimpressive. Joanna couldn't understand Chandler's fascination with wanting her to pose nude. Her models had all been statuesque beauties with unique shapes and contours. She had none of those qualities. She cupped her hands under her breasts and pressed them upward like a push-up bra. She checked her profile in the mirror, arching her back and giving her best impression of a seductive look.

"Yeah, right. That's false advertising. I'm never going to look like one of her models," she said disgustedly and went to dress. She would take herself and her boring boobs out to dinner. She would find a nice quiet little place, order a glass or two of wine and try not to spend the rest of her evening pouting about what had gone wrong with her life. Of course, dinner would be more fun if she had someone to spend it with.

CHAPTER 15

"Is this your idea of hiding?" Macy said softly, coming up behind Deena where she sat on a stool at the counter.

"Oh, hi," Deena slurped down the last of her drink and pushed the glass back. She had a surprised how-did-you-find-me look on her face. Macy ignored it and sat down next to her but Deena said, "I was just leaving."

"No, you weren't. Buy me a glass of wine." Macy unbuttoned her coat and slipped it off, looking to Deena for help that didn't come.

"How did you know where I was?" Deena signaled the man behind the counter and Macy held up two fingers.

"I didn't so you can guess how many places I've had to look.

It's a good thing you haven't been here very long and haven't ventured very far."

"I'm sorry but I've got a previous engagement tonight."

"Yeah, with me." Macy took a sip from her glass. "Drink up," she added, sliding the other glass closer to Deena.

"I don't want any wine."

"Let's get drunk."

"I don't want to get drunk."

"Why not? Are you a lousy drunk?" Macy teased. "Don't worry. I'll help you get back to the hotel."

"I don't need to be drunk to enjoy myself."

"If that's true then you should drink up, sergeant, because you sure as hell aren't enjoying yourself sober."

Obviously fighting against something she wanted to say, Deena stood up.

Macy spun on her stool to face her. "Are you going to pretend you don't know me and run off again?"

"I told you I've got another appointment." She headed for the door. Macy dropped some money on the counter, downed Deena's glass of wine and followed. She caught up to her well down the street.

"Hey, wait up." Macy had to hurry to keep up. "You made me pay. That's a first."

"You wanted the wine."

"Will you slow down? These shoes are for show, not for jogging."

Deena shoved her hands into her jacket pockets and hunched her shoulders to the misty fog.

"Are you catching the vaporetto?" Macy hooked her arm through Deena's.

"Macy, I'm busy. Why don't you run along and we'll talk later." She unhooked Macy's arm then turned down the street.

"Okay, I'll go. But before I do would you tell me something?"

Deena stopped but didn't turn around.

"Tell me you didn't feel the slightest bit of connection between us."

177

After a long moment of silence Deena continued down the street. Macy ran to catch her, grabbing her arm.

"Macy, I'm going to be late. I've got to go."

"Was I nothing more to you than a fuck-buddy?" she demanded.

Deena finally allowed her eyes to meet Macy's but said nothing.

"I was, wasn't I? I was just a vacation fling. You had your fun and now it's time to move on. Hey, I understand. I'm not stupid, you know." They could hear the vaporetto lumbering up to the landing. "You better hurry. You'll miss your ride."

Macy turned and ran through the fog as tears streamed down her face. She had tried to crack Deena's shell, to get her to confess what terrible thing she was hiding behind those big brown eyes. She had tried to intimidate her into honesty but all she had got was the realization Deena had no feelings for her whatsoever. And that hurt.

Macy leaned her forehead against the door and knocked again.

"Are you home?" she said through a shaky voice. Finally, the door opened.

"What are you doing here?" Chandler asked, a cup of something in her hand.

"Can I come in?"

"Since when do you ask?" Chandler stepped back and waved her in then followed her up the stairs. "Are you all right?"

"No, I'm not and I don't feel like being coy about it." She took the cup from Chandler's hand and drank it. "Have you got anything stronger? I need a drink."

"You smell like you already had one."

"I smell like I had two glasses of red wine. It wasn't enough." She dropped her coat and purse in the chair and headed for the kitchen.

"Dare I ask why the need for intoxicants?"

"No, you shouldn't. And don't act so smug." Macy found a corked bottle of wine in the back of the refrigerator. "You should allow me to drink this bottle of Italian swill in peace and quiet. When I crumple to the floor in an intoxicated stupor you can toss a blanket over my inebriated body and step over me."

"I'm fresh out of pity blankets."

"What? No sympathy from my teacher and mentor?"

"You haven't given me any reason to offer any." Chandler leaned against the counter with her arms crossed.

"Isn't it enough to say my poor little heart is broken, crushed, stomped into a withering pile of forgotten dust?" She put the bottle to her lips and downed a swallow.

"Why don't you stop being a verbose writer and tell me why I should care. Although I think I can guess."

"Okay, guess." Macy gave her a dramatically cold stare.

"Deena Garren roped you, hog-tied you, branded you and has now released you back into the herd."

Macy took another drink then said, "You got it, partner."

"Did you really think it could possibly turn out any other way?"

"Don't lecture me, smarty-pants. You and Joanna aren't exactly riding the range together."

"But I went in knowing that it might not work out. I distinctly remember warning you about Deena. Right here in my studio." She nodded up the staircase.

"I hate it when anyone gets to say I told you so." She held out the bottle to Chandler. "Do you want some of this?"

"No, thanks. You may consume until you feel relief." Chandler shook her head and started up the stairs to the studio.

"What are you doing up here? Painting?" Macy followed, carrying the bottle.

"I'm cleaning the studio. I can't find anything. You wouldn't know why, would you?"

"I have *no* idea. I've been too busy being taken advantage of." She raked a pile of rags off a stool and perched on it, watching

Chandler and swigging wine. "Hey, you know sergeant Deena Garren."

"Regrettably."

"What do you know about her being a cop?"

"She's a cop. And in spite of my biased opinion of her personal life, I understand she is a pretty good one. But don't tell her I said that," Chandler admonished.

"Your secret is safe with me. She won't talk to me."

"What did you do? Pry too deep? Ask her about her love conquests? She probably can't count that high."

"Chandler, you are a cruel dyke." Macy saluted with the bottle then took a drink.

"No, I'm not. I offered you sanctuary from your misery. And my last bottle of cheap wine."

"Yeah, I was going to say." She made a face at the label. "Could you get something that hasn't been stomped by barefoot goats?"

"Are you going to need more? Don't tell me. You're going to be a martyr and see her again. You aren't taking no for an answer?" Chandler looked up from a box of art supplies and laughed. There was a knock at the downstairs door.

"Go answer your door. It's probably Joanna here to be understanding and supportive. Something my relationships seem to lack."

Chandler trotted down the spiral staircase and down to the second-floor door.

"Hello." Macy gasped and held her breath in anticipation when she heard Deena's voice.

"Can I help you?" Chandler asked.

"I don't remember how to get to Macy's apartment. I know you probably don't want to tell me but I'd really appreciate it if you'd make an exception this once."

"She's not there."

"Look, could you bury the hatchet. Just tell me how to get there and I'll leave you alone."

"I'm telling you, she isn't there."

"How do you know?"

"Because she's here."

Macy practically fell off the stool. She certainly didn't expect Chandler to tell her that. Although knowing Deena was looking for her was a pleasant, albeit curious, surprise.

"But I don't think she wants to see you," Chandler added. Macy couldn't help choking, coughing loudly.

"It sounds to me like maybe she does," Deena said.

"Macy, you've got company," Chandler called. "Shall I send her up or send her home?"

"Up," Macy said then thought better of it. "No."

"Too late," Deena said, starting up the spiral steps.

"What are you doing here? I thought you had a previous engagement."

"I see you decided to get drunk after all."

"I'm not drunk. I'm just socializing," Macy said smugly.

"Back where I come from, guzzling from the bottle makes you a drunk. And if that's my fault, I apologize." Deena took the bottle from her and set it on the table. "I came to tell you I'm sorry if I upset you."

"Okay."

"I didn't mean to."

"Okay." Macy kept her seat, her knees locked together as she perched on the stool. "Anything else?"

Chandler had meandered back up the stairs to the studio. She returned to sorting art supplies, trying to act inconspicuous, more like a bystander willing to be a referee if necessary. But her presence obviously made Deena uncomfortable.

"You can talk in front of Chandler. She knows all about us." That made Deena frown.

"I'll tell you what," Chandler said, dropping a handful of brushes back in the box. "I think I'll go grab a plate of pasta or something."

"You don't have to leave, Chandler," Macy pleaded. She wasn't sure she wanted to be alone with Deena, not if she only came to apologize.

"Yes, I think I do." Chandler gave Deena a studied gaze then

181

went downstairs. Macy listened to footsteps down the stairs and then the door slammed.

"What exactly did you tell her?" Deena asked.

"Nothing really. But I think she guessed we were having difficulties."

"Difficulties? Is that what you call it?" Deena turned her attention to the canvases displayed around the room, most of them Macy's half-hearted attempts at portraiture. "Are these yours or Chandler's?" She picked up one of a willowy abstract figure with knobby knees and a pointy chin.

"That's mine. Chandler's actually look like something. Mine don't."

"This looks like my cousin in Chicago. She's got that kind of shape." She put it back.

"I'm sorry for what I said, Deena," Macy offered, trying to break the ice.

"That's okay. You were right. I was being a bitch." Deena gazed out the window then slowly brought her eyes to meet Macy's. "I'm very sorry. I don't know what happened."

"I do. I was pressuring you. That's one of my bad habits. I've got lots of them. I should have warned you. Sticking my nose where it doesn't belong is a really big one. Sometimes I try to blame it on my journalistic curiosity. But you have to believe me when I say I was only trying to be helpful."

"I know. I shouldn't have reacted like I did."

"It was my fault for insisting you tell me something you didn't want to talk about. I should have taken no for an answer and stopped hounding you about it."

"It was something I'm not used to talking about. Maybe I should say I'm not comfortable talking about it."

"I understand. You can tell me if you want to or not. Your choice. I just want you to know I'm here if you do." Macy smiled softly.

"No one has ever asked about my work before. At least, not anyone I've dated. Not really asked. They want to know if I'll fix a parking ticket or tell them how to avoid getting pulled over for a DUI. I've had a couple women who told me I looked hot in my uniform or thought being able to frisk some sexy babe would be fun. But no one has ever really wanted to know what I do. The day-to-day, street-by-street details of what I do. I think I was surprised and a little scared when your questions went beyond your research. I don't talk about what it's like being a cop. I mean really being a cop. It's hard enough to do it. I guess I don't want to talk about it and have to relive it."

"How about Joanna? Doesn't she ask?"

"Josie lets me chat up a storm if I bring it up. We have this understanding. She seems to know when not to ask anything. I can tell she wants to but she waits until I'm ready."

"It must have been a real relief to take off your uniform and gun and leave it all behind. I bet you don't do that very often."

"This is my first vacation outside of the Boston area in five years. When I locked my weapon in the drawer and picked up my suitcase I felt naked for a minute. That's how much it influences my life."

"Can you talk about it with your family?"

Deena laughed out loud. "Lord, no. My parents can barely tolerate my being gay. They don't want to know about me being a cop. My dad was an engineer. He thought I should have done something meaningful with my life as he termed it."

"You can't get much more meaningful than being a police officer."

"Yeah, well," she sighed, rolling her eyes.

"You know I didn't mean to pry, Deena. Next time I do that, arrest me. I've never been arrested before." She winked playfully.

"You don't want to be arrested."

"Why? It might be invaluable research."

"Do you want some three-hundred-pound prison matron sticking her fingers up your body cavities?"

"Really? I thought they make you turn your head and cough."

"That's a military physical."

183

"Oh. You mean they actually put their fingers in your—" Macy's eyes got wide as Deena began nodding emphatically before she even finished asking. "Ewwww. Have you ever done that?" Deena continued to nod. "Why?"

"Drugs."

"I thought that was only if you're sent to the big house. They strip search you for just a simple arrest?"

"No, not everyone. But sometimes it's the only way to make a case. We know they've got it on them. We've just got to find it."

"Ewww. Do you at least wear gloves? I don't want to know." Macy clamped her hands over her ears and grimaced.

"And yes, some women can hide a weapon up there."

"Up there?"

"You bet. Small handguns. Single-shot pistols."

"Ouch!"

"We had a prostitute brought in, swearing she didn't have a weapon on her and before we could do a thorough search, it fell out."

Macy gasped and clamped her legs together.

"That sounds like something I could use in one of my books. Talk about a vivid character description. The pro so skanky her pistol fell out of her snatch. Got any more like that? No, wait. I promised not to ask."

"That's okay. Some of this stuff gets tossed around the squad room. Some of it is too funny to be real."

"And I bet some things are too terrible to be real." Macy gave her a tender look.

"Sometimes."

"Those kinds of things must be hard to put out of your mind."

"Sometimes." Deena lowered her eyes.

Macy stepped closer and slipped her hand in Deena's.

"Want to tell me about it?" she said softly.

Deena stood there motionless, her breaths growing rapid and shallow. Macy squeezed her hand and waited, praying this time Deena wouldn't run away from it, whatever it was. Just as Macy decided the silence meant she wasn't going to tell her, Deena took a deep breath.

"I left the squad car at the station," she said quietly. "It needed some work on the air conditioner. Julie offered to take me home but it was out of her way. I told her I'd ride the bus. We had been on a stakeout and I was in civilian clothes. I had a nylon vest on over my shirt to hide my holster. As I was walking to the bus stop I could hear people laughing up the street. I thought it was just someone having a good time. When I got closer I could see two teenage boys and an older woman waiting at the stop. One of the boys was climbing over the bench, horsing around. You know how kids are. I was across the street, waiting for the traffic so I could cross. The elderly woman looked really scared. She was sitting on the bench, holding her purse against her chest and being real still, like when there is a dog growling up at you and you are afraid to move or he'll attack. These kids couldn't have been more than thirteen or fourteen. Nice-looking kids. Clean-cut. Well dressed. Wearing hundred-dollar sneakers and designer jeans. The kind of kids you'd see in a middle-class suburb. Not an inner-city street where winos piss in the alley." Deena turned to the window, looking out as if searching for something.

"I was going to tell them to move along, stop making a public nuisance of themselves, but the kid climbing on the bench started harassing the old lady, asking her for money. I identified myself as a police officer and told him I'd arrest him if he didn't leave. The kid went ballistic. He started cussing and saying no meter maid was going to arrest him. I tried to calm him down but he didn't seem to hear me. He had this wild-eyed look on his face. I knew he had to be hopped up on something. The woman tried to move away from him but he pulled a gun from his pocket and pointed it at her head."

Macy gasped as she said, "Dear God, did he shoot her?"

"He told her to count to five. I tried to get him to put the gun down but he ignored me. He kept screaming at her to count but she was too scared to do anything. I pulled my weapon and ordered him to drop the gun. He wouldn't do it. He pushed the barrel of his gun into her cheek and started counting. The woman was crying and begging me to do something. I told him to drop it or I'd shoot. He was only a kid. I thought he'd listen. When he got to four, the woman screamed. I could see his hand flex around the pistol. He got this cocky look on his face then opened his mouth to say five and I pulled the trigger." Deena closed her eyes and drew a breath. The color had left her face.

Macy wrapped her arms around Deena's waist but she pulled away and went to sit on the top step of the spiral staircase. She buried her face in her hands and cried great heaving sobs.

"Oh, baby." Macy knelt next to her and folded her arms around her, rocking her as she wept. "That's all right. Let it go," she cooed. "Let it all go now." Macy suspected this was the first time Deena had really allowed herself to feel the pain of that terrible day. Joanna was right. Deena was a private person and for her to share this must have been very difficult. "It's okay. I'm here, baby girl. I'm here."

"He was fourteen, Macy," she said through her tears. "Fourteen."

"You did what you had to do."

"Did I try hard enough to talk him out of it? Would he have pulled the trigger when he got to five?" Deena shook her head. "I'll never know."

"You're a cop." Macy wiped away the tears that trailed down Deena's face. "You are trained to make split-second decisions. You did that. You saved the woman's life."

"The kid was fourteen years old. He played soccer. He was an honor student. He had parents who loved him. And I put a bullet right between his eyes." Deena swallowed hard, her chin quivering as she rolled her eyes to the ceiling. "He's dead because of me."

"You can't think that way. You're a police officer sworn to protect. What if you hadn't decided to ride the bus? What if you never crossed that street and that kid shot that poor old woman? She had the right to expect her life be protected and you did that."

"I know." She looked over at Macy with a pained expression. "It doesn't make it any easier."

"Why would a fourteen-year-old boy do something like that?"

"Uppers. Meth. His autopsy showed he was loaded with it. He had been to a party."

"So it was someone else's fault."

"No, it was mine. I shot and killed Steven Blake, age fourteen."

"What was her name?"

"Who?"

"The elderly woman at the bus stop."

"I don't remember."

"When you get home to Boston, you need to find out. That's the name you should remember." Macy touched Deena's face, wiping the last tears from her cheek. "She probably says a prayer every night, thanking God for sending you to protect her." Then Macy placed a soft kiss on Deena's lips and gave her a hug. "Thank you."

"For what?"

"For finding a place in your heart to let me in. How many people have you told what really happened that night?"

"Not many."

"I'm glad I could be one of them."

"Me, too," Deena whispered, lacing her fingers through Macy's hair. "Me, too. Thank you for listening." She pulled Macy to her and kissed her softly.

Macy leaned back, pulling Deena on top of her.

"Kiss me again," she said lovingly. "Forget everything else and kiss me."

Deena lowered herself onto Macy, fitting their bodies together as she kissed her, this time harder and more completely, her tongue swimming in Macy's mouth.

"I've never felt closer to you. Make love to me, Deena."

"Here?"

"Yes. Right here, right now," she whispered. She pulled

Deena's mouth to hers and kissed her urgently, gasping beneath Deena's strong presence.

Deena lifted herself long enough to unzip and remove Macy's jeans. With long fingers and a gentle stroke, she slid her panties off and tossed them aside. Macy hooked a leg over Deena's rear, opening herself to her touch. From the first time they slept together Macy had made her wishes known and Deena had remembered every detail. Macy liked it hard and deep. She wanted to feel Deena against her, commanding her and guiding her to an explosive climax. Even on the cold tile floor of Chandler's studio, Macy could feel the fire building within her.

"More, yes. More," she hissed, her eyes closed tight as Deena brought her orgasm higher and higher. Deena painted kisses down Macy's neck as her fingers delved deeper until Macy's screams meant she had reached her peak. "Yes, yes, yes," she moaned, riding it to the end. Finally she collapsed limp on the floor, both of them breathless. "Damn, you're good," she said, gasping for breath and laughing. But Deena didn't laugh. She looked down on Macy and smiled softly then placed a soulful kiss on her lips.

"Thank you," she whispered. "For being here for me."

"My pleasure, baby," Macy replied, snuggling against her.

"I hate to bother you, but are you done yet?" Chandler called from downstairs.

CHAPTER 16

"I bet you're relieved to have that report done." Deena broke open her croissant to see what kind of filling it had. "What do you think? Lemon?"

"Looks like it." Joanna spread a dollop of cream cheese on a piece of toast. "And yes. Now I can finally relax and enjoy my last few days in Venice."

"By the way, where were you yesterday? I looked all over for you. You weren't working, were you? I thought you were done."

"I went over to Burano on the lagoon shuttle. I wanted to see the handmade lace. I hope you don't mind I went alone."

"No, I don't care. We don't have to do everything together. I'm a big girl. I can entertain myself. So no one went with you?"

"If you mean did Chandler go with me, no. She didn't. I just wanted a little alone time."

"To think?"

"Uh-huh. I had fun. I ate lunch in a little tiny shop that was bright blue on the outside. All the houses and stores are bright colors. They say it was so the returning fishermen could see their houses as they entered the lagoon."

"Interesting." Deena tried to sound interested but she wasn't always good at it. "Have you decided what to do about Chandler?"

Joanna shrugged. "I have no idea and don't you dare say anything," she warned as Deena was about to reply. "I know what you want to say but don't."

"I wasn't going to say a word." Deena gave an impish grin. "So, what page in the tour guide are you visiting today?"

"I'm not sure. First I have to return my key to the basilica."

"You still have a key to Saint Mark's Cathedral?"

"No. Not the cathedral. It's to the lab in the back of the workroom where they keep the equipment. I forgot to leave it when I was finished."

"Keep it as a souvenir."

"I'm not keeping it. I promised I'd return it and I will."

"Why not? They owe you a heck of a lot more than one bent key. It's not as if you're going to steal anything."

"I did my job. I submitted my report. They paid me. I'm returning the key."

"And then I suppose you'll be seeing Chandler."

"Maybe. I don't know."

"Tell me something, Josie. Have you forgiven her for what she did to you?"

"Forgiven? I don't know." Joanna gazed off in thought. "It seems like such a long time ago."

"Have you forgotten how hurt you were?"

"No, I haven't forgotten." She ate the last bite of toast and brushed the crumbs from her hands as the image of Chandler's confident smile floated through her thoughts. "How are things going with you and Macy? Do you have big plans today?"

"I think you know," Deena said and went to refill her cup.

Joanna followed with her cup in hand. "What do you mean?"

"Oh, come on, Josie. Don't play dumb blond with me. You know exactly what I mean," she said, holding the button down on the coffeemaker. "I thought you were going to stay out of it."

"Deena, I didn't say anything. Honestly, I didn't. Macy just guessed."

"And you agreed with her?" She shot her an accusatory glare.

"She just wanted to be supportive. We all do." Joanna followed her back to the table.

Deena took her seat, continuing to frown but it slowly changed to a small smile.

"It's okay, Josie. I understand why you did it."

"You're not mad at me?"

"Naw," Deena said, shaking her head.

"What happened?"

"Let's just say we talked."

"Did you talk about that night?" Joanna asked sympathetically.

Deena nodded.

"Good, I'm glad you did."

"Macy is one of those touchy-feely types who wants to know everything about everyone."

"She's good for you, you know. She has compassion." Joanna leaned in and whispered, "She also strikes me as good in bed. Is she?"

"Among other places," Deena said with a crooked little grin.

"Where?" Joanna couldn't believe she asked that. But what the heck? Deena was a friend. It wasn't the first time they talked about sex.

"Since when are you interested in stuff like that?"

"I'm interested. I may not discuss it but I'm interested. Hey, I'm not dead, you know."

"You surprise me, Josie."

"Yeah, well, sometimes I surprise myself."

"You haven't had sex with Chandler, have you?" Deena asked.

"No." She chuckled. But the idea had crossed her mind. "I think I'll run over and return the key. Want to come?"

"No, thanks. I want to finish my breakfast and wash out some laundry. I'll catch you later." Deena had that devilish look in her eye that made Joanna suspect Macy was going to be her laundry partner.

"Okay, honey. You have fun. And tell Macy hi for me."

Deena grinned and nodded.

Joanna stepped off the vaporetto and followed the tree-lined promenade along the waterfront. It was a beautiful blue-skied morning and the piazza was filled with tourists. The line waiting to get in the basilica was long but kept moving at a steady pace. Once inside, Joanna showed her ID to the guard and climbed the stairs to the workroom. She let herself in and placed the key in the drawer as Francesca had instructed. The computer light was on but the monitor was dark. She pushed the button, expecting to see the familiar aerial shot of the basilica as the wallpaper. Instead a list of the folders on the hard drive was on the screen. She was about to turn off the monitor when she noticed her folder wasn't in the list. She scrolled down, checking for it but it wasn't there. It wasn't in the computer's Recycle Bin either. That was completely empty. The e-mails she had sent had been deleted along with the backup folder she had made. Even the computer's temp files had been deleted. The computer had no evidence she had ever entered a document or even been there. She may have completed her work and submitted her report but she was more than a little surprised that her data had been removed so soon afterward. What if a member of the council had a question about her findings? Joanna checked the hard drive to see if it was nearly full and her data had been deleted to make space available. But it was huge and had over a hundred gigabits of useable space. The more she thought about it, the more troubling it became. Why had her data been removed?

Don't worry about it. You did your job. You e-mailed your report to Francesca and to the council. You are officially finished with your obligation. You no longer have any responsibility. This is their computer. They can erase anything they want.

Joanna took one last look around then closed the door and descended the staircase, trying to put any worry out of her mind. She fell in line and followed the crowd along the roped path toward the front of the cathedral until she reached the baptistery door. Even though it was almost time for the ten o'clock mass she wanted one last look. The door usually stood open before mass with a sign in both Italian and English restricting entrance to only those attending mass. Today the door was closed and the sign was in Italian only. Joanna couldn't read it but she could make out the red circle with a slash mark through it, meaning no entry. Surely Carlo Vittori hadn't begun cleaning and repairing the mosaics already. She pressed down on the heavy door latch to see if it was unlocked. It was. She pushed the door open far enough to peek inside. Stacks of plastic buckets, shovels and long-handled scrapers were scattered around the floor. Two men in work clothes and dust masks were spreading tarps over the altar, crucifix and baptismal font.

"*Signora, no di massa*," the taller man said.

"I know," Joanna said, stepping all the way inside and closing the door. "What are you doing?"

"*No turisti*," he said, shaking his head. "This room is not open." His English wasn't good but it was clear he wasn't happy. "You go now, Signora."

"Where is Signor Vittori?"

He shrugged and went back to covering the altar. Joanna scanned the tools but didn't see those normally used for restoration. There was no mortar, no delicate tools and light bars for the intricate work between the tiny tiles. Only shovels, scrapers and one large sledgehammer, something definitely not a restoration tool.

"Are you going to repair the tessera?" she asked, pointing to the area she had examined.

"*Si*. We remove tessera."

"No, no. No remove. You aren't supposed to remove it. You are supposed to repair it. Put more mortar in, not scrape it away."

"No mortar," the other man said, frowning his disapproval. "We will take away tessera. Take away everything." He waved his hand through the air as if wiping the slate clean. "Next week, we begin new floor."

"No, that's not right. You're making a mistake. The tessera are not to be removed. They are still usable, very old but still usable. You are supposed to repair the rough spots and re-grout the loose tiles. This floor is NOT to be removed." Joanna stood in the middle of the floor, feeling protective of it and the work she had done. "Go ask Carlo."

"Signor Vittori said for us to remove all this floor. All the tessera. He said do it today." He took Joanna by the arm and escorted her toward the door. "You have to leave now. It will not be safe for you."

"Where is he? He will tell you. I turned in a very detailed report two days ago. This mosaic is four hundred years old, at least. It was not part of the nineteenth-century restoration. This is some of the oldest remaining sections of mosaics in the basilica. It can be restored."

Joanna argued with the man all the way to the door, struggling to pull her arm from his grip. The other man had finished covering the altar and had picked up the sledgehammer, as if preparing to begin demolition.

"Wait. Don't do that," she yelled, pulling away but he had already raised the hammer over his head and dropped it, smashing a divot into the mosaic, sending chips of marble flying.

"NO!" She screamed and ran toward him, grabbing the handle before he could strike another blow. "What are you doing?"

"Signora, let go. You have to leave."

"No. I'm not leaving. You can't do this." She fought like a woman possessed, elbowing and bumping them, surprised at her own strength.

One man said something to the other in Italian as if they were arguing over what to do with the irate woman. Finally one of the men grabbed her around the waist and picked her up, pulling her away. She hung on to the handle as long as she could, kicking and fighting, but she finally lost her grip.

"Put me down," she screamed, thrashing in his arms as he carried her to the door. She kicked it closed and braced her feet against it, pushing back. "Put me down or I'll sue you for assault." She knew he probably didn't understand her but that didn't matter. She was frantic.

"Signora, you have to leave or we will call the *polizia*," he said, adjusting his hold on her. One of his hands was now cupped over her breast.

"Get your hands off me," she gasped, his big hand squeezing tighter. "What are you doing? Copping a feel, you pervert." The more she struggled the tighter he squeezed until the pain was too much to bear. Joanna dug her nails into the back of his hand and held them there until he let go, dropping her. She scrambled to her feet and ran back to the man ready to swing the sledgehammer again. She stood in front of him, placing herself in his line of work.

"Move," he shouted.

"NO!"

When she didn't move, he turned, ready to strike another spot. Joanna quickly slid over, blocking him again. He made another turn, the sledgehammer still hoisted over his head and ready to fall. But Joanna moved as well, holding her arms out like a soccer goalie ready to block a shot. The other man was still examining his wounds from her nails and looked as if he had sacrificed enough for the cause. The tool-wielding man was obviously growing impatient. He gave Joanna a shove then quickly readied to strike a blow but she recovered, grabbing the handle again. He responded by shoving her again, this time in the same breast the other man had squeezed.

"What's the matter with you two? Can't you get a date? You have to grab my tits?" she groaned and stomped on his boot. It

195

must not have been steel-toed because he yelped and loosened his grip on the hammer enough so Joanna could pull it away. She immediately placed the handle against the step to the baptismal stage and stepped on it, breaking the wooden handle. "There. Now try smashing the mosaic," she said proudly.

"*Vaffangulo*," he exclaimed, his nostrils flaring. "*Stupido puttana*."

Joanna didn't have to understand Italian to know he had just cursed at her.

"You're an idiot. The basilica has to be protected. Not destroyed, you bastard."

She had never called anyone that before, at least not to their face. She had always been able to remain calm with a sense of refinement and decorum, but this man obviously had no idea what he was destroying. She had never felt this kind of rage before. She picked up another one of the long-handled tools and braced it against the step, stomping it as well. "You are not doing this, not while I have anything to say about it." She kicked a stack of buckets, probably intended to carry away the broken tiles. She could feel her blood pressure soar and her adrenaline pumping as she stomped the last of their tools, splintering the wooden handle into useless kindling. She hadn't noticed Adriana and another guard enter the baptistery until she was finished and looked up at their shocked faces.

"Signora?" Adriana exclaimed, scowling as if Joanna had completely lost her mind.

"Adriana, go find Francesca. Hurry. They are destroying the floor."

"Signora Lucas, you must leave now," the other guard demanded. "We have called the *polizia*. You will be arrested."

"I'm not leaving," she said, taking her stand in the middle of the floor. "They are ignoring my report. This is wrong, wrong, wrong and I'm not leaving until they stop this atrocity."

"I think you are exaggerating, Signora," he said with a sarcastic laugh. He looked over at Adriana and said, "Crazy American."

Two more basilica guards and two police officers, one of them a woman, also entered the baptistery.

"*Qui?*" The woman officer asked.

"This is Signora Lucas," Adriana said, pointing to Joanna. "She is working for Francesca."

"I have a right to be here. I was hired by the Procurator's Council to examine the floor." Everyone was talking at once—Joanna trying to explain her findings, the workmen explaining their injuries and the tools she had broken, the guards telling what they saw and the police arguing over who had the authority over the situation. Occasionally one of the police officers would look over at Joanna and frown. "They aren't supposed to rip out the mosaics," Joanna continued to argue, shouting over the din. "They are just supposed to repair it. I had to stop them."

Everyone finally stopped as one of the police officers, the woman who seemed to be the senior officer present, shouted and raised her hands. The room fell mercifully silent. Every pair of eyes turned to Joanna and stared.

"Signora Lucas," the woman officer said, walking toward her. "You will have to leave the basilica."

"No," Joanna said calmly.

"Signora, you must."

"I'm not leaving while they are here. I know what they are going to do. They are going to smash the floor and carry it away in buckets. I can't let that happen. I submitted a report. You have to ask Francesca about it. She knows."

"Yes, yes. We have sent for Francesca but you have to come with me. You are disturbing these men's work. It is against the law for you to do this. You attacked them."

"I didn't attack them. They attacked me. He grabbed my boob," she said, pointing a finger at the man who had carried her to the door. "And then he pushed it." She pointed to the other man.

"He pushed what?"

"My boob."

"Boob?" She didn't seem to understand the term.

Joanna didn't want to grab her breast to demonstrate then she remembered visiting the Ponte de le Tette with Chandler.

"Yes, *tette.*"

"*Ah, si. Tette.*" She cast a frown back at the men. "I am sorry, Signora, but you must come with me."

"No." Joanna backed up out of the woman's reach, stalling for time, hoping Francesca would hurry up and arrive. "I'm waiting for Francesca."

"*Arresto,*" the man whose foot she had stomped shouted. "*Arresto Americano.*"

"*Si, si,*" the officer said, nodding in agreement then turned back to Joanna. "Come, Signora. I arrest you. You come now with me." She said it as if she assumed Joanna would give in and come along quietly.

"No." Joanna took another step back. She knew she was digging herself a hole but all she could think of was the beautiful floor being smashed to smithereens. She had no choice. She had to take a stand or accept losing this piece of history. She also knew she was outnumbered and it was just a matter of time before she exhausted all her options. "I'm not going. You'll have to carry me."

She had never been a martyr for a cause before but it seemed like the thing to do at the time. She sat down beside the baptismal font and wrapped her arms and legs around the base, hanging on for dear life. The chuckles from the onlookers didn't deter her. "I'm not leaving."

The woman officer rolled her eyes and gave a disgruntled sigh then waved one of the other officers to help her. Joanna wasn't an experienced protestor so it didn't take long for them to attach handcuffs and pull her away.

"You're going to be sorry," Joanna yelled back at the workmen as she was ushered toward the door. "Don't you dare touch that floor. I'm warning you. If you harm even one of those tessera you'll be sorry. Francesca will tell you. I filed a report. The floor can be saved." She continued to shout until the baptistery door closed behind her.

"Those workmen are making a mistake," she said as the police officers escorted her across the square. "You know, these handcuffs aren't very comfortable, are they?"

CHAPTER 17

Chandler waited impatiently for the vaporetto to bump the platform and the gate to be opened so she could charge off and up the sidewalk. She fought her way through slow-moving pedestrians, hopping over anything in her way as she ran toward the piazza. She was out of breath as she rushed through the double doors of the police station and up to the counter.

"*Scusi*," she said, gasping for breath. The man behind the counter was absorbed with his computer and didn't look up. "*Mi scusi*, I'm here about Joanna Lucas. An American who was arrested."

"*Si, si. Uno momento*." He finished what he was typing and looked over at Chandler. "Signora who?"

"Lucas. Joanna Lucas. Blond. Pretty." Chandler held her hand up to show how tall she was. "She was arrested in the basilica."

"Ah, *si*. San Marco terrorist." He laughed. Chandler didn't think it was funny.

"Where is she?"

He nodded his head toward the hall.

"You go down there, turn right." The telephone rang and he answered it, as if that was all Chandler needed to know.

It took three hours of explanations, two hundred euros, a sincere apology and Chandler's promise to assume responsibility for Joanna but she finally gained her release. Chandler was sitting in the waiting area when Joanna was brought through the door. She looked humiliated and embarrassed. Chandler tried not to chuckle at her vulnerable and pathetic smile.

"Hi," she said, helping her on with her coat.

"Hello, Chandler. And thank you," was all Joanna could say.

"Are you all right?" She held the door for her then followed her into the square.

"I'm a criminal, aren't I?"

"Hardened." She directed Joanna down the row of buildings toward a café with rows of tables outside. "I hear they are calling you a terrorist." Chandler bit down on her lip to keep from laughing out loud.

"I'm so embarrassed. Did I really hurt anyone?"

"I understand that one workman already had all the kids he wanted so it's okay."

"Chandler, stop! It isn't funny. I'm really upset about this. I can't believe I did that."

"I should have warned them you are lethal when you're touched." Chandler put her arm around Joanna's shoulder and escorted her through the door of Caffé Florian.

"They said you paid my fine. How much is it?"

"Millions. Two, please," she said to the maître d'.

"How much, Chandler? I want to repay you."

"Don't worry about it. We'll discuss it later. For now, I'm buying you coffee at the first café in Venice to sell it. Florian's."

"Is that what this is?"

"Uh-huh."

"I've read about this place. Established in 1720. Very famous. Even Casanova was supposedly a customer here." She took hold of Chandler's arm. "This place costs a fortune. Let's go somewhere else."

"No." She motioned for her to follow the maître d'. "You have to experience this place at least once. You'll appreciate the art hanging on the walls and the Renaissance architecture."

"I'd appreciate it more if I hadn't been arrested for assault."

"Actually, I'm very proud of you," Chandler said, waiting for Joanna to settle in before taking her seat in the small semi-circular booth.

"What for? Not inflicting injuries that required a hospital stay?"

"No, for standing up for what you believed in. You were sort of like Joan of Arc or Gandhi."

"I don't think so. It wasn't that kind of cause. I just didn't want them to destroy the mosaics." Joanna heaved a regretful sigh. "Now it's too late. They probably had time to smash it and haul it all away. All I got for my efforts was a wrist burn from the handcuffs."

"You got more than that. Francesca heard what happened and came down to stop them. At least temporarily. She said she wished you had sent her a copy of the report though."

"I did. I sent one to her, one to each member of the Procurator's Council, the proto's office and one to Carlo Vittori. I wasn't obligated to send him one but I did."

Chandler put her hand over Joanna's and looked into her eyes. "Joanna, no one got your report. They thought you decided not to send one."

"What?"

Chandler shook her head. "No one got it."

"But, I don't understand. I e-mailed them Sunday. I finished my work and sent the e-mails just before the basilica closed. It was about five o'clock."

"Well, they never got them. They assumed you agreed with Carlo that the floor wasn't salvageable."

"I sent them, Chandler. I *know* I did." Tears were pooling in Joanna's frightened eyes.

"It's okay. Maybe you just copied the e-mail addresses wrong."

"I replied to e-mail addresses I already had. I didn't have to type them in. I just clicked reply. I know they were the right ones. I am sure of it. And I waited to make sure they were sent off the computer before I did a shut down. The outgoing mailbox was clear. I sent a detailed report, several pages with photographs and measurements and everything. I showed the absolute comparison to the tiles saved in the museum that dated to 1640. There is no doubt in my mind the baptistery floor is old, way older than the nineteenth century. It must be saved."

"Francesca was able to intervene but only until tomorrow. The council is growing impatient. Or at least Carlo is and he is pressuring the council. Francesca thought you might have completed your work and just not sent the report yet. But she said your data isn't on the computer. It's as if you were never here."

"I know. I saw that. I was in the workroom this morning to return my key and the computer was on. The folder I created was gone. So were all my photographs, all my data. It wasn't anywhere on that computer. Neither were the drafts of my e-mails. I always make drafts in case just this kind of thing happens."

"Why would anyone erase your stuff?"

Joanna just looked at her, narrowing her eyes. "I think I know," she said.

Chandler leaned back and stared at her. "Carlo?"

Joanna nodded and said, "He has the most to gain by erasing it and the most to lose if that report reaches the council."

"But how could he stop the e-mail from getting to the council? He'd have to be there, waiting at each terminal for the e-mail to arrive. He couldn't do that. He couldn't be in that many places at the same time."

"I think he could. I remember Deena telling me they arrested some guy at MIT for redirecting e-mail from his professor's computer to his. He would change his grades and then send it on the registrar's office. He was some computer wizard but he never went to class. He thought he could get away with it. They might never have found out if he hadn't bragged to his roommate about it."

"You mean Carlo had your e-mail sent to his computer?"

"It's possible. How else do you explain it? Once he got my report, he knew I was finished and he had my data removed from the computer in the workroom. He probably erased any trace of what he did as well."

"But you can't prove it," Chandler said.

"No. Not without a bunch of computer nerds and a lot of money."

"Then he's going to win anyway. You don't have time to redo your work and submit another report."

Joanna's eyebrows went up.

"Maybe. Maybe not. Where is the most secure computer you can think of?"

"I'd like to say mine but my router is down. I can't log on. I don't know. CIA? The Kremlin? The Vatican?"

"No. Caffè Florian." Joanna slid out of the booth and headed up the aisle to the front desk. Chandler had no idea what she had in mind but she followed anyway.

"Why does this café have the most secure computer?"

"What makes a computer at risk?" She stood at the desk inside the front door, waiting for the maître d' to return from seating some guests.

"I have no idea."

"What's on it. If a computer has lots of important data, top-secret documents, codes and credit card names, then everyone wants to crack it and get in. How many people do you think want to get into that computer?" She pointed to the small laptop on the desk. "I bet it has nothing more than reservations and the schedule for which waiters are working and when."

"So?"

"May I help you, Signora?" he asked.

"Yes, sir. My name is Joanna Lucas. I am working for San Marco's Procurator's Council." She held up her ID badge.

"*Si, Signora*." He seemed mildly impressed or at least polite.

"Does you computer have Internet?"

"*Si*."

"May I use it for one minute? I have a very important e-mail to send about the basilica. It is very urgent. Please?" She smiled her radiant and confident smile. The man furrowed his forehead, unsure what to say. "I will pay you twenty euros," Joanna quickly added and placed the money in his hand.

"*Si*. But quickly, Signora. Please." He looked around then allowed her to sit at the desk. He walked away as if he didn't want to be caught with her at the computer.

Joanna quickly logged into her office computer through the Straus Center gateway.

"What are you doing? Asking for more time to redo the work?" Chandler looked over her shoulder as she entered her password and waited for the system to open.

"I won't have to." She scrolled through the hundreds of folders, clicking on one titled Venice Trip.

"You know, Joanna, if you e-mailed yourself a copy it probably didn't go through either."

"I didn't e-mail it to myself. But I did save it to my office computer. I just forgot. I've always backed up my work, ever since my computer crashed in grad school and I lost the term paper I spent weeks preparing."

"You've got the photos and data?"

"Yes." She flipped through the list, her smile slowly growing wider. When she found what she was looking for she pointed to the screen. "And I saved my report. You can save things from just about anywhere anymore."

"Can you send those e-mails again from that computer?"

"Yes, I can. I won't have time to write the polite cover note I used to preface each e-mail but I can send the report."

"Forget the note. Send them," Chandler declared.

"They are being sent as we speak." Joanna's fingers flew over the keys, clicking and sending e-mail. "Francesca's has been sent. I'll follow up with her later to make sure she got it but it looks like she did."

"Signora? Are you finished?" the maître d' asked as he returned to his post.

"One more second."

"Please, you must hurry."

"You are saving a piece of Venetian heritage for your grandchildren, sir," Chandler said, offering to shake his hand. And buy Joanna a little more time.

"*Grazie, Signora.*" He smiled proudly.

"What is your name?"

"Rudolpho."

"May I call you Rudy?" Chandler smiled warmly.

"*Si.*"

"Rudy, some day the whole world is going to celebrate this day as Rudolpho Day. The saints will praise you, sir, for your kind gesture. Because of you, a catastrophe has been avoided." Chandler was laying it on thick but she was running out of material and Rudy was growing impatient. Finally, Joanna gave a thumbs-up.

"Thank you, Rudy," Joanna said, giving him a kiss on the cheek. "I will tell the Procurator's representative how helpful you were."

"*Grazie, grazie.* You have coffee at Caffè Florian now?"

"Yes. Now we'll have coffee."

He escorted them back down the aisle. Before leaving them at their booth he leaned down to Chandler and whispered, "I will tell my wife what you said. His name is Roberto." He gave a little grin then went back to his post.

"What did he say?" Joanna asked.

"He told me his wife's name."

"Oh."

"It's Roberto."

Joanna raised an eyebrow and leaned out of the booth,

looking up the aisle where he had gone. "I thought I recognized that walk."

"Cute butt, huh?"

"Tuxedos will do that for you."

"You don't think his butt is cute?"

Joanna just rolled a smile up to her but didn't answer.

"That's my girl. Still prefers gals' asses to guys'," Chandler mused.

"What were you doing? Testing me?" Joanna teased.

"Just checking." Chandler waited for the waiter to set their coffee on the table and leave before saying, "I have to ask why you had the police call me instead of Deena. After all, she is a cop, even if she's American. Don't all cops have a bond, regardless of country or language?"

"Maybe I should have had them call her. I'm sorry if I put you in an awkward position."

"No, no. I'm glad they called me. I was just surprised. Pleased, but surprised."

"I guess I thought you'd know a little more Italian than Deena. Her idea of speaking the language is ordering pepperoni on a pizza." Joanna stirred her coffee, purposefully avoiding Chandler's stare. "I thought maybe you'd care."

Chandler slid her hand across the table and covered Joanna's. "I do. Very much. I was only sorry I wasn't there to help you earlier."

"Are you ashamed of me for acting like a crazy woman, as the *polizia* called me?"

"Never," she said, squeezing her hand. "I hoped it was just second nature that you had them call me. I wanted to believe you wouldn't call anyone else."

"I knew you'd come and save me but I didn't want to disappoint you. That's all. You had such faith in me."

They sat quietly sipping their coffee but Chandler could tell Joanna was uneasy, as if she had something she wanted to say. Finally she gave in and said, "I'm a little surprised you haven't said anything."

"About?" Chandler asked patiently.

"The ultimatum you gave me."

"What ultimatum? I didn't give you any ultimatum. They always sound so confrontational."

"Well, maybe it was more of a choice. About whether I believe you and am ready to let bygones be bygones."

"Are you?"

"I don't know. I've given it a lot of thought. I haven't slept much because of it."

"I didn't mean to make it so difficult for you." Chandler played with the tiny sugar spoon, threading it back and forth through the handle of her coffee cup and keeping her eyes down. She had something she wanted to say and she desperately didn't want to mess it up. "Joanna, I don't expect you to completely forget what you went through because of my stupidity. Even if we don't get any further than we are right now, I'll have the satisfaction of knowing you still have some feeling for me. That is important to me. And I'll understand if this is as much as you are willing to offer."

"I do have feelings for you. I've always had them, Chandler. That never changed."

"What is holding you back?"

"I'm afraid." She swallowed hard. "I'm afraid of waking up and finding you gone again." Joanna's lip quivered just enough for Chandler's heart to ache. "I don't know if I can go through that again."

"How can I convince you I've changed?"

"I don't know if you can."

"Joanna, I've spent two years dreaming of you, waiting for the moment I could tell you how sorry I was. I've spent every minute of that time kicking myself for being a fool. I hated myself for what I did. All I can tell you is I love you. I want you in my life. I want to make a home for us. I want to grow old with you and enjoy art with you and take care of you when you're sick. And make love with you. I can't tell you what things will be like in twenty or thirty or forty years. Maybe you'll hate me by then. I don't know. But I know I'll only ever love one person. And that's you. And I will spend the rest of my life showing you that. It's up to you. But if you don't want that, I'll understand. I did a terrible dreadful thing to you and I can't say I'm sorry enough. Deena is probably right to hate me."

Joanna looked into Chandler's eyes, swimming in them as if searching for the truth and what to say.

"I don't want you to decide now, Joanna. I want you to think about it some more. This is too important a decision for both of us."

"Do I sound childish if I say I don't know what to do?" Joanna asked softly.

"No. You sound like a woman who has been hurt and are only protecting yourself. And it's understandable."

"I guess I should go tell Deena what happened at the basilica and let her tease me about it. She'll be worried I didn't meet her for lunch."

"She probably already knows. I called Macy while I was waiting for you to be released. I didn't want her to think I was blowing her off today."

"And I'm sure she told Deena."

"No doubt. She was going to cook for Deena today in her dinky little apartment. It makes mine look like a palace."

"Is that why she spends so much time at yours?"

"Exactly. That and Macy is a people person. She'd make a terrible hermit."

"I think she is good for Deena. She isn't intimidated by her being a cop."

"They do enjoy some of the same things," Chandler said with a twinkle in her eye.

"No kidding. I accidentally walked in on them."

"Me, too." Chandler laughed.

Joanna shifted in her seat, crossing her legs as if getting comfortable. Chandler noticed her blouse was unbuttoned enough to show the pale skin nestled between her breasts and the lace on her bra licking at it. Joanna was relaying how she walked in on Macy and Deena in the hotel room. Chandler smiled and chuckled appropriately but she didn't care about Deena's and Macy's naked sweaty bodies. All she could think about was Joanna's. There was an innocent sincerity in Joanna's blue eyes so real and so deep Chandler thought she could easily fall inside and drown a happy woman. "Yep, that's Macy," Chandler said, draping her arm over the back of the booth, her thumb resting against Joanna's back. "She doesn't care if she is a top or a bottom, so long as she is one or the other."

"Chandler, this is lovely. I really enjoyed Caffè Florian and visiting with you but I have to excuse myself. I really need a shower. You have no idea what that jail was like. Maybe it was just the fact I was in the slammer, so to speak, but I feel filthy. Do you mind?"

"No, that's okay. I understand." Chandler walked Joanna to the vaporetto stop. "How would you like a homemade spaghetti dinner tonight? I bought the stuff but I hate to cook for just myself."

"Are you sure you want to cook for a felon?"

"I assumed responsibility for you while you're in Venice. That's the only way they'd drop the charges. I'm obligated to feed you."

"Okay. What can I bring? Wine? Crusty bread? Bibs?"

"Just yourself," Chandler said, buttoning Joanna's top coat button. "Six o'clock?"

"I think I can clear my calendar," Joanna said with a warm smile. The vaporetto cruised up to the dock and the railing opened. "Thank you again for rescuing me, Chandler. I'm forever in your debt. And you still have to tell how much the fine was," she said, as the disembarking passengers pushed them apart.

"We'll discuss it later," Chandler shouted over the crowd. "Six o'clock."

"Six o'clock," Joanna replied then stepped onboard and stood at the railing. The breeze off the lagoon was playing with a lock of her hair that had come free from her ponytail. She held it out of her face and smiled, her eyes never leaving Chandler's. Chandler blew her a kiss, not expecting to get one back. But she did.

CHAPTER 18

Joanna hurried down the hall and into her room, humming to herself as she stood over her suitcase. What to wear to Chandler's? Slacks? Skirt and blouse? But that was what she always wore. Business clothes. Maybe Chandler would expect something more casual? Jeans? Yes, the new ones with the flaps on the back pockets, the ones Deena said made her ass look sexy. Joanna didn't think so but if Deena did, maybe Chandler would, too. Joanna snapped the wrinkles out of her white sweater and spread it out on the bed.

She made a quick call to Francesca to check on the report, then turned her full attention to getting ready. She had just enough time to shower, dress and get to Chandler's before six. It had been a long time since anyone cooked for her. That last evening she had spent with Chandler in her kitchen in Boston, the two of them cooked one of their favorite meals together. She remembered how the sautéed vegetables had gone from tender and delicious to burnt in the pan when Chandler's kisses along the back of Joanna's neck sparked a different kind of heat.

The door to the bathroom was closed and just as she was about to open it she heard voices coming from inside. Macy and Deena. Joanna gave thought to knocking and waiting for a reply but something Macy said stopped her in her tracks.

"She's going to be sorry if she doesn't pose for her. I'm telling you, if she really cares about Chandler she'll forget her stinking pride, take her clothes off and put her ass on that stool. My God, Deena. What's the big deal? They've had sex, haven't they? Oh, wait. Is she one of those women who leave their top on and turn out the lights?"

"Josie is self-conscious. That's all. She's always been like that," Deena said.

"Yeah, well, she needs to get over it. She doesn't understand what Chandler has put herself through. She hasn't painted in two years. She won't pick up a brush. That shit she paints to pay the bills is nothing. Whatever happened between the two of them has put Chandler in a creative funk. I don't know if she'll ever come out of it. I can't believe Joanna won't get past her stupid modesty. Chandler is wasting her talents on me and those damn Venetian postcards. Joanna is the only one who can help her."

Joanna heard the door into Deena's room close and the voices fade. She stood with her hand on the doorknob, too stunned to move. She had never considered Chandler not painting because of her or what happened between them. It had never occurred to her. She just assumed it was a phase she would eventually come out of, ready to put brush to canvas and create those breathtaking images that had won her so much acclaim. Was her guilt over what she did so deep it crippled her creativity? To think she might never do that again would be a crime. But posing nude for her? Allowing critical eyes to examine every curve and line? Joanna could barely stand to look at herself in the mirror. How could she pose nude for an artist, even if it was Chandler? She opened the door and stepped into the shower, trying to scrub away the guilt she felt.

"Hello," she said brightly as Chandler opened the door and gave her a welcoming kiss on the cheek. She wore a white shirt tucked into her jeans.

"Come in. I was thinking I said seven instead of six," Chandler said, looking at her watch.

"No. You said six. I'm sorry. I had to wait my turn in the bathroom then I took a wrong turn off the vaporetto. Something smells good."

"*Pasta pomodoro con polpette e pane*," Chandler said with her best Italian accent as she followed Joanna up the stairs.

"Which is?"

"Spaghetti and meatballs and bread." She took Joanna's coat, her eyes drifting down the white sweater and back up. She looked pleased. "Nice."

"Thank you. You look nice, too. I like the pushed up sleeves. You look very French."

"And you look very sexy."

Joanna blushed but that was the look she was going for, if she did say so herself.

"Turn around," Chandler said, stepping back for a better view.

Joanna was self-conscious but she did so.

"I like the jeans. You've got a great butt. No, it's more than that. It's a great ass."

"And there is a difference?" Joanna asked, subconsciously placing her hands over her back pockets.

"Yes, there is. A great butt means you have a nicely rounded, well-formed derriere. A great ass means you have a bottom everyone wants to touch and hold and look at." Chandler winked then went into the kitchen to stir the sauce.

"I never knew that and I thought I knew all the artist terms." Joanna followed, her eyes on Chandler's rear. *Great ass, Chandler. Great ass.*

"That isn't an artist's term. It's a physical one. Pure and simple. Taste?" She held up the spoon for Joanna to taste.

"Oh, that's good, babe. Very good." The term of endearment seemed only natural and it didn't go unheard. "What can I do to help?"

"Go put something on the CD player. There's a stack of CDs over there on the desk. Since I don't have TV I like to play music."

Chandler's music collection wasn't very extensive. kd lang, Indigo Girls, Mood Music for the Spa and Melissa Etheridge. Joanna slipped in the Mood Music CD and pushed the power button. While she was in the living room she noticed the pink sweater draped over a chair. Joanna's picture was in a small frame nearby.

"When was this picture taken?" she called.

"The one of you in a rainbow T-shirt and sunglasses?"

"Yes. I don't remember that."

"That's because I took it without you knowing."

"Where was it taken?" Joanna came back to help.

"Boston Commons, during the Gay Pride weekend. You were sitting under a tree eating an ice cream cone."

"But?"

"I know. It was three months after we broke up." Chandler smiled over at her and handed her the bread to slice. "Don't cut yourself. The knife is sharp."

"I didn't see you there."

"That was my act-invisible phase."

"Were you stalking me, Chandler Cardin?" Joanna asked wickedly.

"No. I had promised to donate a painting for the silent auction to benefit AIDS research. I was delivering it."

"So you did paint after we broke up."

"Actually it was one of my old paintings."

"Which one?"

"The one I titled *Sierra Sleeping*."

"Oh, I liked that one. You gave it away?" Joanna asked disappointedly.

"I understand it raised sixty-two hundred dollars."

"I wish I had known. I would have bid on it. But I don't know that I could have gone that high."

"I didn't hang around."

Chandler tested a strand of pasta then said, "If you really want to know, I didn't stay because you were there. I took your picture then left. I didn't want you to see me and be uncomfortable."

"I'd like to say I wouldn't have been uncomfortable."

"But you can't. I know, baby." Chandler stroked Joanna's arm as she went to set the table.

"It was too soon. I was still in a fog about everything." Joanna heaved a remorseful sigh.

"So we had something in common." Chandler went back and forth with dishes, glasses, wine bottle and silverware.

"When did you leave Boston?"

"The month after Gay Pride. I got a good deal on this apartment and saw no reason not to take it."

"Do you think you're ready to go back to painting? I really think you should."

"We'll see." There was a heavy dose of indifference in her voice.

"Chandler, you need to be painting."

"You sound like Macy. She hounds me about it all the time. I'll tell you what I told her. I'll paint when I'm ready. But right now, our dinner is ready. Come sit down in my huge dining room." Chandler seated Joanna in the better chair, the one that didn't wiggle. She leaned the other one against the wall and sat down carefully.

"I don't remember you ever cooking spaghetti for me before." Joanna dipped a crust of bread in the sauce and tasted it. "Oh, Chandler. This is yummy."

"I decided if I was going to live in Italy I better learn to cook pasta with tomatoes and garlic." Chandler held up her wineglass for a toast. "Cheers."

"Cheers," Joanna said then took a sip, their eyes meeting over the rim of her glass. "I'm sorry this has been so hard for you, Chandler."

"Cooking isn't hard. You just have to experiment until you find what you like to cook."

"I don't mean that and you know it." Joanna rolled her wineglass against her cheek as she studied Chandler. "I meant the guilt you have heaped upon yourself."

"I deserved it," she said, ladling sauce over her pasta.

"Isn't it time to move on? I have."

"I have, too." She looked up and smiled.

"How about move on enough so you can paint again?" Joanna wasn't going to let it drop if she could help it.

"Joanna, let's talk about something else. How about the report? Do you know if they all got the e-mail?"

"Yes. I called Francesca from the hotel. She was on her way out and we didn't have time for a long conversation but she received my report and so did the council. They rescinded Carlo's work order and are hiring a different company to complete the repairs on the mosaic," she said proudly.

"That's great. The mosaic is saved. I bet Carlo isn't a very happy camper."

"I bet not." Joanna gave a lusty laugh. "I would love to have been there when they fired him. I guess it all happened within twenty minutes of them receiving my report. Now, let's go back to you and why you aren't painting."

"Baby, I'd really rather not."

Joanna went to get the salt and pepper from the counter. She needed time to plan what she was going to say next. She remained standing and looked down at Chandler.

"I have changed my mind. I want to pose for you."

Chandler nearly choked on her bite. "You?" She looked up at her in shock.

"Yes, me. I want to be your model. I'll be here three more days. That's enough time, isn't it?"

"Nude?"

"Yes, nude," Joanna said, wringing her hands.

"Sweetheart, thank you, but no. You don't really want to do that. I understand." Chandler pulled her down into her chair. "Now eat your dinner."

"But I do, Chandler. I want to be your model. I've decided."

"Joanna, it was wrong for me to ask two years ago and just as wrong the other day. You're not the model type."

"Yes, I am. I like to try new things. To take risks."

"Baby, you're not exactly a risk taker. For you, wearing jeans without underwear is living on the edge. I'm talking posing nude, completely naked and sitting there for hours." Chandler leaned over and gave her a forgiving kiss on the cheek. "But, thanks."

"I want to do it. Don't you want me to?"

"Sure, I do. You know I do. But I can't ask you. Eat your pasta before it gets cold."

Joanna sat up straight. It took all her courage as she said emphatically, "I want to pose for you, Chandler. I want to start tonight." Chandler stopped in mid-bite when she looked over and heard the determination in Joanna's voice. "I mean it. You asked me to pose and I'm saying yes. I want to do this."

"You want to pose nude for me, up there in my studio, tonight?"

"Yes." Joanna drank the last of her wine then folded her hands in her lap to wait for instructions.

Chandler stared at Joanna for a long moment, digesting what she said. But a small curl at the corner of her mouth told Joanna she wanted this as much as she ever did.

"Could we at least finish our dinner first?" Chandler said, swallowing.

"I don't know if I should. I might bulge."

Chandler laughed and said, "You will not bulge. Eat your dinner, sweetheart." Chandler thought a moment, twirling her pasta on her fork then muttered, "Wow."

Joanna didn't have much of an appetite. Her knees were shaking, her palms were sweaty and her heart was pounding in her chest. She poured herself another glass of wine and drank it. It didn't help the butterflies. Chandler seemed to know she was nervous and did her best to talk about other things. But there was definitely an enthusiastic tone to Chandler's voice and a brighter twinkle in her eyes. They finished dinner and carried the dishes to the kitchen. Joanna washed while Chandler dried and put away the leftovers. Joanna's eyes kept darting up the spiral staircase, her mind wondering what she would have to do.

"I'll be right back," Chandler said, nodding toward the bathroom. Joanna pushed the play button to start the CD over again and turned it up a little. Maybe it would help distract her. When Chandler returned she was wearing paint-splattered shorts and T-shirt.

"Aren't you going to be cold in that?" Joanna asked.

"No. I'm going to turn the thermostat up." Chandler smiled, took Joanna by the hand and led her into the bedroom. There was a robe lying on the bed and a pair of slippers next to it. "Take your time, sweetheart. I've got a few things to do upstairs." She kissed Joanna's cheek and pulled the door closed on her way out.

Joanna stood staring down at the robe as she stepped out of her shoes and peeled off her socks. She then unzipped her jeans and slid them down, hesitating at the knees before stepping out and folding them across the bed. The sweater was next. She pulled it over her head and placed it neatly next to her jeans. Here she was, a Summa Cum Laude college graduate with three degrees but she couldn't decide what should come off next. Panties or bra?

Joanna finally stepped out of the bedroom wearing only the flimsy robe Chandler had given her. It was white and nearly transparent. She was certain of it. She took a deep breath then climbed the stairs to Chandler's studio. She stood at the top of the stairs, clutching the robe against her chest as Chandler busied herself getting ready. She had placed a fresh canvas on the easel, blank and awaiting Joanna's image. Chandler had placed a small chair on a raised platform and was arranging a chocolate brown satin sheet over it. The fabric draped over the back of the chair and down onto the floor as if it had just slid off a bed in luscious folds. The platform was surrounded by floodlights in every conceivable position. The thought that she was not only going to pose nude for Chandler but she would be illuminated from all sides, gave Joanna a chill. All of her fears and self-doubt about her body and its flaws were screaming at her.

"One second, babe," Chandler said, arranging things on the platform. She was right, she had raised the thermostat. Joanna could feel a bead of sweat running down her spine. Chandler stepped back and looked but didn't seem to like what she saw. She pulled the chair off the platform and replaced it with a round hassock then draped the sheet over it. "That's better."

"Are you going to use all those spotlights?" Joanna asked, holding onto the railing to steady herself.

"No, I don't have to. Would you be happier if we just used ambient room lighting?" Chandler asked, studying her face. "We can do whatever you are comfortable with." She patted the hassock. "Why don't you sit down and relax while I adjust the lights."

Joanna lowered herself onto the hassock, still clutching her robe. She pulled it closed over her exposed leg, holding it there. She wondered if Chandler could just paint her face and use her imagination for the rest. After all, Chandler's fingertips had traced every inch of Joanna's body and more than once. She should know what she looked like by heart.

Chandler dimmed the lights, all except one small spotlight over her easel. Joanna was busy arguing with herself, defending what she was doing as good for Chandler. If this is what it took to convince Chandler to resurrect her career, then it would be worth it. Joanna kept telling herself that. She was doing this for Chandler.

"Let's have you turn sideways. I want your legs extended slightly off to the left." She showed her. "How are you doing?" she asked softly.

"I'm okay." Joanna knew she didn't sound that way.

"You're doing great. Now, I want you to turn your shoulders like this. Very good. And one more thing, baby. I want your hair down." She waited while Joanna pulled the ponytail holder out and gave her hair a toss. "Yes, just like that." Chandler arranged it to flow over her shoulder, part of it around to the front.

"I should have let it grow longer," Joanna said, trying to make light of it, but right now she would sell her soul for six more inches of hair to cover her breasts.

"It's gorgeous. I hope I can capture the way it shines." Chandler was fussing with Joanna's hair and the angle of her shoulders and chin. She placed a small painting sponge on the floor a few feet away. "I want you to look at that sponge. I want your eyes down there. Your chin just like this but your eyes down. I want to capture the subtle Joanna. You feel a quiet reluctance about this and I want to capture that. Okay, sit just like that while I see how the shadows fall."

Chandler stepped back and studied her, squinting one way then the other as she circled. She continued adjusting things, prolonging the inevitable.

"Pull one foot back and extend the other one. Yes, like that. Good."

Joanna didn't know what to do with her hands. Chandler hadn't said anything so she kept one at the neck of the robe and the other holding it closed over her knees. She couldn't help fidgeting on the hassock.

"Sorry," she said, quickly reassuming the pose Chandler had chosen.

"You're fine. Relax a minute while I get things ready. I'm going to start with a charcoal sketch to get an overall composition. Normally I take a few digital photographs for reference. It helps when we come back to it tomorrow. But I think you'd rather we skip that part."

"Yes, thank you."

The closer Chandler came to being ready, the tighter Joanna held the robe and the wider her eyes got.

"Okay, let's see if I remember how to do this." Chandler rubbed her hands together and took a deep breath. "I'm a little nervous."

"You're nervous?" Joanna said with an anxious twitter in her voice.

"Yes, me. All you have to do it sit there and be gorgeous. I've got to try and capture magic on canvas." With that, Chandler stepped up onto the platform and looked down at her. "Ready?" She smiled reassuringly.

"I think so."

Chandler untied the sash and tossed it aside.

"We're going to let the robe drop and become part of the draping." She gave Joanna's hand a comforting pat then pushed it down, opening the robe and sliding it over her shoulders. As soon as it fell Joanna felt a blush race over her entire body, tweaking her pale nipples and warming her face. She folded her hands over her lap trying to hide her patch of curly blond pubic hair. Even that wasn't thick and dark and sensual like Chandler's, she thought.

"Rest one hand back here and this one on your other thigh." Chandler positioned them. "Open your hands, babe. Relax your fingers. You're doing great. Your hands are delicate and fragile. That's what I want to capture."

"I should have gotten a manicure," Joanna joked nervously.

"No, you're fine." She laced her fingers through Joanna's long hair, bringing it over her shoulder and partially hiding her face. "Good, perfect." She gave a long look, repositioning her shoulders a fraction of an inch then climbed down and went to the easel, leaving Joanna alone on the platform, naked and feeling utterly exposed.

Joanna knew she wasn't facing front. The turn of the shoulders and the drape of her hair offered some privacy but she was still naked, bare-breasted and bare-bottomed.

"Chandler?"

"Yes, baby," she said, sorting through her box of charcoal sticks.

"Did you lock the door?"

"Yes, I did." She looked up. "It's just us."

"Good. This isn't as easy as I thought."

"Are you uncomfortable? Do we need to change the pose?"

"No, it isn't that." Joanna swallowed hard, fighting her fears that wanted to clamp her hands over her chest and make her scream.

As soon as Chandler selected a stick and looked up, ready to begin, Joanna felt her body start to shake. Perspiration formed on her upper lip. Her heart raced. She felt like she had run a marathon, unable to catch her breath.

"Move your hand over, babe. Back where I showed you. That's it."

Joanna moved it but it snapped back to her lap. She looked over at Chandler, her eyes pleading for help. She wanted to do this. She wanted to rescue Chandler just as she had rescued her, time after time. But she couldn't do it. She couldn't stop the tears that streamed down her face either.

"Chandler, I can't," she whispered, closing her eyes.

"Joanna? Are you all right?"

"I'm sorry, but I can't do this." She folded her arms over her exposed breasts as she began to cry.

"Oh, sweetheart." Chandler dropped the charcoal and rushed to her side, pulling her into her arms.

"I wanted to. I wanted to do it for you but I just can't. I don't know why, but I can't." She leaned into Chandler, sobbing against her shirt. "I can't. I can't."

"Oh, baby, I knew you couldn't. I was surprised you got this far."

"Then why didn't you stop me?"

"Because you wanted to do it so badly. But this isn't you. You know it and I know it. And that's what I love about you." She stroked Joanna's hair and held her as she cried.

"I wanted you to paint again. If I'm the reason you aren't, I wanted to fix it," she blubbered.

"I know you did. But it isn't your fault. It's mine. But I

appreciate what you tried to do. It must have been very hard for you. I love that you would do that for me."

Joanna looked up at her, her tear-swollen eyes stained with sorrow. Chandler wiped her tears and kissed her softly.

"I'm so sorry," Joanna whispered.

"Sweetheart, it'll be all right. You don't have to do this. I love you anyway. You never have to do this, ever," she said, stroking her face. Then Chandler kissed her again.

Joanna folded her arms around Chandler's neck and returned the kiss, pressing herself against Chandler's chest. There was no hesitancy, no regrets in this kiss. Joanna opened her mouth and allowed their tongues a sultry dance. She felt her nipples harden as they pressed into Chandler. Chandler eased Joanna off the hassock and onto the carpeted platform, laying her amid the folds of the sheets. Joanna no longer felt nude. She was naked in the arms of her lover. And that was exactly where she wanted to be. Why had she waited so long to allow it? Chandler was her lover. She had always been and would always be. She wanted to feel her, experience her, consume her and be consumed. Chandler's hands had already begun stroking and exciting her skin, arousing those feelings she thought were dead. Joanna tugged at Chandler's shirt, searching for skin to touch. Chandler peeled it off and allowed Joanna to unhook her bra. She then lowered her nipples against Joanna's, softly brushing them against one another until all four stood swollen and erect.

"Shorts," Joanna muttered between kisses, fumbling with Chandler's waistband. They too, quickly came off. "You aren't wearing any panties," she whispered.

"Just for you," Chandler replied, fitting herself against Joanna's body. The feel of Chandler's thick patch of hair brought on another soft moan and Joanna began to move against it.

"I need to feel you, Chandler," she said softly, stroking her hands down Chandler's lean body. "All of you."

"I'm here for you, baby. Whatever you want, I'm here for you."

"Paint me," she said breathlessly. Chandler seemed to know

what she meant and lowered her mouth to Joanna's nipple licking it and sucking at it.

"Like this?" she whispered, drawing her tongue down Joanna's cleavage then back up.

"Yes, just like that," she sighed, closing her eyes. "Just like that." Joanna gave little whimpers and moans as Chandler's tongue painted soft brush strokes across her nipples.

Chandler moved down her body, flicking and painting feather strokes with a curious tongue until Joanna's moans grew too loud to ignore.

"Touch me, Joanna. Show me where you want it, baby. Show me."

Joanna cupped her hand over Chandler's breasts massaging her nipple. Chandler did the same. Joanna moved down, her hand flowing over Chandler's tight abs and curling over her mound.

"Touch me here, sweetheart. Touch me, here."

As Joanna's fingers entered Chandler, Chandler's entered Joanna, both of them moving slowly, intimately, tenderly. They moved in unison, exploring, delving, giving to the other. Joanna pulled Chandler down to her, until their breasts touched then closed her eyes and rode with the feeling she was giving and receiving. As if in perfect tune with the other, they each felt the intensity building inside at seemingly the same moment. Reaching for their own orgasm, they continued to share and please the other, deeper and deeper until only gasps and screams filled the studio and their senses. Joanna had never felt such attachment to anyone as she did to Chandler at that moment. She wasn't sure where her body ended and Chandler's began.

As their breaths slowed and they cuddled together among the folds of the sheet, Joanna lay her face against Chandler's chest and listened to her heart race. She wanted to ask Chandler why they had wasted two years but there was no answer for it.

"Promise me something," Joanna said softly, her mouth touching Chandler's skin.

"Anything."

"Promise you'll paint again."

There was a moment of silence then Chandler pulled her closer.

"I promise." She kissed Joanna's forehead then said, "Stay with me tonight."

There was nothing to think about. Of course, she would. There was nowhere else she wanted to be. With only a few days left before she returned home, she had some decisions to make and this is where she needed to be to make them.

CHAPTER 19

In the last few minutes before dawn Joanna could feel a warmth flow over her as stood at the windows in Chandler's studio. She had left Chandler sleeping peacefully, a relaxed innocence to her lover's naked body as she slipped out of bed and made her way up the stairs. They had slept in each other's arms, barely moving but to sigh and snuggle a little closer. It felt good to be in Chandler's arms. They seemed even more tender than she remembered, if that was possible.

Joanna flipped on the light over the platform and looked down at the satin sheet, the imprint of their bodies still visible in the folds. Joanna hugged the robe Chandler had given her around herself as she stepped up on the platform and lowered herself onto the hassock, just as Chandler had positioned her.

It seemed easier this morning, easier to find that pose and make it her own. The decision over what she should do about Chandler seemed to have been made without her even realizing it. Of course, she wanted Chandler back in her life. She couldn't imagine not having her there to turn to and comfort her and love her and accept Joanna's love in return.

Joanna loosened her hold on the robe and allowed it to slide down her shoulders. She lowered her gaze, remembering Chandler's gentleness and understanding, and let it slip to the floor, pooling at her feet. She was once again naked. When she looked up, Chandler was standing at the top of the spiral staircase, watching her. She too was naked. But she had a confident presence about her and Joanna admired that.

"What are you doing up so early?" Chandler asked.

"I couldn't sleep. I had some things to think about." Joanna didn't reach for the robe. She didn't need it.

"Good things, I hope." Chandler picked up the charcoal stick where she had dropped it yesterday, holding it like a cigarette in her fingers.

"I don't know about you, but I think they're good things." Joanna sat sideways on the hassock, leaning back on one arm. She knew her breasts were exposed to Chandler's view but it was all right. There was softness in Chandler's eyes that told her she could be trusted with it.

"Should I be worried?" Chandler stood within reach of the easel, nonchalantly making a stroke on the canvas then another.

"I think you know my decision, sweetheart. How could you not? I think I showed you enough last night." She grinned sheepishly.

Chandler continued to sketch, moving closer to the easel. Her eyes darted back and forth from Joanna's body to her work as she drew line after line.

"I have a question for you." Joanna swept her hair to the side and looked up at her. Chandler seemed to like it and scrambled to draw it.

"What?" she asked distractedly.

"When is your lease up on this apartment?"

Chandler hesitated, smiled at her over the top of the easel then went back to sketching.

"This coming weekend. The day after you go home."

"Chandler, how did you know I'd want you back in my life?"

"I didn't. But I was hoping." She sketched at a feverish pace, her attention now completely on her work, her eyes narrowed and focused.

"Is it okay if I'm not ready to live in Venice?"

"I didn't want you to. I want us to live in Boston or wherever your work takes you. I can work anywhere. We'll come here on our anniversary. We'll ride Marcello's gondola and kiss in the moonlight."

"I'd like that."

All Joanna could see was Chandler's bare legs from the knees down and the top of her head. Occasionally her shoulder and one breast popped out the side as she took another look at Joanna.

"Will I get to approve what you're working on?" Joanna couldn't help ask.

"Don't you trust me?" she teased.

"Yes, I trust you. It's my body I don't trust. I'm not sure I want to see the truth, the whole truth and nothing but the truth."

"You are the most gorgeous woman I have ever painted, bar none." Chandler gazed over at her with a sincere look in her eyes. "Tell me, am I going to have to do this all in the nude, too?"

"I like that idea but no, you don't have to," Joanna replied demurely. "Besides, I have a pretty good imagination and a great memory." She winked, bringing a delightful smile to Chandler's face. "Would it be okay if I take a look? I'm still a little nervous about seeing myself on canvas like this."

"Sure. It's just a rough sketch though. I did it in pastels to get an idea of the color palette. The finished painting will be in acrylics."

Joanna stepped down and cautiously came around the easel for a first look. It wasn't what she expected and she gasped.

"It's just a rough idea," Chandler reminded her. She applied

227

another stroke here and there, then stood behind Joanna, looking over her shoulder.

"But, I thought," she stammered, completely taken by surprise.

"See," Chandler said, wrapping her arms around Joanna and kissing her neck. "I told you pink was your color."

Joanna had expected to see herself on the canvas naked, exposed and raw. But Chandler had sketched her wearing the pink sweater. The sleeves were pushed back. The sweater hem draped down, covering her lap and bottom. Her legs were all that seemed seductively nude, long and slender from her thighs to her feet. Her long blond hair fell over one shoulder, framing her face. Her eyes were cast to the side with an innocent confidence.

"Do you like it?"

"Yes, very much." Joanna could barely speak.

"You did something wonderful for me by posing. I wanted to do something for you. No one will ever know unless you want to tell them. Anyway, I'm not sure I want anyone else to see you naked," Chandler whispered in Joanna's ear then bit it playfully.

Joanna leaned back into Chandler.

"Should I pose with the pink sweater on?" she asked, still touched by Chandler's generosity and compassion over what she had sketched.

"No," she moaned softly.

"What's it worth to you, Ms. Cardin?" Joanna turned around within Chandler's arms and grinned up at her.

"I'd be glad to tell you but I'd rather show you." She kissed her on the nose then the lips, holding Joanna's bottom in her hands.

"Please, do." Joanna kissed her back. "Could I interest you in accompanying me to the conference room on the lower level?"

"I'd love to."

Chandler swatted her bottom. Joanna responded by giving her mound a pinch then hurried down the stairs to get away, giggling all the way. Chandler followed, threatening to tickle, but just as they got to the bottom of the stairs they heard a key in the lock at the bottom of the stairs. Before they could react, the door opened and Macy and Deena started up the steps. The only thing Joanna could find to put on was the pink sweater draped over the chair in the living room. She slipped it on, though backwards and tugged at the hem to cover herself. It wasn't nearly as long as Chandler had sketched it. Chandler snatched the tablecloth off the table and held it up like a beach towel, keeping her back to the wall.

"See, I told you they'd be here," Macy said, not yet noticing what they were wearing. "Oh, and yes they did," she added with a chuckle.

"Hey, there, Josie," Deena said, grinning devilishly. Her eyes immediately scanned up and down Joanna's body then moved to Chandler. "Nice tablecloth, Chandler. What size do you wear in those?"

"Don't you ever knock, Macy?" Chandler scowled.

"And miss this?"

"What do you want? We're busy."

"I can see that." They both laughed, making Chandler's and Joanna's blushes all the redder.

Macy noticed the light on in the studio and went to the railing to look up.

"Have you been painting, Chandler?" she asked hopefully.

"Maybe."

"I want to see," Macy said and trotted up the steps. Deena remained in the living room, grinning at Joanna and Chandler's predicament.

"No, wait," Chandler called. "It isn't finished. It's just a sketch."

"I don't care. I want to see what the master has created."

"Macy, please." Chandler did her best to dissuade her but it was too late. Macy was already up the stairs. After a moment of silence there was a loud *wow*. "All right, you've seen it. Now come down."

"Deena, come see this. It's really good," Macy declared enthusiastically.

"No, Deena, you don't need to," Joanna begged. "It's not finished."

That seemed to be all the prodding Deena needed to trot up the stairs and have a look for herself. And like Macy, the first thing she said was *wow*. Chandler looked over at Joanna, as if apologizing if she was embarrassed.

"Hey, Josie," Deena called. "How come you didn't go totally naked? How come you wore the sweater? You've got a great body."

"Yeah, Joanna," Macy added. "It's nice but why not go all the way and be totally nude?"

Joanna went to the railing and looked up, still holding the hem of the sweater down to cover herself.

"How do you know I didn't?" she said.

Deena's and Macy's faces appeared at the top of the stairs, both of them with wide-eyed curiosity.

"Did you?" Macy asked.

Joanna shrugged and said, "I'll never tell."

"She'd never do that, would you, Josie?" Deena scowled down at her. "Would you?"

"I consider that none of your business, sergeant Garren." She smiled up at her mischievously.

As the two of them started back down the spiral staircase, Deena said, "She'd never do that. I know Josie."

"Now you've seen it so why don't you tell me what you are doing here and then leave," Chandler said, moving back to where she was standing against the wall.

"I don't get it. Joanna is wearing the sweater and you are in the nude?"

"It's a new technique so I could be in touch with my inner creativity," Chandler smirked. "What do you want?"

"I want to tell you I won't be taking any more classes from you. I'm officially giving up my artistic endeavors, at least the painting ones. We only had a few more anyway."

"Do you want a refund?"

"No. I don't expect a refund. I just wanted you to know so

you wouldn't be sitting here wondering where I was."

"What are you going to do?" Joanna asked, although from the smug look on Deena's face she had a pretty good idea.

"I'm going back home. North America, here I come. I'm Veniced out. No pun intended."

"You're going back to Toronto?"

"Well, in a month I am. I'm going to Boston for a month first. I have some research to do," she said, smiling over at Deena. "I'll have to see how things work out. I may want to set one of my books in Boston. Maybe a whole new series set in Boston."

"Good for you," Joanna said fondly. "And good for you, too, Deena. I've happy for you."

"I'm just research material," Deena replied, wrapping her arm around Macy. "By the way, are you dragging her back to Boston with you to keep you from getting lost and out of jail?" She tossed a little grin Chandler's direction.

"What? You approve?"

"Yeah, I guess so." Deena extended her hand to Chandler. "You're okay, Chandler." She waited while Chandler fumbled the tablecloth under her arms and accepted it. "I guess we can get along, so long as you take care of my Josie."

"I plan on it. And I expect the same from you. Macy may be a crappy artist but she's a keeper, Deena."

"I think so, too."

Chandler and Deena smiled at each other, something that warmed Joanna's heart all the more. She never thought she'd see the day they would get along.

"Do you want to meet us for dinner this evening? Tavolino?" Macy asked.

"No, I don't think so. We're going to be busy," Chandler said, winking at Joanna.

"Yes, we're going to be very busy," Joanna agreed, and went to Chandler and kissed her, the hem of the pink sweater riding up over her bottom. But she didn't care. She wanted to feel Chandler's lips on hers, bare bottom be damned.

231

Publications from
Bella Books, Inc.
Women. Books. Even Better Together.
P.O. Box 10543
Tallahassee, FL 32302
Phone: 800-729-4992
www.bellabooks.com

THE GRASS WIDOW by Nanci Little. Aidan Blackstone is nineteen, unmarried and pregnant, and has no reason to think that the year 1876 won't be her last. Joss Bodett has lost her family but desperately clings to their land. A richly told story of frontier survival that picks up with the generation of women where Patience and Sarah left off.
978-1-59493-189-5 $12.95

SMOKEY O by Celia Cohen. Insult "Mac" MacDonnell and insult the entire Delaware Blue Diamond team. Smokey O'Neill has just insulted Mac, and then finds she's been traded to Delaware. The games are not limited to the baseball field!
978-1-59493-198-7 $12.95

WICKED GAMES by Ellen Hart. Never have mysteries and secrets been closer to home in this eighth installment of this award-winning lesbian cozy mystery series. Jane Lawless's neighbors bring puzzles and peril--and that's just the beginning.
978-1-59493-185-7 $14.95

NOT EVERY RIVER by Robbi McCoy. It's the hottest city in the U.S., and it's not just the weather that's heating up. For Kim and Randi are forced to question everything they thought they knew about themselves before they can risk their fiery hearts on the biggest gamble of all.
978-1-59493-182-6 $14.95

HOUSE OF CARDS by Nat Burns. Cards are played, but the game is gossip. Kaylen Strauder has never wanted it to be about her. But the time is fast-approaching when she must decide which she needs more: her community of Eda Byrne.
978-1-59493-203-8 $14.95

RETURN TO ISIS by Jean Stewart. The award-winning Isis sci-fi series features Jean Stewart's vision of a committed colony of women dedicated to preserving their way of life, even after the apocalypse. Mysteries have been forgotten, but survival depends on remembering. Book one in series.
978-1-59493-193-2 $12.95

1ST IMPRESSIONS by Kate Calloway. Rookie PI Cassidy James has her first case. Her investigation into the murder of Erica Trinidad's uncle isn't welcomed by the local sheriff, especially since the delicious, seductive Erica is their prime suspect. 1st in series. Author's augmented and expanded edition.
978-1-59493-192-5 $12.95

BEACON OF LOVE by Ann Roberts. Twenty-five years after their families put an end to a relationship that hadn't even begun, Stephanie returns to Oregon to find many things have changed... except her feelings for Paula.
978-1-59493-180-2 $14.95

ABOVE TEMPTATION by Karin Kallmaker. It's supposed to be like any other case, except this time they're chasing one of their own. As fraud investigators Tamara Sterling and Kip Barrett try to catch a thief, they realize they can have anything they want--except each other.
978-1-59493-179-6 $14.95

AN EMERGENCE OF GREEN by Katherine V. Forrest. Carolyn had no idea her new neighbor jumped the fence to enjoy her swimming pool. The discovery leads to choices she never anticipated in an intense, sensual story of discovery and risk, consequences and triumph. Originally released in 1986.
978-1-59493-217-5 $14.95

CRAZY FOR LOVING by Jaye Maiman. Officially hanging out her shingle as a private investigator, Robin Miller is getting her life on track. Just as Robin discovers it's hard to follow a dead man, She walks in. KT Bellflower, sultry and devastating... Lammy winner and second in series.
978-1-59493-195-6 $14.95

LOVE WAITS by Gerri Hill. The All-American girl and the love she left behind--it's been twenty years since Ashleigh and Gina parted, and now they're back to the place where nothing was simple and love didn't wait.
978-1-59493-186-4 $14.95

HANNAH FREE: THE BOOK by Claudia Allen. Based on the film festival hit movie starring Sharon Gless. Hannah's story is funny, scathing and witty as she navigates life with aplomb -- but always comes home to Rachel. 32 pages of color photographs plus bonus behind-the-scenes movie information.
978-1-59493-172-7 $19.95

END OF THE ROPE by Jackie Calhoun. Meg Klein has two enduring loves—horses and Nicky Hennessey. Nicky is there for her when she most needs help, but then an attractive vet throws Meg's carefully balanced world out of kilter.
978-1-59493-176-5 $14.95

THE LONG TRAIL by Penny Hayes. When schoolteacher Blanche Bartholomew and dance hall girl Teresa Stark meet their feelings are powerful--and completely forbidden--in Starcross Texas. In search of a safe future, they flee, daring to take a covered wagon across the forbidding prairie.
978-1-59493-196-3 $12.95

UP UP AND AWAY by Catherine Ennis. Sarah and Margaret have a video. The mob wants it. Flying for their lives, two women discover more than secrets.
978-1-59493-215-1 $12.95

CITY OF STRANGERS by Diana Rivers. A captive in a gilded cage, young Solene plots her escape, but the rulers of Hernorium have other plans for Solene--and her people. Breathless lesbian fantasy story also perfect for teen readers.
978-1-59493-183-3 $14.95

ROBBER'S WINE by Ellen Hart. Belle Dumont is the first dead of summer. Jane Lawless, Belle's old friend, suspects coldhearted murder. Lammy-winning seventh novel in critically acclaimed cozy mystery series.
978-1-59493-184-0 $14.95

APPARITION ALLEY by Katherine V. Forrest. Kate Delafield has solved hundreds of cases, but the one that baffles her most is her own shooting. Book six in series.
978-1-883523-65-7 $14.95

STERLING ROAD BLUES by Ruth Perkinson. It was a simple declaration of love. But the entire state of Virginia wants to weigh in, leaving teachers Carrie Tomlinson and Audra Malone caught in the crossfire--and with love troubles of their own.
978-1-59493-187-1 $14.95

LILY OF THE TOWER by Elizabeth Hart. Agnes Headey, taking refuge from a storm at the Netherfield estate, stumbles into dark family secrets and something more… Meticulously researched historical romance.
978-1-59493-177-2 $14.95

LETTING GO by Ann O'Leary. Kelly has decided that luscious, successful Laura should be hers. For now. Laura might even be agreeable. But where does that leave Kate?
978-1-59493-194-9 $12.95

MURDER TAKES TO THE HILLS by Jessica Thomas. Renovations, shady business deals, a stalker--and it's not even tourist season yet for PI Alex Peres and her best four-legged pal Fargo. Sixth in this cozy Provincetown-based series.
978-1-59493-178-9 $14.95

SOLSTICE by Kate Christie. It's Emily Mackenzie's last college summer and meeting her soccer idol Sam Delaney seems like a dream come true. But Sam's passion seems reserved for the field of play…
978-1-59493-175-8 $14.95

FORTY LOVE by Diana Simmonds. Lush, romantic story of love and tennis with two women playing to win the ultimate prize. Revised and updated author's edition.
978-1-59493-190-1 $14.95

I LEFT MY HEART by Jaye Maiman. The only women she ever loved is dead, and sleuth Robin Miller goes looking for answers. First book in Lammy-winning series.
978-1-59493-188-8 $14.95

TWO WEEKS IN AUGUST by Nat Burns. Her return to Chincoteague Island is a delight to Nina Christie until she gets her dose of Hazy Duncan's renown ill-humor. She's not going to let it bother her, though…
978-1-59493-173-4 $14.95